MIRAGE CITY

BOOKS BY LEV AC ROSEN

THE EVANDER MILLS SERIES
Mirage City
Rough Pages
The Bell in the Fog
Lavender House

OTHER FICTION
Depth
All Men of Genius

FOR YOUNG ADULTS, AS L.C. ROSEN
Emmett
Lion's Legacy
Camp

FOR CHILDREN
The Memory Wall
Woundabout (with Ellis Rosen)

LEV AC ROSEN

MIRAGE CITY

MINOTAUR BOOKS
NEW YORK

Please note: This story contains content that some readers might find disturbing, including period-accurate homophobia and conversion therapy.

This is a work of fiction. All of the characters, organizations, and events portrayed in this novel are either products of the author's imagination or are used fictitiously.

First published in the United States by Minotaur Books, an imprint of
St. Martin's Publishing Group

EU Representative: Macmillan Publishers Ireland Ltd, 1st Floor, The Liffey Trust Centre, 117–126 Sheriff Street Upper, Dublin 1, D01 YC43

MIRAGE CITY. Copyright © 2025 by Lev AC Rosen. All rights reserved. Printed in the United States of America. For information, address St. Martin's Publishing Group, 120 Broadway, New York, NY 10271.

www.minotaurbooks.com

Endpaper art by Colin Verdi

The Library of Congress Cataloging-in-Publication Data is available upon request.

ISBN 978-1-250-32247-0 (hardcover)
ISBN 978-1-250-32248-7 (ebook)

The publisher of this book does not authorize the use or reproduction of any part of this book in any manner for the purpose of training artificial intelligence technologies or systems. The publisher of this book expressly reserves this book from the Text and Data Mining exception in accordance with Article 4(3) of the European Union Digital Single Market Directive 2019/790.

Our books may be purchased in bulk for specialty retail/wholesale, literacy, corporate/premium, educational, and subscription box use. Please contact MacmillanSpecialMarkets@macmillan.com.

First Edition: 2025

0 9 8 7 6 5 4 3 2 1

For Lucy,

No one else I'd rather storm Hollywood with

MIRAGE CITY

ONE

It's early when she walks up to the bar. The band hasn't started playing yet, and the Ruby is half empty, so the only sound besides her footsteps is the echoed murmuring of people in corners, like whispered gossip in church. Her footsteps are heavier than they need to be, each one landing with annoyance, or maybe an attempt at authority.

Or maybe she's just scared, I think, taking her in as she approaches me; sometimes anger is easier to wear than fear. The woman's face is carved of stone, with high cheekbones and a wide jaw. She looks maybe fifty, with short dark hair pulled back from her face, and she's not dressed like people usually dress at the Ruby. The matching gray skirt and jacket aren't fashionable or flashy, not even masculine. She looks like the sort of woman who marches up to inform policemen about teenagers down the street who are loitering on the corner and smoking cigarettes. Except she's marching up to me, in the best queer bar in San Francisco.

"You're the detective?" It's only a quarter of a question. The rest of it is a demand, loud enough to startle my drink into my face.

I glance across the bar at my boyfriend, Gene, who's the bartender and manager. We'd been flirting a moment ago. She didn't mind interrupting. He raises his eyebrows at me and hands me a towel.

"I am," I say, wiping my face. "Evander Mills. You can call me Andy."

She doesn't seem impressed by my charm. Or maybe it's that I just spilled my drink. Though she seems unfazed by that, too.

"You have an office upstairs, but you weren't in it." An accusation, a deep moral failing on my part.

"People usually wait."

"How nice that they have time for that." She looks me up and down. My face is dry now, so I think she finds me barely acceptable. "Well? I have business to discuss and I don't want to do that . . . here." She looks around, almost instinctively, as if someone is about to leap out and try to frighten her.

"You lead the way," I say, wondering if she's going to go for the elevator or the stairs. Stairs. Her heels echo like boots on them.

When I close my office door and sit down, her expression eases for the first time. Not by much, but enough I can tell this is what she was expecting from a private eye—me behind a desk, taking notes, her telling me what to do. She glances around and frowns slightly at the vase of flowers Gene left me. He likes to make sure the office looks nice for me, and I like that he brings me flowers. Apparently it's too festive for a PI's office.

"So how can I help you, Miss . . ."

"Bolton. Myrtle Bolton."

She waits.

"Miss Bolton," I say. She wanted me to finish the sentence.

"Mr. Mills, are you familiar with the Mattachine Society?"

I nod. "In passing. Group of gays who have secret meetings and try to . . ." I almost make a joke and say overthrow the government, but it's clear Myrtle wouldn't appreciate that. "Get political rights for folks like us. They paid for the lawyer for that entrapment case last year in '52, got one of us off. Or so I've heard."

"We pursue equality for the homophile movement." She nods, like she's pleased, but her mouth turns down, too. She didn't want me to have the right answer. She doesn't want to be here at all. "Are you perhaps a member?"

"No," I say. "And I know members are supposed to keep themselves secret."

"Well, that's true. For everyone's safety, you understand. But I'm going to"—she takes a deep breath—"trust you. I am such a member."

"Well. thank you for that," I say, managing not to smirk. "Is that why you're here? To ask me to join?"

"No," she says immediately, her lips a perfect O, surprised both by the question and how quickly that answer came out of her. "I am here to hire you. For the society."

I raise an eyebrow. "For the society?"

"Yes."

"I didn't realize the Mattachines hired anyone. You keep everything off the books for privacy, I thought. You organize in . . . cells, almost, like spies. There are passwords to get into meetings."

"All true." She nods. "Though that is changing . . . somewhat. It does worry me to know that all of that is public, though."

"Well, not public. I hear about it. You probably have some members who come here"—she frowns at that, pulls down her jacket—"maybe try to recruit people. That's how you get members, right?"

"Yes, I suppose," she concedes. "In any case, I hope you keep all of it private."

"I am a private eye." I smile, trying to be charming again. It misses the mark again, too, a bullet flying past the target by a foot.

"And that's why we need you. The circumstances are . . . unusual, as you say. The society doesn't really do anything like this, but I—" She flounders for a moment, her mouth quivering.

"That is, we . . . need help. And we know how you've helped people before. Blackmail especially."

I nod. I helped out some blackmailed folks, no charge, a while back, and more recently tried to help out a beloved pair of bookshop owners. That didn't go so well, but the bookshop is still standing.

"Is the whole society being blackmailed?" I ask.

"Not blackmail, no. It's not like that. I just meant . . . you seem trustworthy."

She says it like she's not being paid enough to and looks around my office again, annoyed. She wanted a nice investigator with a well-decorated, expensive office, not some shady room over a club where you can hear the band through the floorboards. As if on cue, they start to play. She flinches.

"Well, thanks. So what can I do for the society?"

Myrtle pauses, the thing she's been waiting to say suddenly stopping in her mouth. The band keeps playing, and Ava, one of the girls who performs dressed like a girl, starts singing "You Belong to Me." She likes songs about longing and sings them well. The room suddenly feels like it aches, and I think of Gene downstairs.

"Some of our members," Myrtle finally says. "They're missing."

I raise my eyebrows at that. I'm not sure exactly what I was expecting, but this wasn't it.

"Missing?"

"That is, they haven't been to meetings. Our meeting. My discussion group's."

I nod and start taking notes. Her eyes dart to my pen.

"I won't use names, don't worry," I say.

"Well, we don't use names either. Not real ones. Although that's changing now. A lot is changing. . . ." She pauses, as if unsure how to feel about that, but then she nods, assuring herself it's for the best. "Some of us just used our first names before, too. Most people know I'm Myrtle—" She shakes her head, she's getting off the point. "Just be careful," she says, looking at the pen again. She leans back slightly, folds her hands in her lap. "As I said, some of us are missing. Three, precisely. They haven't been to a meeting in months."

"Is that unusual? I didn't think attendance was mandatory."

"It's not, and certainly we have our share of members who just drop in from time to time." She frowns, a little annoyed by that. "But not these three. They'd been members since the first chapter started in San Francisco. Missed a meeting here and there, yes, but not like this. And there was . . ." She sighs. "I should tell you. This is all very private, you must understand."

"I promise, I can keep a secret."

"The society, we had two conferences back in May."

"Conferences?"

"Members from across the country. We have chapters everywhere. More than one in San Francisco."

I nod. The music is still humming.

"And we're large enough we thought there should be a conference. To discuss policy, process, how we will achieve our goal of equal rights. The organization of the group. One of the conferences was in Los Angeles, some of us took a bus down for it."

"Sounds fun."

"Well, it got a bit . . . divisive." She blushes at the word.

"How so?"

"The Fifth Order—that is, the founders, the ones who started the organization—they're from Los Angeles, and while many of us appreciate what they've done, starting the group, and their work for homophile rights, all well and good . . . But a lot of the membership had differing ideas on what that might look like."

"What ideas?" I'm curious now.

"The Fifth Order believe that we homophiles have a unique . . . *culture*, they call it."

They. So she's not with them. "Culture?"

"Female impersonators, women who wear suits, swishy . . ." She sneers, her face turning red. "They think there's something unique about us besides our attraction."

"And you don't?"

"No," she says quickly, almost offended. "The only thing which makes us different from heterosexuals is our attraction to the same sex. Otherwise, we are completely normal, and saying otherwise will only hurt the cause. As will . . ." She frowns again. "It turns out some of the Fifth Order—they unmasked themselves at the end of the second conference, here in San Francisco . . . they're communists." She whispers the last word. "We can't have people like that in the group, you understand. Not the sort of people we want to associate with!" She nods, some fierce combination of fear and fortitude in her expression. "We must prove to society we're just like anybody else. Assimilation is key to obtaining equality. And that's what the majority of the membership at the conference agreed upon."

"So the founders were overruled?"

She nods once, with a little pride. "Yes. And they chose to leave the society."

"I see," I say, taking more notes. Who knew the Mattachines had all the drama of a pulp novel? My friend Lee will love this. "The missing members, they were at these . . . divisive conferences?"

"One of them was. Edward. He came to one meeting after the conferences, but since then, he and his boyfriend, Hank, haven't been back. He was very vocally opposed to the founders. Pointed out they made all homophiles look bad. How they were the ones ruining our chance at assimilation." She sighs. "He's a good boy, Edward, so thoughtful and forthright. Really understands the purpose of Mattachine."

"That his real name?"

Her eyes widen a little. "I . . . well, I don't know. I think so."

"I understand. And who's the third missing member?"

She blushes slightly and looks down, trying to cover it. "Daphne."

Ava's voice rises up through the floorboards again; the room feels cooler, closer, like something is missing.

"Was she at either of the conferences?" I ask.

"No, Daphne is dedicated to the cause but she's shy, and the conferences were going to be large, so she chose to avoid them. She came to meetings for a while after the conferences, but she vanished a few weeks after Edward and Hank."

"And is that her real name?"

"I . . ." Myrtle's never considered that it isn't. Her eyes open wider, a little horrified at the thought. "Yes, it must be."

"You know anything else about them?"

She shakes her head. "Edward mentioned they'd moved up here from LA a few years ago. Said he used to work in the movies. And Hank he said came from a good family."

"A good family?"

She shrugs. "That's how he put it. I assumed he meant rich."

I nod. Sounds right. "How about last names? Parts of town they live in?"

She shakes her head. "We don't want to know those things, in case one of us is brought in by the FBI. They'd consider us some sort of communist cell, the way the papers paint us. That's why it's so important we stay private, so we can't name names, if asked. And why it's so important we achieve these rights, so we can start meeting more publicly. So we won't need to meet at all."

"Not at all?"

"Well"—she shrugs—"I suppose for . . . companionship, or something. A social club. But not a political one, like we are now."

I nod again and don't mention most people I've heard talk about Mattachine say it's a great place to pick up guys.

"So three missing people, whose names you don't know, and a meeting where one of them was strongly opposed to the founders of the Mattachine."

"Vocally so. Edward believes very strongly in assimilation to achieve equality."

"But if that's why he's gone missing—if someone is angry at him for his views—why has Daphne?"

Myrtle blushes again, but this time draws her face up in a sneer. "You're the detective. Figure it out."

"But you do think that Edward, and maybe his boyfriend, Hank, vanished because of something at the conference. That is, the society believes that?"

She glances away. "Just find them, please."

This isn't a job from the society. Just Myrtle. Missing Daphne. Using the name of the organization to give her authority. Maybe none of it is connected with the conference at all. Sometimes, people just leave. But, three around the same time, after a falling-out . . . people don't always just leave.

"All right," I say. "I'm fifty a week, plus expenses."

"That's fine." She stands up, ready to go.

"And I'll need to come to a meeting."

"What?" She looks confused. "Whatever for?"

"You don't know their real names, or anything about them

except that they went to these meetings. Someone else might know something. That's the best way to find them."

She sits back down, annoyed, but considers it for a moment.

"Unless there's somewhere else you think I should start?"

"Well . . . I thought you could go see the founders. They have a new organization down in LA. A magazine."

"You want me to drive to LA and ask them if they're kidnapping members in San Francisco?"

"Well . . ." She looks down. It's exactly what she wanted. But out loud, it sounds absurd.

"It's more likely it's something local. Maybe another member of your chapter."

She looks horrified at that. "No, that can't be. Everyone is very sensible."

"Or they appear to be. Let me come to a meeting—just one. I won't tell anyone what I'm doing there. I can pretend to be a new member. Though if the society is hiring me, maybe everyone will know?"

She frowns at that. "No, no. Only I know . . . and some key people who won't be there."

I nod, letting her have that lie.

"But . . . fine, I see your point. We have a meeting tomorrow." She rattles off an address in Sunset. "We have to stagger our arrivals, so you'll come last; which will be at . . ." She does the math in her head. "Six thirty-four. Exactly. Go to the side door. Say you're there to pick up a package for your wife."

"What do the women say?"

"We say we're there for the cooking lesson."

I nod.

"If anyone asks, say you're grabbing a casserole your wife's friend Eleanor made for her. Be discreet. Dress . . ." She looks me up and down. I'm wearing a bright red tie over a baby blue shirt. "Discreetly. This isn't a nightclub. It's a discussion group. At someone's house. Be careful."

"I promise I will." I try to sound reassuring, but judging by her expression, I fail.

"And don't bring anyone. And burn that when you've memorized it." She nods at my notes.

"I'll be good," I promise. "Do you have any photos of these missing members?"

She pauses, as if it hadn't occurred to her she'd need them. But of course she does. She shakes her head. "We don't take photos, that could be dangerous."

"All right." Not ideal, but understandable. "So you want me to find these folks without knowing what they look like or their real names?" I try to keep my voice even.

She nods, simply, like she doesn't realize how impossible this sounds.

"Can you tell me what these missing members look like, then?"

She makes a face, as if she were being asked to name names in front of Congress, but then she nods. "Daphne is . . ." She looks at her hands. "About thirty. Brown hair, sort of fawn-colored. Pale skin, hazel eyes. She's small, maybe five feet, around there, and slim. Oval face. She has a birthmark on her jaw right . . ." Myrtle tilts her face to point at a spot on her cheek, but then meets my eyes and looks away, straightens her shirt. "Edward is in his twenties or thirties, light brown hair, tall . . . I'm not sure how tall, maybe not quite six feet. Blue eyes. He looks like a poster for a young man just out of college. Hank is taller than him, dark brown hair and eyes, broader than him, too. Muscular. He's a big fellow."

I nod, writing it all down. "Big enough he'd be hard to take down?"

She shrugs. "I suppose. I'm not really sure how . . ." She shakes her head. "Hank is quieter than Edward. I don't know if he can fight if that's what you're asking. I would think not."

"And they're all white?"

She looks surprised by the question, but gives a nod. "Is that all?"

"Unless you can think of anything else that might help me."

She shakes her head and stands up. "No. And I suppose I'll see you tomorrow night if I think of anything in the meanwhile."

I stand up and extend my hand, which she shakes, still wary, then drops and goes to the door. "Thank you," she says softly, without looking back. Then she leaves.

I pull on my earlobe. The Mattachine Society had a breakup. That's interesting.

I head back downstairs. Now that the band is playing, the place is starting to feel alive. Ava is onstage in a blue dress, belting "You You You" with a lot more attitude than the Ames Brothers. She's good, Elsie should move her to a later slot, with more of a crowd. Not that it's entirely empty. Plenty of people have poured in, out of the muggy summer heat. San Francisco usually isn't so bad. Cool ocean breezes sweep away the worst of it. But this summer has been brutal for some reason. The air sticks to you the moment you go outside, and it makes you feel like you're in a sauna in a winter coat. Gene has been ordering extra ice since May. The crowd that's starting to fill up the place is dabbing at their brows with handkerchiefs, ordering the coldest drinks, sweat making long arrows down the backs of their shirts as they dance real slow. Too hot to dance fast. At least not until later.

Gene is busier now, mixing drinks, so I just take my seat at the end of the bar and wait. Elsie, the owner, probably won't be in until later, because she normally spends her days outside town with the family now, playing with her baby, Rina. And Lee isn't on for a few more hours, so will probably be coming in . . . I glance at the door. He comes in on cue.

I've been here over a year now, the detective over the Ruby, the queer detective, and I've definitely found my place—my own seat even, which people leave empty for me. But sometimes I do wonder if I have it a little too figured out at this point. Too routine. Too—

"Comfortable?" Lee asks, sitting next to me. His shirt is unbuttoned enough I can see his undershirt. He puts his hat on the bar and wipes his brow with the back of his hand and meets eyes with Gene. "Just ice water," he says. Gene nods. Lee turns back to me. Sweat pools on his dark brown forehead. He'll go upstairs in a bit, powder his face, put on lipstick. and come down the most perfectly put-together woman in the room. But for now, he's just a sweaty fella like me. "You haven't had to go outside today, have you?" he asks, maybe aware of how disheveled he looks. "It's a beast."

I smile. "Nope, today everything came to me."

Lee smirks as Gene puts ice water in front of him. Gene briefly grazes his hand over mine as he does, cold and wet from the ice, then vanishes to pour someone else's drink. Lee presses the glass to his neck, then drinks deeply.

"You know a couple, in their twenties or thirties, white, Edward and Hank?"

Lee pauses for a moment, going through the address book of his mind. "I know a lot of Edwards and Hanks, not sure how many are together. Certainly no regulars here."

I nod. That makes sense, based on what Myrtle was saying. Too much "queer culture" here, if Edward and Hank are anything like her. Not every Mattachine member is. "Weird case came in."

"Matchmaking?" Lee helps run our little matchmaking business, pairing up queer people in heterosexual-looking relationships to appease work or family, and crafting stories for them: how they met, how they ended it. It's half my business at this point. I like it, it's easy and helps people out. But it's not especially interesting these days.

"No, much stranger," I say. "Woman hired me on behalf of the Mattachine Society."

Lee's eyes go wide. "Well, la-di-da, someone is moving up in the world."

"She was just trying to sound more impressive. I think it's just her hiring me. But some members have gone missing, and apparently there was a big break in leadership a few months back. You hear about this?"

"Bits and pieces. But I don't pay much attention to the Mattachine. Secret names, code words, masks—too much trouble, if you ask me."

I nod, agreeing, but I also understand why the Mattachine Society does it. Organizing for gay rights is exactly the sort of thing the government would label an un-American activity. They're probably being spied on, so it's smart to keep things anonymous. Being queer is trouble enough—trying to work for queer rights? That's dangerous.

"Well, I'm going to a meeting tomorrow night."

Lee laughs. "Better break out your old gray suit."

"She was really just interested in the missing girl, Daphne. Sounds like they had something going on. Except the client, she never knew anything real about Daphne because she's clearly a stickler for Mattachine protocol. Flinched when I asked her to describe the missing folks."

Lee laughs. "Hey, that's one way out of a relationship—never give them your name in the first place."

I laugh with him, shaking my head. At least with Lee asking around for Edward and Hank, something might come up. Or at the meeting tomorrow.

Gene comes back over, free for a moment, and takes my hands. "That lady hire you?"

"She did. Some missing Mattachine members."

"Oh." Gene nods. "I know a few of them. They seem like good folks."

"Well-intentioned, anyway."

"But remember, your case cannot interfere with your birthday."

I sigh. "Gene, I don't need a—"

"Birthday?" Lee asks. "We doing a party?"

"He had only just moved in last year when he turned thirty-six, none of us knew it was his birthday. Elsie has this plan where we're going to start the party the night before and ring in his birthday at midnight, like it's New Year's. And I gotta do what the boss says." Gene winks at me.

"Will I be performing at this party?" Lee asks. "I do a fantastic 'Happy Birthday.' I'll wear my silver dress."

"No," I say. "We don't need a party. I am happy with my annual call from my mother and a few people maybe buying me drinks, but we don't need to do more than that."

"You drink free," Lee says. "We all drink free."

"Even better," I say.

Another patron calls Gene for a drink and he hurries over. I turn to watch Ava onstage and Lee follows.

"She's good," Lee says.

"Yeah, not as good as you though."

He grins. "You always know the right thing to say." He puts the water to his neck again, and I almost laugh, thinking of Myrtle, who clearly didn't think I ever said the right thing. "You really all right with a party?" he asks suddenly. "You know Elsie can go real big."

I shrug. "I don't know how big she could go with a birthday party. I'm not sure who would show. You, Gene, Pat. No one from Lavender House would risk being seen here. Maybe my old friend Helen, but Elsie has some kind of rivalry with her, so I don't think she'd send the invite."

"Oh, Elsie'll make it big somehow, trust me. Better tell her exactly when you're expecting that call from your mother so she doesn't interrupt."

"Between ten and noon, same as Christmas and Easter. Mom's a nurse, likes to keep things on a regular schedule."

"She still works?" Lee spins the ice in his now-empty glass.

"Oh sure. She was a nurse before the war, didn't see a reason to stop after. She's got what Dad left her, but I think she does it to keep busy, and because she likes it. She likes . . ."

"Helping people? Family trait, I guess."

I laugh. I hadn't ever considered it that way until now. "Guess so. She switched to a private clinic a few years back, too. Says it's fancy, quiet, with better hours."

Lee nods. "Mary Mills, nurse in LA. I bet she's swell."

I smile, thinking of Mom. Always a little too close growing up, like a plastic wrap you can't quite pick off, but since I moved away, we only really talk a few times a year. I've gotten enough distance to see her as her own person. "Some people think of their mothers as these little fragile things knitting or something, but my mom never did. I mean, she can knit, sure, but she's always ten steps ahead of everyone around her, organized, efficient. Not cold. Just . . . prepared."

"She know about you? About Gene?"

My smile falls. I sip the mostly empty drink I'd been nursing since before Myrtle showed up. "No. I don't think she'd . . . No."

"What does she know about your life?"

"Just that I'm a detective. What does your mom know?"

Lee laughs, but his eyes are sad. "Oh, she knows everything, it's why we haven't spoken in almost a decade. She wrote me when my daddy died, which was kind of her, though. Said not to come to the funeral, but I could stop by his grave later, if I wanted. So it's nice yours still calls you."

"Yeah. Sorry about yours."

He shrugs. "Life is what it is. But if we talk more about this, I'm going to need more than water, and I gotta go put on my face, so let's drop it."

"All right."

"You want anything for your birthday?" he asks, standing up from his barstool.

"Just be nice to see you."

"That you can count on."

He winks, then walks away, headed to the dressing rooms upstairs to change for his act. I turn back to Gene just as he sets down a drink in front of me. It's a vibrant blue, in a highball glass with a slice of lemon.

"Testing something?" I ask.

"I had this idea, we could create unique drinks just for the Ruby, all named after gemstones. This is sapphire. The color is from blue curaçao. Try it."

"You're not starting with ruby?" I bring the drink to my lips. It smells of orange and citrus.

"Ruby would be the one we wouldn't have, because that's the name of the club."

I sip. It's orange and lemon, but something else, too. I cough. Gene raises an eyebrow. "No?"

"Too sweet. Tastes like a kids' drink."

He tilts his head, considering. "Some folks would like that, but . . . maybe something to mellow it. . . ." He takes the drink back and sips, making a face, then mixes something from another bottle into it, then sips.

"Elsie isn't really planning a big to-do for my birthday, is she?" I try not to sound too worried as I ask it.

He smiles and hands me the drink. "I think it's like an anniversary party, really. A year of you, working here. More than that, I know, but she wants to celebrate . . . a lot."

"And you're not stopping her?" I sip the drink. It's better now, less like sugar water.

"She's my boss." Gene puts his hands up and shrugs, like he's powerless in this situation.

"You're my boyfriend. You're supposed to tell her how I won't like anything big."

"I did." He leans forward, smiling, chin in his hand. "How's the drink?"

"It's good. How convincing were you when you told her?"

"Not very."

I sigh.

"I've managed to keep her from going too all out. She was going to have Lee write a song about you."

"Well, thanks for that."

"Why don't you want a big party anyway? When all your friends want to throw you one?"

"I just..." I shake my head. One year of being a PI for the queer folks in town doesn't make up for the years I was a cop and wasn't helping them. "I want something small. Just some friends. You and me, maybe, going out to eat somewhere nice where we can hold hands under the table."

He smiles and takes my hand. "We can do that, too."

I squeeze his hand and we look at each other a moment as the band plays, but then someone calls out to him and he's gone. I finish the blue drink watching the band, and Lee comes down a while later, dress and lipstick on, and starts her set with "Love Me or Leave Me." I watch her sing, and when another bartender shows up, I even get to have a dance or two with Gene. Maybe I'll let Elsie throw me her ridiculous birthday/anniversary party. I may not deserve it, but my friends do. And after a year of this, living openly in the shadows, it might be good to mark that. One year of having a real life, or something that looks a lot more like it than when I was a cop. I might not quite have made amends yet, but I have had a good year.

Tomorrow I have to try living the old way again, though. Putting on a gray suit and showing up with a fake name. It's not quite the same, but the Mattachine folks know how to lead secret lives. So who's been taking them out one by one?

TWO

The sound of Gene turning on the shower wakes me. He stayed over last night, slipping into my bed after I was already asleep, and curling his head onto my chest. I woke up briefly to smile down at his face, lit pink by the Ruby's neon sign just outside the window, and wrap my arm around him before we were both asleep again. He still has his own place—mine is too small to keep all our stuff together—but he's got a key to mine, too, and he stays over a few nights a week. We've talked about getting a place somewhere with a landlord who wouldn't ask too many questions, but then I won't be right across from the office anymore and easily available to Elsie if there's trouble. Besides, I think Gene likes only having to walk upstairs after a long night of managing the bar. So I've tried to give him some space in my little studio apartment. Moved some of my records and clothes into the office. It's working out all right.

    I stretch in bed and then get up, going into the bathroom and pulling aside the shower curtain to watch Gene, naked under the spray of water, his bronze skin gleaming. He grins at me, inviting me to join him. Mornings are like this a lot now. Not that I'm complaining. After we've moved back to the bed, and then back to the shower again to clean up for real, we run out and grab breakfast at the greasy spoon down the street, before returning to the Ruby, where he starts his day, and I start looking for Myrtle's missing people.

    Without their real names, it's a long shot, but I call in to various police stations pretending to be a reporter and asking about missing persons. There are a lot, but none of the names are Edward, Hank, or Daphne. Then I try the coroner, but the only unidentified body they have is that of an old woman they found in the street. I call Lee at the music store he works at and ask him to grab a bunch of missing posters from the police station today on his way over, tell them he works for a lawyer if anyone asks. He knows I can't exactly swing by the police station without one of the boys in blue recognizing me and trying to finish what they started when they found me in a gay club the first time. I spend the rest of the day before the Mattachine meeting going over a few matchmaking clients we have, creating whole dramas they have to perform just to keep their jobs or homes.

The band starts practicing around five, and Lee shows up with my missing person posters a little after that. I thank him and flip through their faces as I shave and put on my old gray suit, white shirt, black tie. Most of the missing posters are of women, less than half of them white. Myrtle had been most descriptive of Daphne, so I pull out the posters that might fit her description—only four of them—and put them in my briefcase. Of the few missing men, five could be one or the other of the men, so they go in the briefcase, too.

I straighten my tie and head downstairs, giving Gene a kiss and letting him tell me to be careful, before I hop on the trolley and take it to Sunset. The sun is still bright and hot, and though the trolley windows are open, the air coming through doesn't do anything to cool me down. By the time I find the house, I can feel the sweat streaking down my spine. I wipe my face with my handkerchief and find an out-of-the-way place to sit until it's my time to knock on the door.

Sunset is a nice little residential area. The houses are cheerful shades of yellow and white, and there's a mix of hedges and white picket fences between them. I find a bench next to a small playground and watch men pulling into their driveways, waving at one another, meeting women at the door, a peck on the lips before going inside, maybe a kid calling out for Daddy. They all look so deeply similar, these lives. I wonder what they'd do if they knew a secret meeting of gay organizers was happening just next door.

The house I'm going to is white with pale blue shutters. They're closed, which in this heat is suspicious enough I start to think that maybe these Mattachine members aren't as good at hiding out as they think they are. Inside must be like an oven. I watch a pair of women go up to the door, each of them in plain dresses, hair in nearly identical curls. One wears cat-eye glasses. They're both in heels and are carrying trays of food, like for a potluck. One knocks on the side door, and it opens slightly. They whisper a few words and go inside.

If I were a neighbor, I might think it's a little strange, but not worth reporting to anyone. If I were a Fed, though . . . I look around. Down the street, there's a black Packard parked at the curb, not in a driveway like a local, and I can see two silhouettes in it. Could be nothing, just two guys waiting for a friend, or checking a map. Or it could be a stakeout.

I glance down at my watch. It's my turn.

Careful to keep my face turned away from the Packard, I head to the side door and knock. It opens very slightly.

"Yes?" asks a voice. Myrtle. I see one of her eyes staring out at me, waiting. She recognizes me, but I still need to give the password, apparently.

"I'm here to pick up a package for my wife," I say. She opens the door just wide enough for me to slip inside.

It's not as muggy as I feared it would be. The windows in the large living room open onto the backyard, green curtains drifting in the breeze from a ceiling fan. The house is beige, like the background of a movie—and the people are like extras. About a dozen others are already here, all dressed conservatively, the men in plain suits, the women in skirts or dresses. Some chairs have been placed in a semicircle in the center of the room, and by the windows is a table with some plates and some dishes—it really is a potluck.

"Nice place," I say to Myrtle. "You live alone?"

She frowns. "We try not to ask too many personal questions," she murmurs. Then she makes her face a smile and turns to the others, who have been eyeing me with curiosity. "Everyone, this is the new member I told you about." She looks at me expectantly.

"Hello." I nod at them all. "Thank you for having me. I'm Andy."

A flicker passes over Myrtle's face, doing the math—it's my name, but it's short for Evander, not Andrew, so it's half a disguise.

"That's everyone here," Myrtle says. "Why don't we get started?"

I'm not sure what getting started means. But everyone takes a seat, and I join them. Myrtle stands up and begins the meeting by going over the usual sort of organizational stuff: roll call, the address to write if anyone would like to sign up for the newsletter, with promises of anonymity. Then there's a reminder to pay dues, and a report on statewide goings-on, of which there are only a few, mostly larger lectures. A young woman raises her hand and Myrtle nods.

"Since we have a new member, shouldn't we all take the membership pledge?"

Myrtle's eyes flicker over to me, then back. "Oh, well, I wasn't sure if, after everything, we were still going to do that. It might be a bit . . ."

"I like it," says a young man in a gray suit that matches mine. "I don't think there's anything wrong with it."

I see some people nodding, and Myrtle glances up at me, her eyes almost apologetic for a moment, before turning hard again. "Very well, let's all gather up. Andy, I have a copy of the pledge right here. Don't worry, we'll all say it together."

I swallow, wondering what it is I'm about to pledge, then swallow again when I see everyone holding hands in a circle. There's a music stand in front of Myrtle, my lines on a piece of paper on it. I take her hand and the hand of the gray-suited man on my other side, and start to read. Everyone else apparently has it memorized, chanting in unison in that listless way people do in church. I mumble along. It's okay to fake it, I think, as long as it's in service of finding these missing people.

"I swear to conduct myself in a way that will reflect credit upon myself and the organization. To respect the rights of all racial, religion, and national minorities." I look around the crowd of white faces. "To observe the generally accepted social rules of dignity and propriety at all times, in my conduct, attire, and speech." I try not to smirk thinking of my wardrobe at home. I own a pink tie. And a lavender one. And I work at a gay bar with female impersonators. Not sure how much propriety these folks would think I had left. "To unconditionally guard the anonymity of all members of the Mattachine.

"We are resolved that our people shall find equality of security and production in tomorrow's world." Well, that part is nice. "We are sworn that no boy or girl, approaching the maelstrom of deviation, need make that crossing alone, afraid and in the dark ever again." That part is nice, too. Language is a little over the top, but it's nice. Everyone around me is smiling as they say it. "In these moments we dedicate ourselves once again to each other in the immense significance of such allegiance, with dignity and respect, proud and free."

By the end of it, I feel a little misty-eyed. Maybe I was wrong to judge these folks. They want the same things everyone at the Ruby does. The same things I try to get people, if only in small doses.

We break hands and Myrtle looks at me, catching the emotion that's welled up, and for the first time, she smiles at me. Really smiles in a way I haven't seen, her whole face glowing. She squeezes my arm, and then motions for everyone to sit.

"Well," she says, "now that that's settled, let's get started. Dr. Bryner?"

I return to my seat in the back, a few of my now-fellow Mattachines offering me handshakes or pats on the back. Up front, an older man steps forward. He hadn't been part of the circle, I realize. He'd been standing to the side. Myrtle introduces him as their special guest, a psychiatrist, who will be speaking about homophilia.

Everyone listens attentively as he speaks. He talks about Kinsey and "the pathology of sexual deviance," a phrase that makes my hair stand on end, but everyone else nods along to it. I try to tune most of it out.

"What about swishy men, or men who dress as women?" asks a man in his forties after the lecture is over.

"Or the women who wear suits?" asks a woman next to him.

"That's a different pathology entirely," Dr. Bryner says. "Though interlinked with homosexuality in some cases, it speaks to a deeper deviance. One that should be treated."

Everyone smiles, relieved. The good feeling I had from the second part of the oath leaves me in a shudder. This is not the Ruby. Lee and Elsie, my closest friends, wouldn't be welcome here. These people may be queer, but they're not my people. Maybe the missing members just got disgusted and left.

"And what do you say to the idea of integration for homosexuals who conform to proper society in all other aspects?" asks a woman.

"Well," the doctor says, "if the deviance cannot be rectified, then society ought not discriminate against them any more than it would someone unfortunate enough to be born blind, or unable to use their legs. Such people are to be pitied, not ostracized. I believe many homosexuals can live good and productive lives and be a boon for society." He smiles magnanimously, and the crowd applauds.

After the lecture, Myrtle thanks the doctor, and only then does the potluck portion begin, and I can finally get to work. Mingling isn't hard; the guy in the matching suit is next to me before I even get a look at the drinks, offering me a beer, cold from the fridge.

"Too hot to wear a suit inside, right? But we can't exactly strip down in front of the ladies." He grins.

Well, I know why he's here. "It is hot," I say, taking the beer. It's already slick with sweat.

"I'm Carl. Andy, right?"

"That's me. My friends Hank and Edward asked me to join." I look around, as if confused. "I guess they couldn't make it tonight, though."

He looks around, then turns back to me and shrugs. "Yeah, they haven't been in a while. Good guys."

"You know them outside the meetings? That allowed?" I grin

like it's a funny question and take a swig of the beer. It's bitter, but at least it's cold.

He laughs, takes the moment to lean in so close I can smell his cologne. "Sure, sure, plenty of us hang out outside meetings. You weren't supposed to mention it, but seems like rules are changing."

"Yeah, I heard about that." I sip my beer again, waiting for him to go on.

"It's all above my head." He drinks from his own beer. "Before, we kept secrets from each other, but then they were sending mailers out to politicians. Now that we've kicked out the commies, we won't talk to politicians, but you can know I'm Carl. Honestly, seems like a safer policy to me."

I nod. "Edward mentioned that. You know, I haven't seen them at all, come to think of it. Not even at the bar." I take a sip, then snap in the air in front of me. "You know, the one they're always at."

"The Silver Jay?"

"That's it." I know the Silver Jay. Blue-collar guys and white-collar guys hoping to meet them. Sleazy manager, too.

"Never seen you there, though. I'd remember." Carl lifts his eyebrows, inviting, and I laugh politely.

"My boyfriend and I haven't been going out as much lately."

He nods, pursing his lips to hide his frown. I feel bad for a moment, leading the guy on, but I got what I needed. Now I just need something on Daphne.

Carl and I exchange a few more pleasantries before he excuses himself, and I check out the food as a reason to sidle up next to Myrtle, who stands watching the buffet like a lifeguard in case anyone takes more than their portion.

"Who here was close with Daphne?" I ask her quietly. "Who did she talk to the most?"

Myrtle blinks, first annoyed, then considering the question. "Me," she finally says, with a shrug.

"There must have been someone else. Did she ever get a lift from anyone?"

"We leave in pairs, male and female, for appearances. Or groups. Daphne . . . she usually left with Hank and Edward, actually. I remember they gave her a ride home once because it was raining and she didn't want to walk to the trolley."

"So they'd know where she lives?"

Myrtle considers this, looking sad. "I suppose so. I don't know why I never . . ." She shakes her head. "Secrecy. I made an oath. We all did." She reaches out to squeeze my arm as she did before. "I saw how it affected you, Andy. It's a powerful thing, belonging."

"Just playing my part," I say. "Did they always leave together?" I'm wondering if that's why they would be the missing ones—someone going after one of them, but ending up with all three. A personal motive and someone being in the wrong place at the wrong time strikes me as more likely than some conspiracy by the Mattachine founders to pick off the folks who have spoken out against them.

"Not always," Myrtle says.

So they could be unrelated. But if Hank and Edward knew Daphne's address, or at least her neighborhood, they can point me in her direction. And right now, I can go check out their local watering hole.

"I have something for you to look over. Can I give it to you?"

She looks around, then says too loudly, "Come help me refill the ice bucket, would you?"

I nod and follow her into the kitchen, a little white-and-yellow affair. She starts filling the ice bucket, and I take out the envelope with the missing person posters in it.

"I just want you to look at these and tell me if any of them are the missing members," I say in a low voice.

"Now?"

"It can be after everyone has gone home. I left my card in there, too, so you can call. It's discreet."

She nods, then hands me the ice bucket, eyeing the envelope like it might sting her. Then, shoulders back, she takes it and tucks it behind some cans of beans in a cupboard. "I'll remember it and look later. I can call late?"

"Yeah. I'm going to head out, try another lead, but I'll be back in the office later. If someone else picks up, you can leave a message."

She frowns at that.

"Just say no if they aren't there, and the names if you do. You can say you're MB, if you need to."

She considers that, then nods. I've never had to be this cloak-and-dagger, but it seems to be the only way she'll help.

"Right. Then I'm off. Thanks for having me."

"Oh." She looks a bit surprised. "You don't want to stay? These are good people, Andy. Knowing them might . . . improve your state of life a little."

I shake my head. It was a long oath we took, holding hands. Some parts I liked. Others not so much. And I've already seen what it is to live a life in just parts. To try to become what you think will help you fit in. It's like wearing a gray suit, same as everybody else's. You start to forget who you are and just focus on the we. These aren't bad people, but they're not my people either.

"I like my life just fine. And you hired me to find your people, so that's what I'm going to do." I pause. She means well. "Thank you though." I nod my goodbyes at people and then grab my hat and head for the door.

Outside, the black Packard is still parked down the street. The sun is low now, glinting off the windshield, so I can't get a good look inside. I keep my face turned away as I walk.

THREE

I've been to the Silver Jay maybe a dozen times. It wasn't one of my preferred spots when I was still a cop, and I've only come here as a detective, never socially. It's a dive bar in the Tenderloin, out of sight behind the shops, marked on the door with a black bird that must have been gray at some point. All the shops are closed now, the streets quiet, and the boys who drive the trucks and load stock come here to mingle with guys in suits from the financial district, or guys in denim or leather from the industrial district. They have performers sometimes. Lee worked here once, female impersonators dressed like movie stars who tell raunchy jokes and mingle with the patrons for laughs. But it's not like the Ruby. There's less dancing and more pawing; the whole place feels like a growl and a stare across the bar.

It's hot tonight. The few windows are closed, covered in black wood, and it's stuffy, smelling heavily of sweat, cigarettes, leather, and smoke, smells that can be good, but here have turned stale. The tinny jukebox plays Peggy Lee, "Black Coffee." The dim wall sconces turn the smoke that hangs in the air yellow and dark. When I walk in, a bunch of guys at the bar look over, evaluating. A few smile and lean back in invitation. Everyone has stripped down because of the heat, or at least they're using it as an excuse. Shirts are unbuttoned, and some guys are down to white undershirts or tees, dark runs of moisture on all of them, turning the white transparent, showing skin and hair underneath.

There's a young guy behind the bar, all muscles, blond hair a little shaggy. Behind him is the same sign I remember—

WARNING: YOU ARE SUBJECT TO A RAID AT ANY TIME. Other places have systems: red lights, switching partners. Not the Silver Jay. Here you just get what you get.

"What'll it be?" the bartender asks.

I think about asking for the manager, Bert. I helped him out when I returned blackmail photos. But what I need now is information on the regulars, and I've never seen Bert outside his little office in the back. So I settle onto a stool and ask for a Scotch. The bartender brings it to me and I pay him, then put a hefty tip on the table.

"I'm looking for some guys I know. Haven't seen them in a while. They mentioned coming here though."

The bartender eyes the cash, still folded between my fingers, then snatches it without looking up. "You a cop?" he asks, pocketing the bills, finally meeting my eye. He pushes his shoulders back a little so I can see the full swell of his muscles.

"Not a cop. Bert can vouch for that."

He softens at the mention of Bert's name, seems more curious. "Just looking for friends?"

"Hank and Edward." I briefly describe them the way Myrtle did. "Haven't seen them in a while."

The bartender nods. "I remember them."

A guy sits down a few stools away, and the bartender's eyes flash over to him. The bartender looks at me for a beat, then sidles down the bar and gives the guy a beer before coming back to me. He walks slowly, still considering.

"What do you want them for?" he asks me.

"Just looking for them. Worried because I haven't seen them in a while."

He smirks at that. "Yeah. Well, I think Hank, the tall one—I think you won't see him again for a long time."

I feel a shiver down my back, but keep my face still. "Why's that?"

"He took off."

"Took off?"

"Yeah, with"—he leans forward and lowers his voice—"some motorcycle gang."

"What?" I immediately think of the Hollister Riot from six years ago—a rally turned sour, violent. It was all over the papers, that photo of the guy leaning back on his motorcycle, hat askew, shirt open, defiant, drunk, smashed glass all around him. The press went so mad for it I couldn't tell what was true, but all the papers painted a nasty picture. That's what's stayed with me—stayed with everyone. Even the ad with the kid giving a nun a ride on his Harley-Davidson couldn't change how the public thinks of motorcycles now. Certainly not the sort of thing a boy from the Mattachine Society should be involved in. Not much "generally accepted social rules of dignity and propriety" in that kind of thing.

"He took off with a motorcycle gang?" I ask, still trying to figure it out.

"I think so. Those two used to come in, every couple days or so. Then this gang rolls in. I was pretty scared when they first showed up, honestly. Thought they were here to hunt fairies or something." He smirks. "And I guess they were, just not like that."

I feel my eyebrows raise. "They were gay?"

"The whole gang." He nods, happy to be telling this outrageous story. "I heard them say they were up from LA, on a trip."

I nod, not wanting to interrupt.

"So, they pull in, and your friends spot them, and they all start sitting together, chatting, flirting. That first night, they all left together."

I smirk. Not very Mattachine at all, boys.

"Then they're all back here every night for a week, drinking, flirting. Except after night three, it's just the tall one. And no one seems to notice his boyfriend is gone. Or least, no one seems to mind it. A few more days of that, and then they're all gone. Back to LA, I guess. Haven't seen any of them here since."

"Thanks," I say, working through this information. "How do you know they were a gang, and not just some guys who like motorcycles?"

He smiles, proud of himself. "The patches on their jackets. All the same."

"Patches? What kind?"

"Just patches like on a jacket. They looked like a . . ." He reaches behind him and takes down a coupe glass with a rounded bottom. It's covered in dust; people don't order martinis here. "This, in purple and black. That's it."

"Huh. No words? A motto?"

He shakes his head.

"Well"—I hand him another dollar—"thanks. You've been helpful."

"Sure thing." The bartender goes to another patron, glad to have told his story, and I sip my Scotch. It's cheap, tastes like tires, but it warms me up. Hank and Edward were fooling around with a gay biker gang. That's one hell of a sentence. But if the bartender isn't pulling my leg, then sounds like Edward got bored with it. Or maybe they got bored with Edward. Could they have killed him? I scratch behind my ear. If they did, they've hid the body well, I already checked the morgues.

Either way, I only have one lead left—these bikers, whom Hank left with. Or, if he didn't, they're the last ones to see him. Myrtle already wanted me to visit LA, to check out the ousted

Mattachine founders. Her theory, that they're picking off the folks who were against them, still doesn't hold much water. But if they knew this gay biker gang and sent them for Edward, and they... had some fun first? Maybe convinced Hank to help them, if the relationship was unhappy? I take another sip. It's hard to make these two pieces fit.

I drink the rest of the Scotch in one swallow, letting it burn on the way down, then I head back to the Ruby. I go upstairs to change first, the gray suit stiff and uncomfortable.

My office phone is ringing. "Hello? Amethyst Investigations."

"Andy?" Myrtle asks cautiously.

"Yes, hi, Myrtle. I've found some things out."

"Oh." She sounds relieved. "But be careful with your language. Never know who's listening." I remember the car parked outside the Mattachine meeting. It's possible her phone is tapped. "Did you find Daphne?"

"No." I frown a little and sit down in my chair. I can hear the music and laughter from the club below me, the chatter of the drag performers in the hall. "I assume you didn't recognize anyone from the missing posters."

"No." She sounds nervous. "That's good, right?"

"Could be." All it really means is no one else has noticed them missing. "I did get a lead on Edward and Hank, though."

"What?"

I take a breath. This one might shock her. "They were hanging around with a motorcycle gang from LA."

She gasps and is silent for a moment.

I wait a beat. "I know that's a lot to take in."

"But LA—could they have been sent by"—she pauses, finding a code word—"the founders?"

"I'd thought of that, too." Though it still sounds a bit out there. "They seem to have gone back to LA and taken Hank with them."

"Kidnapped him?"

"Not the way it was told to me. But I think it makes sense for me to head down to LA, try to find them. It's the only lead I have right now."

"Then you must investigate the founders while you're down there, too. I have—" She sighs. "I know of a meeting, like the ones we have, in LA, run by my friend Samuel. I'll give you his phone number. He knows I was thinking of hiring someone, so you tell him that you're the PI Myrtle hired and then tell him . . ." She thinks for a moment. "Tell him his mother's recipe for apple pie had too much cinnamon. That should prove to him you are who you say."

I take a few notes, then write down the number as she gives it to me. "All right. I don't know if the founders are involved, but it'll be good to have a contact there. Maybe he can direct me to this motorcycle gang."

"Oh no, I don't think so. Samuel wouldn't associate with those types. I didn't think Edward and Hank would, either, but maybe it was blackmail, or threats. If the founders sent them, there could be all sorts of reasons."

I don't say that it sounded like there was only one reason—sex. "I'll head down there tomorrow. It'll take me a few days. I'll call in to let you know if I find anything."

"Thank you." She pauses. "This will lead to Daphne, right?"

Daphne, not Edward and Hank. They're just collateral to her. "If nothing else, they know her address, which should make finding her a lot easier." I hope. If the bikers haven't killed them—either at the orders of the Mattachine founders, or just for fun.

Myrtle says good night and I hang up the phone. There's

a knock on the door and Lee strides in, now dressed and in makeup, ready to go on. Her lipstick is on, so she, not he.

"You look tired," she says. "Those Mattachine folks drain the life out of you?"

I smirk. "Sort of. They have a narrow vision of who should be getting equal rights."

"Not people like me, you mean?" She flutters her eyelashes and pats her elaborate hairdo.

"No." I frown. "But they said some good stuff, too. About making sure no queer person felt alone, especially when they're young and figuring it out."

"Well, sure, they're probably not all bad. And I don't mean some of them are bad, I mean all of them are some mix of good and bad, same as the rest of us."

"I think some of them are just scared. Running for their gray suits, trying to blend in, hoping it'll save them from something."

"Straight people," she says, then sits down opposite me. She's in a dark blue satin dress, nearly purple, and has white flowers in her hair. "You're wearing your old gray suit."

"I came up to change."

"You thinking about what it was like when you were a cop?"

I nod. I've felt that old Andy following me around all day like a shadow. "A little."

"I remember you from then. You're not the same."

"I know, that's why I think I feel"—I search for the word and find it immediately—"sorry for these Mattachine folks. I pity them. Their fear. They want to blend in so much. I used to want that, too. Would have given anything for this suit to really keep me safe. Wouldn't think about folks like you at all."

Lee raises an eyebrow, skeptical. "I don't think you give yourself enough credit."

"I was scared back then. You remember. Never made a friend."

"Well, you have friends now."

I nod. "I'm glad I didn't become like them. So determined to blend in they turn against all of us who aren't. But then they're also organizing. They're staging political actions. So that's brave, and part of me admires them. I feel like if I could just bring them all down to the Ruby, they'd change their outlook."

Lee grins. "That's a real foolish idea, Andy. But a nice one."

"I changed, right?"

"You're not everyone."

I smile, it's nice to hear. And she's right, I'm not everyone. And not everyone can do the penance I'm trying to do, trying to make up for who I was. Even if everyone is telling me all's forgiven, it never quite feels that way. "That's why I gotta find these folks, even if they're not exactly . . . our folks."

"I know." She nods. "And who would you be if you decided some queer people were worth saving, and some weren't?"

"I'd be too much like them."

She laughs. "No. That's not the same. But you wouldn't be you."

I laugh, too, and stand up. "Well, I guess I'm going to LA then."

She raises an eyebrow. "Really?"

"Yep." I loosen my tie. "To chase a motorcycle gang."

Her eyes go wide, like I hoped they would. "What?" Lee loves the excitement of my cases.

"Let me change, and I'll tell you as much as I can before you go on."

With my lavender tie, holding a green drink Gene called an Emerald, I feel back to myself. I tell both Lee and Gene about what I found out. When I'm done, Lee is thrilled, but Gene is frowning.

"You're going to LA?" he asks. "When will you be back?"

"Depends what I find there, I guess."

"So you'll miss your birthday?"

Lee sips her drink, eyes flicking between the two of us.

"Maybe?" I offer. "I'll try to be back by then."

Gene sighs. "Andy . . ." Then he glances over at Lee. "Aren't you on next?"

"Stan has to finish," she says.

"He's just about done," Gene says, nodding at the stage, as Stan belts out "No Other Love." "Lee, please?"

She sighs and stands up. "It's not like you're in a private corner."

"Little different than having someone watching us like we're *I Love Lucy*," Gene says.

Lee shrugs and walks toward the stage, and I turn back to Gene. "It's not a big deal."

"You're not just doing this to get out of the party?" He takes my hand. "I know you don't want it, but I do think you'll like it."

"A big loud thing with Lee singing 'Happy Birthday' and a bunch of strangers there for free booze?" I shake my head. "I don't need that."

"That's not what it'll be. How long will you be in LA?"

"If I leave tomorrow, stop at some cheap motel on the way, I should get in before the next night."

"And then how long will the case take you?"

I shrug. "I really don't know. I gotta find this gang, talk to the founders, find this couple . . ."

"Do you want me to come with you? I can ask Elsie for some time off."

I smile and squeeze his hand. That's sweet. This will be the first time we're apart for a while since getting together. "You gonna miss me?"

He raises an eyebrow. "I'm more worried you're going to miss me and my medical skills. I need you to come back in one piece or Elsie is going to be very annoyed about having to cancel the party."

I laugh. "You want to tag along as my nurse?"

He raises his chin a little. "Yes. Don't act like you haven't needed a nurse before. It's how we met. And now you're going after a biker gang?"

"Don't worry, if I get beat up, I'll go see my mother."

He looks offended. "Your mother?"

"I wasn't planning to tell her I was in town, but in an emergency . . ."

"You're just going to show up at her door, bruised and bloody?"

"It's how I first showed up at yours."

He narrows his eyes. "And she'll just bandage you up?"

"She's my mother."

"Without any questions?"

I sigh. "Well . . . she's my mother."

He nods.

"But she knows I'm a PI now. I'll just tell her I'm working a case I can't talk about. She'll patch me up, make me chicken soup."

He scoffs. "My *arroz caldo* would be better."

I bring his hand to my lips. "I know it would. And I'd love to bring you. But you have a job here, and where I'm going could be dangerous."

"That's why I should come." He sighs. But I can tell he's given up. He knows he can't leave Elsie so suddenly with no one to manage the bar while he's gone.

"When I get back, how about we go on a trip, just the two of us? Somewhere no one will ask questions."

He smiles at that, then takes his hand back. "Maybe. We'll see if Elsie will let me."

"Let you what?" asks Elsie, who hops onto the stool next to me. "Oh, good, just in time." She's facing the stage, where Stan is taking his third bow to very light applause. But behind him, Lee steps out, and the applause grows into a roar. Stan, thinking for a moment it's for him, grins hugely, patting his red wig and blowing kisses to the crowd before he realizes, and the smile turns forced as he nods at Lee and exits. Lee turns to the band, taps her finger in the air, and then they all break into "Your Cheatin' Heart."

Gene hands Elsie a highball when she turns back around. "What am I letting you do?"

"I wanted to take Gene on a little vacation, when I'm back," I say.

"Back from where?" She sucks on the straw in her drink, eyes narrowing.

"My case is taking me to LA."

"And when will you be returning?" she asks, her voice cool. I glance at Gene, but he's edged away from us, is making a drink for someone else.

"I'm not sure."

"You'll be back for your birthday," she says. Not a question.

"I will try." I give her my most winning smile.

"I am planning quite the shindig, Evander. You're the guest of honor. No bailing."

"You don't need to do all that."

She smirks. "Andy, I do. And I will. And you'll be here for it."

"It's a long drive to LA, and then I'm not sure how long it'll take to find this motorcycle gang, but I will try, promise."

She doesn't even flinch at "motorcycle gang," like I'd hoped. She just keeps staring me down.

"Why is it so important? It's just a party, right? You throw one every night." I gesture at the crowd.

"You're part of the community, now, Andy. Part of the Ruby. You've helped a lot of people—no, I see your mouth opening, don't interrupt me with your sad-sack-haven't-helped-enough-people-to-make-up-for-who-I-was nonsense right now." I close my mouth. "You've helped people, and that should be celebrated. You should be celebrated. You've come a long way, and you need to have a spotlight on you for that, for just one night, because it'll show other people that they can come a long way, too. It's not about you."

I sigh. "I get it. I'll do everything I can to make sure I'm back."

"Good. Because it'll also help you drum up more business."

I shake my head, smiling. "How's Rina?" Rina is her daughter. Well, hers and everyone else's at Lavender House.

"She's good. She's starting to talk."

"Isn't she a little young?" I'm not sure, but Rina can't be more than nine months.

"She's advanced. She went 'El' when I came into the room today."

"El?"

"Well, sort of an *ellllll* sound, but she's trying."

I laugh. We talk a bit more about the family and Lee sings some more, and Gene dances with me a little, before we go upstairs to bed and I feel the comforts of his body next to me all night. Tomorrow, I'll be leaving this place, going farther away than I have been in a year. I haven't left San Francisco since '46, when I drove down to see my mother after the war ended.

I lie on my back, Gene asleep on my chest, and wonder if I should stop in to see her. No, I decide. Our relationship is better since it was whittled down to just letters, phone calls. Why ruin that? It's a case. I run my hands up and down Gene's shoulder and he shifts slightly, still asleep. I'll be back soon. It shouldn't be long.

FOUR

I take the Pacific Coast Highway down. It winds close to cliffs, the ocean on my right, the gray pavement cutting through the green landscape, hugging the coast like a needy lover. I'd left early, giving Gene a long kiss goodbye before taking my old Buick sedan out of the garage under the Ruby and easing her along the roads out of town. Now I have the windows rolled down, and it smells like salt water and sand and those little patches of dried-out grass that grow all along the rocks. About twenty minutes out of San Francisco, Bing Crosby starts singing "Don't Fence Me In" on the radio and I smile. It's nice to be outside the city, following the road, so much sky ahead of me.

I drive most of the day, stopping only to stretch my legs, refill the tank, and eat lunch at one of those little highway diners. The coffee is bad, but the hamburger isn't. When the sun goes down, I stop for the night at a hotel just far enough from the ocean I can't see it, but I can hear it. I call Gene, something he'd made me promise to do this morning as I was leaving. A call every night. He's tending bar, there's already a crowd and I can hear the band playing, but he's glad I'm still alive, and we exchange *I love you*s before I have dinner at another burger joint, then turn in early. The next morning, I let myself sleep in a little, sad to wake up alone in a bed I don't know. The open road had seemed like a nice change of pace yesterday, but today it just seems lonely.

As I get behind the wheel again, I wonder what it's like doing this drive on a motorcycle. I've never ridden one, but I imagine with the wind, it feels good, and probably terrifying. I roll the windows all the way down, but I know it's not the same.

I get into LA as the sun is going down. The walls of the Hollywood Freeway are jarring, I haven't seen them before. They almost look like the walls of a fortress, the white peak of City Hall visible just beyond them, gated, inaccessible—feels like the whole city is. Then I turn off onto Santa Monica, and I'm suddenly in the streets again, and there's a sort of itch of memory in the back of my skull, from when I was a kid, riding shotgun in my dad's Buick, which was a mustard yellow and always covered in dust. LA was a new city then and had felt like it had had some kind of growth spurt from frontier town to metropolis, buildings rising out of the sand almost overnight. Plenty of places, like Boyle Heights, where I grew up, were still essentially small towns, suburbs around the city. There was a main street with a few shops and a movie theater, and then rows of houses going back, lawns on some of them. It wasn't Peoria—too many different types of people for that—but it was quaint.

Dad would drive me into the city proper, with tall buildings and the trolleys, and it was like a whole other world. I didn't do much, really, mostly followed him around as he followed other people around, spied on them, asked questions about stolen or broken goods, just to make sure the insurance claims weren't fraud. They usually weren't. It never got really dangerous, but sometimes it felt that way, sitting in our car, waiting for a guy to pop out of a warehouse, maybe hauling a crate that had supposedly fallen off the back of his truck. Times were tough, especially after the stock market crash. People did crazy things. But Dad caught them at it. It felt bad, sometimes, turning in folks down on their luck, trying to scrape together some money with cons or thievery, but Dad always said if he didn't turn them in, it was his job on the line. Us or them. And he was determined to keep himself, and his family, safe. And so I always felt safe with him.

It doesn't feel that way now. Maybe that's just since he died, or since I knew what I was, or maybe it's just that the city feels just different enough I don't know it anymore. The buildings feel taller, all red, tan, and gray, solid-looking things like desert plateaus and painted caverns. Billboards with celebrities' smiling faces and neon signs pop up in unexpected swathes of concrete, too-wide streets, islands between them. It's not San Francisco, with its sloped roads and tight alleys. Here everything feels flat, open, pulled apart like the rib cage of some rotting animal, vultures overhead and blood fertilizing the pavement, willing some new building to grow.

I stop at a hotel on Temple, just past a giant neon sign for the exterminator Doc Kilzum: a man in a top hat and red bow tie holding a suitcase, his arm moving up and down as rats scurry toward him, each one flipping over, dead. In bright green, under him, it says, "His Patients ALL DIE."

The hotel is nice enough for a PI from out of town. There's some parking in front, and the concierge is an old lady with cat-eye glasses and a cigarette in her hand. The desk has a fan of brochures: "Welcome to Los Angeles," "Grauman's Hollywood Egyptian Theatre," "Quick Facts About Southern California's Climate." They're all yellowish, even the new ones, the corners curling. The clerk takes my money with a hacking cough and hands me the key to my room without asking any questions.

"There a pay phone around here?"

She nods at the front door. "Around the corner."

"Thanks."

I bring my suitcase upstairs, put my stuff away in the closet. The room has slatted blinds, which I close, but they don't block out all the light from Doc Kilzum. Stripes of bright green fall on the bedspread.

I grab a handful of quarters and go out to the pay phone she directed me to and call Gene. It's expensive, but I promised him. He picks up from the bar phone, and I hear music in the background.

"The Ruby."

"Hey," I say, my voice soft. My throat hitches slightly. It's strange, we don't spend every night together, but we have also never been so far away physically. It makes the separation different, sharper. "I'm here. Found a hotel. There's even a neon sign outside so I feel at home."

"Red?" I can hear the smile.

"Green."

"Too bad. The drive was all right?"

"Mostly. There was a spot when the radio went out for a little bit, but I found a new station a little while later."

He laughs. "Andy without music. That would be hard." He pauses, and behind him I can hear someone singing. "Weird being back?"

"Yeah. It's too different to be really familiar, but it's like there's some lingering perfume or something. Started thinking about my dad soon as I got here."

"You never talk about him."

I lean against the glass of the phone booth and look out the side at the street. It's totally dark now, aside from streetlamps, lights in windows, and Doc Kilzum. "Not much to say. He was a good dad. You don't talk about your parents much either."

"Yeah."

"Should I go see my mom?"

"I thought you said you weren't going to. That your relationship is better when you're far apart."

"It is, but . . ." I shake my head. "It is. Just thought it might be nice to see her face. But I don't know if I want her seeing mine."

"Well, you are a PI. You're good at spying."

I laugh. "Maybe."

"That Andy?" I hear Elsie's voice, yelling loud enough to be heard over the din. "Tell him to stop talking to you and finish the case so he can get back here."

I laugh. "Tell her I'm going to call my contact here next. Just wanted to tell you I made it. And I love you."

"I love you, too," Gene says. "Be safe."

I hang up the receiver and take a breath. Spying on my own mother? Maybe I could at least drive by the old house.

I put a bunch more quarters in and call Myrtle next. She picks up on the first ring.

"Hello?"

"It's Andy. I'm in LA."

"Good."

"I'm going to call your friend Sam next, ask if I can come around and meet him."

"Samuel, he hates Sam."

"Samuel, then. You want me to report in every day I'm here or just when I find something out?"

"I think . . . just if you find something out. I don't need to know all the sordid details. I just want you to find all . . . my missing friends."

"Of course." There's a click suddenly on the line, a faint sort of tapping noise. Could just be the long distance. "I'd better go. I'll be in touch."

"Good luck, Andy."

"Thanks. Good night."

She hangs up and I get out my change again, but only put in enough for a local call. Then I call Samuel's number.

"Hello, this is Samuel Blanchard."

"Hello, Mr. Blanchard," I say, making my voice sound more energetic than it feels. "My name is Andy, I'm a private investigator hired by our mutual friend Myrtle, who's asked me to look into some missing people."

There's a beat. "Ah." He sounds tired, wary. "She's finally done it, has she?"

"She has. She said you might not believe it, and I'm to tell you your mother's apple pie recipe had too much cinnamon in it."

He laughs, a high falsetto tinkle. "Oh yes, that's a message from Myrtle all right. I suppose you want to come by?"

"I would. Maybe drop in on one of your"—I pause, thinking of the clicks—"gatherings?"

"Mmm. Yes, well, if you know about those—"

"I've been before." He might think I mean I'm Mattachine myself, which is fine. As long as he knows I'm gay, I think he'll trust me more.

"Really?" He sounds shocked. "A private eye?"

"It takes all kinds to survive the *maelstrom*," I say, choosing a memorable word from the oath. Everything feels like a test with these Mattachine people, but I'm getting used to it.

"Well, then, come by tomorrow. I'm hosting a little gathering."

"There a password or anything?"

He laughs. "No, no. We're not like that. Let me give you the address." I write it down. "Come by tomorrow at six. Bring a bottle of wine. But now I must go, I need to take this roast out of the oven."

"Of course. Thank you, Mr. Blanchard."

He hangs up, and I'm left wondering if he's quite as serious with all the secrecy as Myrtle is. I suppose I'll find out tomorrow.

I resist the urge to call Gene back, just to say good night, then walk around the corner to the hotel. I shower off the road and fall into bed, the green light like strange cuts over my body, and I go to sleep remembering the LA I grew up in, buried somewhere under all the concrete.

The next morning, I head out into the city to find something to eat. On foot, it looks even more different than it did last night. Buildings shooting up where I don't remember them, freeways cutting away whole neighborhoods I used to drive around. It's uneasy, this new LA. Like it keeps finding new parts of itself and isn't sure how to feel about them.

I find a pharmacy with decent coffee and a breakfast counter, and I buy a map, looking it over as I eat. Samuel's place is in Echo Park, but I don't know where the founders, or their new magazine, are, and I'm not sure where to start looking. Maybe someone at the meeting tonight will have a lead on them, as well as the biker gang. But as I eat, I realize I don't know anything, not really. This is a new city to me in many ways, and I'm lost in it. The only other address I know is my old one, where Mom still lives, in Boyle Heights. I think about what Gene said last night, about maybe driving by, seeing if I spot her. She's probably already at work by now, and I don't remember the name of the new clinic she's at.

I tap my finger on the map and then fold it up. I have nothing to do until the meeting tonight. I don't even know which gay clubs are still around if I wanted to try asking about the motorcycle gang or magazine. I feel fidgety with nothing to do, and I know ordering another cup of coffee won't help, so I pay the bill and get in my car and drive home.

Boyle Heights isn't so different from how I remember it, and for a moment I feel back on familiar territory, my foot falling into old footprints left in the dust. It's gotten a little bigger, more buildings down the street, a movie theater showing *High Noon*, a few retirees lined up to see it. And the people are different. It used to be everyone came here—Blacks, Jews, Mexicans, immigrants from all over. A funny little hodgepodge of people Mom said was just a small version of America. Now there are a lot more white people. But it's not like the other folks are gone. I spot Mr. Garcia, the barber, through the window of his shop. He's got a toupee now, but that's him. And I see Mrs. Goldstein, from two doors down, walking her poodle—a new one, I assume, not Frizi, the one she had when I was growing up. I almost stop to say hi, but she'd tell my mother for sure. I feel back home, or close to it. Until I see the house.

She must have repainted it. Just a simple two-story Victorian with a porch that curves around it, and a nice lawn, lined in bushes and flowers. It used to be white, plain, same as all the other houses, with light green trim. But now it's a lemon yellow, and the trim is red. It looks like a flower maybe, or the circus. I drive slow, wondering if the door will open and she'll spot me, but the car isn't even in the driveway, so I pull up alongside and just look at the house. The garden is different, too, new flowers, new bushes. It looks nice. Just not the place I grew up. There used to be a broken rail on the porch railing, too. I would climb up on it and launch myself off, pretending to be Tarzan. Landed badly more than once, went running to Mom, who always bandaged me up and then read me more Tarzan stories. As I got bigger, the push off on the rail got harder and harder, splintering the wood, and then cracking it. She never replaced it though. She said it kept me from jumping off it again. It's fixed now.

I spot Mrs. Goldstein and her new poodle in the rearview mirror, walking closer, so I take off before she recognizes me.

The rest of the day I spend driving around to places I remember, and seeing if anything is the same. Nothing really is, but I see glimpses of the past in most of it. I buy a bottle of wine at five thirty and then drive over to Samuel's place. It's above a beauty salon, in a squat brick building with big glass windows showing off women sitting under hair dryers, reading Hollywood gossip magazines. I look around at the parked cars, but I don't see anyone waiting, like I did outside Myrtle's. Inside the stairwell is stuffy, and as I climb, I can hear music and laughter from above. I knock, and the laughter cuts off suddenly.

Then the door bursts open to a smiling little man. "Are you the detective?"

I look down at him. He's short, maybe five-four, in a blue polo shirt and brown pants. He's got brown hair with a gray streak through it, and he's a little wide at the waist.

"Samuel?" I ask.

"Just bring him in," calls a voice behind him. I look out at the apartment—a bold striped-pink-and-gold wallpaper, and a white rug, a white sofa, and some tan leather armchairs. Only four other people are inside.

"They're impatient," Samuel says to me, as if it were a little secret, but he walks back in and motions for me to follow. I close the door behind me. A record player is in the corner, a 48 RCA on a stand with speakers, and Eddie Fisher's "Wish You Were Here" is playing, uneasy strings vibrating in the air. A bar cart is in one corner, a coffee table in the center. There are some stools at a counter, past which is a small kitchen. And scattered, all lounging comfortably, are the other guests: another man, maybe forty, with black curls parted neatly on the side and deep brown skin, who stands by the record player, and three women—two older, with dyed-blond hair to their shoulders and simple dresses, sitting on the sofa, and one in her late twenties, gorgeous with a messy red bob, perched on a barstool, legs crossed in a pencil skirt. She's holding out a martini glass, which she toasts me with as I enter.

"The man of the hour," she says, half smiling like it's a mean joke. I feel suddenly like I've entered an old Roman coliseum and they're the lions.

"Don't mind Vera," Samuel says. "She thinks it's funny, you being a detective."

"The only detectives around here are on-screen," she says. "I wasn't sure they existed in real life anymore."

"That's the fun of having him," one of the older women says. "Find out what's true."

"Especially for a gay detective," says the other older woman.

"This is Marie and Ethel," Samuel says, not clarifying which is which, "and the handsome fellow is my Leo. What was your name again?" Samuel goes and sits on the sofa.

"Andy," I say, still wary. I stand in the center of the room, not sure where to sit.

"And you're really a detective?" Leo asks.

I nod. "Looking for some missing Mattachine members from San Francisco."

"Yes." Samuel rolls his eyes. "Myrtle is such a drama queen, isn't she?"

I try not to smirk. This Mattachine meeting is very different from the last one I went to.

"Don't be mean, Samuel," Vera says, sliding off the stool and walking over to the bar cart. "She's worried about her friends. You saw how high tempers ran at the conferences."

"Yes, but now it's fixed." Samuel throws his hands in the air. "The Fifth Order can go start their little magazine, and we can go on trying to actually integrate into society."

"So you don't think the founders could be coming after people who spoke out against them?" I ask.

The room goes silent, everyone exchanging looks before they all burst out laughing.

"Darling, no," Leo says.

"They're socialists, sure," Vera says, mixing herself a martini, "but they're the kind who think newsletters cause revolutions. *ONE* magazine? The One Institute? What does that even mean? They're not dangerous. And if they were, they wouldn't go after Mattachine members. They'd go after politicians." She smiles, arches an eyebrow at me.

"The whole thing was just a little tiff, really," Samuel says. "Bound to happen, and a more interesting story than it was an event. Certainly not a melodrama."

"More like a breakup," Vera says. "All that yelling and then everyone goes their separate ways and forgets about each other until they stumble on an old photo or hear that one song." She shrugs. "Can I make you a drink?"

"Oh, where are my manners?" Samuel says, taking my hand and pulling me over to the leather armchair, which he pushes me down into. "Sit down. Vera makes a mean martini. We want to know all about you. You're our special guest speaker, after all."

"Am I?" I ask, looking around.

Marie and Ethel nod, eagerly. "It's exciting," one of them says. "We want to know what you do, your cases."

"It's a shame Milton isn't here," Leo says. "He loves those noirs."

"Crush on Bogart," Vera says.

"Why isn't he here?" Ethel or Marie asks.

"Blackmail," Samuel says. "Someone found his love notes to an old beau and was extorting him or they'd tell his job at UCLA. He couldn't afford it, so he moved. St. Louis of all places."

"Such a shame to go out like that," Leo says, as though their friend had died.

"You must deal with plenty of blackmail," Vera says, handing me a martini. I sip it. It's extremely good. She could give Gene a run for his money. "If we had one of you around, Milton might still be with us."

I nod. "Blackmail comes up a lot. Missing persons, too, like this one. Sometimes those are murders."

"Really?" Samuel asks, eyes going wide. "You've solved murders?"

"A couple. More when I was a cop."

"You were a cop?" Vera asks. "So masculine. Exactly the sort of people Mattachine is looking for, you know. Role models. So when we go public—"

"If we go public," Samuel interrupts.

"If and when we go public," Vera continues, "we'll have strong, upstanding members of society to show off. To demonstrate how we're just like everybody else."

I sip my martini. Probably best not to mention the reason I was kicked off the force.

"Oh, but we interrupted you with tedious politics," Samuel says. "Tell us more about your business."

I look them over; they're all leering at me like vultures, smiles pinching the edges of their mouths. Vera brushes a strand of red hair out of her face and takes the olive out of her martini with her fingers, popping it in her mouth.

"Well, like I said, lots of missing persons," I say. "Right now I'm looking for three people. Daphne, Hank, and Edward." I describe them like Myrtle did, looking around the room for sparks of recognition. Samuel narrows his eyes.

"You know, I think we do know them—well, the men. But they haven't been around in years."

"Yes," Leo says. "They were with us a few times but they moved—to San Francisco, seems like. I didn't remember that."

"You don't remember anything outside the Basin," Vera says.

Leo chuckles. "Why would I bother?" He toasts the air and sips.

"The shorter one, he worked for Mannix, I remember," Samuel says. "Scary man."

"Edward?" I ask.

"No, Mannix. He's a fixer for the studios. When something goes wrong, a star is in trouble or something, Mannix fixes it. Edward helped him, but he was always coy on how. I saw him walking around the studio sometimes, delivering notes, talking with actors, crew, doctors, whoever. He was probably spying. That's what most of Mannix's boys did."

I nod, not sure if this means anything. "But you haven't seen either of them recently?"

"Mannix? I saw him a few weeks ago."

"He meant the couple," Leo says, laughing.

Samuel's eyes go wide and he laughs a little jingle. "Oh."

"We haven't seen them in years," Leo says. "Sorry."

I nod. Not so helpful, then. "I guess I'll try the founders, then. You know where they are?"

"They're working out of Harry's place in Silver Lake," Vera says.

"How do you know that?" Leo asks her, hand on his hip.

"Martha is working with them," Vera says with an eye roll. "I met her there to give her back some stuff."

"I still can't believe how that ended," Marie or Ethel says.

"After everything you did for her," Ethel or Marie says.

"It's fine, I knew she wasn't a long-term prospect," Vera says. "I just like a project sometimes."

"Well, you definitely transformed her. From bulldagger to beauty queen. That first time she walked properly in heels, oh, I was so proud." Samuel puts his hand on his chest. "She was so close to elegant."

Vera tilts her head. "She was, wasn't she?" Her eyes go off for a moment, remembering something, but then land on me. "But let's not talk about me when we have such an interesting guest. So what's next in your case, Detective? Shake down the founders?"

"Ask them some questions, maybe. And try to find this gay motorcycle gang."

"Motorcycle gang?" Samuel leans in. "Really?" He's practically drooling.

"Yeah, they might be connected. Any of you ever encountered them? They have a patch on their jackets that looks sort of like one of these"—I hold up my martini glass—"a purple glass." I look around the room, seeing if anyone has a reaction. They're all staring at me aside from Vera, who's stirring her drink. "Anyone know them?"

Leo laughs. "We're not really motorcycle people, Andy. We stay out of Long Beach."

I nod, like I already knew that, but Long Beach is a good lead.

"What on earth does a motorcycle gang have to do with missing Mattachine members?" Marie or Ethel asks.

"I'm not sure yet. Just a lead. I shouldn't talk too much about it." I watch Vera get up and down the rest of her martini before starting to mix another.

"Well, then tell us about another case," Samuel says. "Something scandalous."

I laugh and shake my head. "I don't really do much scandal these days. Most of my business is setting up fake relationships for folks to keep their jobs or fool their parents."

"That's what I do, too!" Leo says, thrilled. He sits on the arm of the chair I'm in and leans down. "Isn't it fun?"

"You make up relationships, too?" I ask.

"I work for a studio. Mum's the word on which. But creating lavender couples for tabloids is my raison d'être!"

"Darling," Samuel says, "you plan the weddings, you don't create the couples."

Leo waves him off. "Well, sure, Mannix might pair them off, but I'm the one who puts together the wedding, the press, the love story for the tabloids!" Leo looks at me expectantly. "You know, to cover up things like Barbara's lesbian orgies or Clark's pining over Billy."

"Oh, now you've started him." Vera walks back over with a fresh drink. "Leo drops names like he drops hairpins."

"There's handsome Monty, and poor Ramon—he hires streetwalkers you know," Leo says, ignoring her. "Marlene everyone knows about, of course."

"And Barbara," Ethel or Marie adds. "I was invited to one of those orgies once."

"You never told me that," Marie or Ethel says, eyes wide.

"Well, I didn't go, of course! That sort of thing is exactly the image Mattachine is trying to get away from. We're just normal people. Not deviants throwing lesbian sex parties."

Everyone laughs in unison. The record ended a while ago, but for a moment, it's as if they were a chorus.

"My favorite is Kate and Spencer," Samuel says. "Whoever set that up knew what they were doing."

"How do they feel about it?" I ask. "The gay stars."

Leo frowns a little and looks down at his drink. "Well, with these marriages, plus some blackmail and threats, the studios make sure the general public doesn't know about the stars being gay, so they can keep being in movies."

"Better than being left out in the cold," Samuel says. "Fired, not making movies, their sex life splashed on the cover of *Confidential*. The studio taking care of them means they still have a career and private life."

"Do you know what happens to someone who's gay *and* famous?" Vera asks. "I don't, but it can't be good."

I nod. I narrowly avoided that particular combination earlier this year when a reporter wanted to write about me.

"Cary and Randolph are still my favorite couple," Leo says, his voice light again, changing the topic. "Not lavender at all."

"That's so long ago," Vera says, unimpressed.

"They got *Modern Screen* to do a piece on their happy life together, and before the war," Leo says. "Audacious if you ask me. Even if Cary did have to date Phyllis because of it." He looks at me, lips pressed together to hold in his smile, eyes wide, waiting. I know what he needs from me.

"Cary?" I ask.

"Grant." Leo's smile shows how thrilled he is to have been asked.

The next hour continues like that, a who's who of supposedly queer Hollywood stars, names I only half recognize. I'm not part of this world, and they're not really inviting me to be. Drinks are refilled often and start to spill over the rims of tilted glasses. Laughter grows louder. My case is forgotten, and so is my presence for the most part. I think I have what I came for, though. An address for the founders. A neighborhood to start looking for the motorcycle gang. I wasn't really expecting more. Although . . . I look at Vera again. She sees me looking and raises an eyebrow, smiling.

"We should get going," Marie or Ethel says, rising for the first time from the sofa. "But as always, it's been a lovely time."

"That's my cue, too," Vera says. "C'mon, Detective. Let's leave Samuel and Leo to their dinner."

I thank them all for having me, and the information, and follow the ladies out the door. Vera threads her arm through mine when we're outside. "Let's go to dinner."

"We're going home," Ethel or Marie says. "Nice meeting you, Andy."

They walk away together and I look down at Vera, whose eyes are twinkling, either from alcohol or mischief, I can't tell.

"There's a diner near here." She pulls me down the street. "I always go there after meetings. Leo and Samuel have good liquor. That's most of the reason I go. But I tried driving home like this once and smashed my own mailbox, so now I get a grilled cheese and a cup of coffee before I get behind the wheel. Some man always hits on me, though. A woman eating alone. So come be my protection from that, would you?"

It's not really a question, we're already walking together. She sways a little as she leads me down the street and around the corner to a diner with big glass windows and a man in a soda jerk hat and a red apron behind the counter. There are few families in the booths here, and some single men, who turn and leer as we walk in. Vera raises her chin a little, apparently thrilled to have me as a shield, then takes me to a table far in the corner.

"Just get a grilled cheese and a malted," she says, after a waiter has given us menus. "That's what I always do." She laughs. Her hair has fallen slightly into her face, one strand over her eye and ending at her bright red painted lips.

I order as she commands and she leans back in her chair, across from me, now studying me.

"You don't talk much, do you?"

"At the meeting? I was a stranger, didn't understand half of what you were talking about."

"You mean all the Hollywood names?" She blows the strand of hair out of her face. It floats in the air a moment before falling back down where it was, so she uses her hand to pull it back behind her ear. "It's just gossip. You should have asked who everyone was talking about, Leo would have loved it. They would have thought you were a hick, but they thought that anyway. They think that about anyone who doesn't work in the movies. Most people do."

"Do you work in the movies?"

She laughs again, but it's different this time, a low chuckle. "No." She tilts her head. "I'm a pharmacist. Though I've certainly helped some Hollywood types find a cure for whatever ailed them. But that's it. Normally my days are spent doling out Tuinal and pep pills to housewives—one to knock them out at night, one to keep them awake during the day."

"And you never gossip about your Hollywood patients?"

She snorts. "I mean, I don't really know who they are. They send over some kid with a prescription made out to them, oral morphine for the pain from an injury or disease they obviously don't have. We all know it's for some star with a problem, but they hide who it is. Don't want me talking to the tabloids."

The waiter comes back with our milkshakes and Vera happily puts the straw to her lips and starts drinking.

She stops and leans back, bliss on her face. "I love a milkshake, don't you?"

I sip mine. It's pretty good. I don't usually drink them; last one I had was when Gene convinced me to get one after the movies, holding hands in the dark, and remembering that makes my hand ache for a moment, lonely. I squeeze it tight at my side. I'll get home soon.

"When I mentioned the motorcycle gang, you looked like you knew them," I say.

Her eyes go wide for a moment, taking that in. Then her face turns wary, her expression more guarded. "Noticed that, did you? I didn't want to say in front of all of them, they'd act like it was such a scandal, but, yes, I've seen the patch you mentioned." The hair has fallen back in her face, and this time she catches it between her fingers and pulls it back to join the others on her head. "There's a guy who comes in, has a prescription for allergies he has to refill regularly. I thought he was just some businessman, always wore a plain suit." She pauses to lean closer to me. "But then, a few months back, he came in on a weekend, and he was wearing a leather jacket with one of those patches. A few other guys in jackets were waiting outside, too."

"So you know his name?" I ask, trying to keep the excitement out of my voice. "If you have his prescription, I mean."

Her face goes even more still. "I could get it. But that would be illegal. I'm not supposed to disclose patient information."

"I'm not a cop."

She tilts her head, face still a mask. I get the impression she's not nearly as drunk now, or maybe she never was. "This will really help the case?"

"It could. The motorcycle gang is the only real lead I have."

"Then . . . maybe I could be persuaded to look up the name for you. Get an address. But I'll need you to promise it won't get back to me."

"It won't."

"And . . . I need a favor. Tit for tat, right?"

"What kind of favor?"

She looks over her shoulder at the door, then turns back to me. "If tonight goes like most nights I come here, then in about half an hour, a guy is going to come in. He's not a pleasant man, always hits on me and sits right by the door so he can make a grab for my ass as I walk out. When he comes over tonight, I'm just going to go over there and make it clear how much I dislike that and then tell him you're my husband, just back from Korea. You're a tough guy. Just stay here, glower, look mean."

I wonder how much of this she's had planned. Did she fake that look of surprise about the gang, or did she only come up with this as we were leaving? "You don't want me to just tell him all that?"

"No, I think it's good for a woman to speak up for herself. Plus, you won't always be here, and I don't want him thinking that if you're not around, it's okay to play grabby-hands again. You're going to be like a gun I show him and then holster. I want him to remember you could always be there."

I don't buy it. Something else is going on; maybe she's not exclusively gay and the guy is an ex or something. But it also doesn't seem like much trouble for me.

So I nod. "Sure."

The waiter puts our grilled-cheese sandwiches down in front of us.

"Oh, thank God," Vera says. "I'm starving." She bites into the sandwich, her face again showing incredible pleasure, then calls the waiter back to ask for another milkshake. I start eating, too, and the food is good, but apparently not as good to me as it is to her.

"So you're going to visit the founders tomorrow?" she asks after a moment.

"That's the plan. I don't think they have anything to do with it either, but the client does, so I should check it out."

"Here." She takes a pen out of her purse and writes an address on a napkin. "You'll see Martha," she says, almost to herself, as she writes. Then she hands it to me.

"You want me not to mention your name?"

Her eyes flash to mine. "Oh no, tell her I say hi. It might be the only way anyone there will trust you. I'm your referral. Just tell me how she looks after. You can come by the pharmacy afterwards, and I'll look up that address. If you do your part . . ." She glances back at the door. No one new has come in yet, and she turns to me. "Dahlia Pharmacy, in Los Feliz. You know LA?"

I nod, then shake my head. "I grew up here, but . . ."

"It changes." She bites into her sandwich, nodding.

"But I know Los Feliz. I can find it."

"Big green sign, you can't miss it."

"Dahlia is a funny name for a pharmacy."

She tilts her head, a smile on her lips that she might give a small child. "No, it isn't. Los Angeles loves dahlias. We name everything after them. Movies, drinks, dead girls, drugs. I think the idea is to make things prettier, glamorous. It's such a big, beautiful flower, like a firework. But, you know, the thing about dahlias—they don't have any scent. You can cover a body in them, and it'll look gorgeous, a mountain of those honeycomb petals. It'll still smell like rot, though."

The door to the diner opens and my eyes flicker to the man walking in. He's rough, but not big. Vera turns and spots him, then looks back at me, her mouth a thin line, and nods. She puts her sandwich down and walks over to him. He's put himself at the door, like she said he would, leaning against the window, one elbow on the table. I watch as she slides into the chair across from him, and he straightens up, already worried. Not wolfish. She leans forward and speaks softly. I can't make out anything. He glances over at me, and I do my best to look intimidating. I glare. He looks more nervous and turns back to her. He says something, but she cuts him off, and then he nods, fast, his head bobbing. When she gets up and starts walking back to me, he darts out the door. She doesn't look back at the sound.

She sits back down and picks up what's left of her sandwich, takes a bite, and smiles. "You want to split an order of fries?"

"That guy looked scared of you."

She looks for the waiter and waves him over. "That was the point," she says, as he gets there. "Can we get an order of fries, too? And a coffee."

The waiter nods and leaves.

"But he was scared of you, not me."

She smiles and watches me for a moment, considering. "You probably don't know this. You're a man, and one who doesn't really interact with women the usual way. But when a man hits on a woman like that, is aggressive, if the woman turns it back around on them, they find it unsettling. It reverses the power dynamic." She spins her straw in her milkshake and takes a deep sip. "My approaching him wasn't his dream come true—his dream come true was, I don't know, him grabbing my ass and me giggling, and then giving him my number or something. But me sitting down before he even did anything? That was strange for him. And then you were the icing on the cake. He's not going to bother me again. Thank you for that, really." She drinks her milkshake again until the straw makes that hollow sucking noise at the bottom of the glass.

I bite into my sandwich, and a moment later the waiter brings the fries and coffee, as if he'd just been waiting for her to ask for them. She squirts some ketchup onto the plate and dunks a fry in. "Some people dip these in their milkshakes," she says, shaking her head. "I tried it. Not for me." She talks a little about the city as we eat; where she went to school, where she worked, how the Dahlia is better than the last one, even pays a few cents more per hour. She downs the coffee when it's lukewarm, in a few long sips, like it's medicine. The man who ran out the door is forgotten.

When the bill comes, and I take out money to pay, she shakes her head and puts cash on the table from her purse. "You were such fun tonight. Samuel really should have bought you dinner, but since he's not here, I will. Thank you for dropping by and being so entertaining."

We leave, and I can see a thin line of sweat between her shoulder blades, coming through the back of her pale yellow shirt. Maybe it's just the heat, thick and oppressive. Or maybe talking to the man was scarier than she said, and she's putting on a front. I'm not sure. Only thing I know is that she used me tonight, had a whole plan, and lied about it elegantly. She walks perfectly straight now, her heels don't wobble at all, and she stops in front of a new bright blue 1952 Roadmaster convertible. I'm not much of a car guy, but even I stare as she opens the door. It's an expensive car. Too expensive to have crashed into her mailbox. Or to afford on her new few-cents-more-an-hour job.

"It's nice, isn't it?" She strokes the side. She stands in front of it proudly before sliding in and patting the seat next to her. "You want a ride?"

I shake my head. "Thanks, but I need to get back to my hotel, check in with a few people."

She shrugs. "Suit yourself. Tonight's the kind of night you want the top down, get some air on your skin to cool down."

"Well, you enjoy it for both of us, then." I put my hands in my pockets.

She closes the door and waves, a sly smile on her face, then drives off. I feel like I've been played with, but I still don't understand the game.

Back at the hotel, I push some more quarters into the pay phone around the corner and stare at Doc Kilzum. It rings a few times before Gene picks up. It's noisy in the background. Not just music, but people talking. It's Saturday night, the Ruby must be packed.

"Andy?" Gene shouts.

"Yeah," I shout back, wondering how ridiculous I look on the street.

"How are you?" I can picture him, a finger in one ear, smiling.

"Confused. How are you?"

"It's packed." I'm not sure if he heard my question to answer it. "You all right?"

"Yes," I shout back, louder.

"Good. I can't talk, but I love you."

"I love you, too. Good night."

"We'll talk tomorrow." There's a click as the line goes dead, and I feel my chest drop. I step out of the booth, wishing I could have talked to him more, not sure what anything I learned today meant, and wondering what Vera whispered to the man in the diner. The heat is thick. The sun's going down hasn't changed that—made it worse, maybe. It sticks to my face and makes all my clothes stick, too.

In the hotel, I take a cold shower before lying down. Tomorrow, maybe, I'll have some real leads. Maybe I can even find these missing people. And then I can go home.

FIVE

I wake up hoping to feel better, but the heat hasn't abated, and I tossed and turned under the sheets all night, trying to get cool. Washing up helps a little, and breakfast helps a little more, but I still feel sluggish, limbs rusting in the humidity, by the time I make it over to the offices of the One Institute, or the publisher of *ONE* magazine, or whatever the new venture of the Mattachine Society's ousted founders is called. Except it's not really an office, as Vera said last night. It's someone's house on Cove Avenue, which is up a hill so steep I feel like I'm back in San Francisco. There's a long flight of concrete stairs up the side, cutting into the thick green foliage. It's a nice neighborhood. Suburban. I think of Myrtle's house, the neighbors, the men in the car. I look up and down the street. There's a Packard parked several houses away, someone still behind the wheel, but so far away I can't make out a face. Which means hopefully they can't make out mine, either. Just to be careful, I turn away, keeping my face turned from them as I climb the stairs and then turn onto a small path with the address.

It's a plain house. It doesn't have a sign out front or anything marking it as the One Institute, but it's the address Vera gave me. I go up and ring the bell. A young Black woman opens the door. She's got short hair and is wearing a fashionable version of Rosie the Riveter's utility jumpsuit.

She looks at me, suspicious. "Can I help you?"

"I heard this is the One Institute?" I say, half a question. "I'd like to talk to you."

"Are you a cop?"

I shake my head quickly. "No, no, I'm, uh, part of the movement."

Her expression changes, much more welcoming. She steps back to let me in. "You're a volunteer? I could use a hand moving these boxes."

"I was just hoping to ask some questions."

She nods. "All right, well, go ahead, I'll answer best I can."

Inside, it's a home, but also clearly an office for a magazine. There are papers all over, a desk by the fireplace, a coffee table shoved against the wall. On one side of the room is a corkboard with pages pinned to it. In the center is a bright green cover with white lines all over it, the words *HOMOSEXUAL MARRIAGE?* at the top, and a logo that just says *ONE* at the bottom, next to *August 1953, 25 cents*. I walk over to it, fascinated by the words, suddenly imagining getting down on one knee in front of Gene.

"Next month's issue," she says proudly. "I didn't write anything in it, but I helped set the lettering and proofread."

"Quite a cover."

"If we want rights, we gotta ask for them, and there's no need to start small. You have our other issues? That why you want to help?"

"Oh." I turn and put on my best smile. "No, sorry. I heard about you from the Mattachine Society."

She frowns a little at that. "And you decided you actually wanted to get something done? Then you're in the right place."

I look back at the magazine. "How do they even let you sell that?"

"Through the mail, a few special vendors sell it under the table. Feds haven't stopped us yet, but . . . probably they'll try." She puts her hands on her hips. "And we'll fight them in court."

"That's brave."

"Like I said, we actually get things done here. That takes bravery. I'm Mattie, by the way." She extends her hand.

"Andy." I shake her hand. "I was hoping I could talk to some of the founders. The Fifth Order."

She laughs and walks over to a large stack of boxes. "Help me move these?" She picks up a box and I do the same, following her down a blue-carpeted hall to another room. This one has a few desks in it, typewriters, more papers. She puts the box down in a corner and I stack mine on top.

"The Fifth Order is gone. There's just One. But if you're looking for Dale or Harry, who used to be the Fifth Order, they're not here right now."

"Any idea when they'll be back?"

She shrugs. "What is this about?"

She starts walking back to the room with the corkboard.

"I know this will sound a little hard to believe," I say, following, "but I'm a private eye."

She pauses, turns around, and looks me up and down, evaluating. "All right."

We're in the hall, the walls close. "I'm from San Francisco, where some Mattachine members have gone missing. There is some concern that after the split, there were some hard feelings, and—"

She holds up her hand. "We have been focusing on putting out a magazine. Harry and Will are out looking for real offices, so we don't have to crowd into this place anymore. We want to make a center, a public center, for gay life. Do you know how much work that takes? And it doesn't pay, it's all volunteer. Why do you think I'm here on a Sunday? No one, none of us at One, have time for petty grievances because Mattachine decided they wanted to be a little social club instead of doing real activism." She turns and keeps walking.

"That's what I figured, moment I walked in." I follow her. "But just in case, you ever meet anyone named Daphne, Hank, or Edward?" I describe them as she moves another box.

"No, none of those people sound familiar." She pauses, as if realizing something. "A gay detective. Working for gay people."

"That's the idea. Helping folks like us."

"Well, I respect that, I do. But if you really want to help, join up with us. One is helping a lot of people." She points at the magazine cover for the August issue. "Talking about how to get what we want. It's not like Mattachine, it's not about becoming what society wants you to be and then asking if they can forgive just this one little thing. That approach is never going to work for someone like me. So what I'm doing, what One is doing, is saying, 'Hey, here we are, and we're just as human as anyone and deserve to be treated that way.' Telling the world that—that's helping. Helping everyone, not just paying clients." She smiles slightly. "And a PI means someone tough, someone who can find stories, talk to people, right? You'd be a great addition."

I laugh. "I appreciate the pitch, but I have to get back to San Francisco soon."

She sighs. "Well, I tried. If we end up opening a branch up there, I'll look you up, though, don't think I'm dropping this. You have a card?" I give her one and she looks at it. "The Ruby? I've heard of that place. Didn't think Mattachine would hang out there."

"I'm not really Mattachine. Just working for them. Although, one of them last night told me to say hi to Martha. She around?"

"That's me. I prefer Mattie though. Who said to say hi?"

"Oh." I try to hide my surprise. After what they'd said last night, I was expecting heels and a dress, plenty of makeup. Mattie is in boots and her outfit is definitely not Mattachine approved. "Ah, Vera, she said to say hi."

Her face immediately shadows. "You're friends with Vera?"

I shake my head quickly. "Just met her last night. She knew where to find One."

Mattie nods. "All right. Yeah. Well, tell her hi back, I suppose. Be careful with her."

"Why's that?"

"I thought she and I were of the same mind—equal rights. But all she really wanted was equal pay. And she's fine telling me and every other lesbian to put on a skirt and heels so she can get it." Mattie twists her hands together in front of her, then realizes what she's doing and tries to make it look like she's just massaging her fingers. "She . . . she sneaks up on you," Mattie says, eyes firmly on her hands. "A little favor here, a little favor there. Or, 'Mattie, just try the heels, everyone will be so happy. Just try on the dress for me, you're so pretty in it,' and then one day you've done her so many favors you don't recognize yourself in the mirror." Mattie looks up, her expression sad. But she shakes her head and it vanishes.

"I'll be careful," I say, thinking of the favor I did for her last night. Simple, just glowering at some guy across the restaurant, but I still don't know why. "I just need one more thing from her anyway."

"Well, if she asks, tell her I was in this jumpsuit." Mattie grins, then wider as she thinks of something. "No, tell her I was in denim overalls, flannel shirt underneath. That'll horrify her."

I laugh. "All right, I will. But can you do something for me?"

"A favor?" she asks, suspicious.

"Just, ask if anyone else around here knows any of those missing folks I described? I doubt they will, but if they do, you can call the number on the card and leave a message. Someone will let me know." I take out a few bucks and hand them to her. "Here, it's long distance."

"What if no one knows them?" she asks, looking at the money.

"Then consider it a donation to One." Then I glance up at the bright green cover. "And send me one of those when it's done."

She takes the money. "Three dollars will get you a yearly subscription."

I hand her another dollar. "And you're really going to ask about the missing people?"

"I promise," she says, in a way that makes me believe her. "But now you gotta tell Vera I had an oil stain on my overalls."

I laugh, walking for the door. "Deal. And if you do set up something in San Francisco, I'd be interested in helping."

"I know." She smiles. "Here." She writes something on a notepad on the desk and tears off the page and hands it to me. "My number. Call in when you're back in San Francisco, confirm your subscription, see what we're planning. Careful what you say, I'm pretty sure the line is tapped. But we should stay in touch. You're one of us, Andy. I can tell."

I smile and take her number, not sure what to say to that. Then I turn and walk back down to the stairs, the sun hot on my neck. One of them? I don't know. This town has me turned around. Mattachine here is all gossip, and One has a plan, an agenda, that puts them squarely in the crosshairs of anyone who might not like that plan or agenda. I'm not sure I fit in anywhere here. Not like the Ruby.

As I reach the sidewalk again, I spot the car with the silhouette inside. Still there. I turn my face away and get in my car, driving off. I glance in the rearview, and the car has pulled out, too, and is coming my way.

This isn't the LA I grew up in, this is new territory. I'm not entirely sure how to lose them, if they're following me. Might just be a coincidence. I take a turn to see what happens. They take it, too, staying one car behind me. I try another, and they follow again. I think as I drive, heading downtown, hoping it's the best place to lose someone. I pass Pershing Square and the Biltmore, not sure exactly what to do. If they're the Feds, they probably just want to see if I'm heading somewhere else, another meeting, another link in a chain. I don't want to go to the pharmacy yet. Vera could take them back to the Mattachine meeting. If they're not Feds, then I don't know who they are or what they want, and I need to lose them anyway.

Downtown is crowded, at least that hasn't changed since I left. People swarm the streets, going into the various shops and theaters. Neon letters stick out from the side of every building writing store names, some I recognize, and some I don't. I pull into a lot and wait a moment, to see if they care that I've spotted them. They don't. They pull in after me, and I turn away, trying to keep them from seeing my face again. Then I walk out onto the street and join the throngs of people.

The crowd is good for getting lost, but not good for moving. I glance back and two men in matching dark suits have just come onto the street from the lot and are looking around. There's a department store—SILVERWOODS in bright neon down the side of the building. Five stories to get lost in, a big corner lot, huge windows under carved garlands. I duck into it.

My heart is going pretty fast and I can feel my face is wet with sweat, not just from the heat. I'm used to being the one doing the tailing, not the one tailed. And I'm in a city I barely know anymore, with no friends around. No one will even notice if I'm gone. I'll just blow away like smoke in the wind.

Inside, the store is a little less crowded, the walls lined in suits and shirts. I head for the stairs and glance back once. I can only see the bottom of the door, but two pairs of shoes come in just a minute after me.

The next floor is shirts and ties. They line the walls in stripes of color, most of them staid; black, gray, blue, but in one corner are some red, purple. Someone with some daring must work here. I hear footsteps on the stairs again, so I walk up the next flight. Shoes. Brown, black, shiny as bullets. I keep walking up. The next floor is pajamas and underwear, and I think I might have a shot at hiding here. The pajamas are on mannequins, hung on racks, making walls and curtains. I duck around behind a few mannequins and pretend to look at the boxer shorts, my back to the stairs. I listen for the footsteps. A pair of them coming up, one just after the other, slightly out of beat, a leaky faucet that sputters instead of doing a steady drip. They stop when they get to the top of the stairs. They're looking around.

I'm not the only man perusing the pajamas. At least a dozen guys are up here, plus a salesman working the floor. I carefully move over to the socks, trying to keep shelves and clothing between me and the footsteps, which are slowly spreading out, going in different directions. When they're both far from the stairway, I carefully turn, head down, and walk back toward it, keeping my feet as light as possible.

Back in the ties, I look around. There's one salesman here, adjusting the merchandise, keeping it tidy on the hooks. His tie is a red, leaning toward pink.

I walk over to him. "You're the buyer for this floor?"

He nods. "May I help you with something?"

"You can actually." I wonder how to quickly communicate with him, check. I let my wrist go limp and extend a pinkie. It's cheap, but it should get the idea across. He watches my hand, his eyes flitting to mine, wary. "I love your tie."

He nods, careful. "Thank you. Did you want one? They're right over here—"

"Maybe another time," I say quickly. "Right now, there are two men in dark suits following me. If they come down, can you slow them down? Get in their way and try to sell them something? Just a minute or two?"

He tilts his head back and forth, unsure for a moment, then nods.

"Thanks," I say, and head farther downstairs. I don't know how long he can hold them off. That might have been a bad move, with the time it took me to get him to agree. I hear steps on the stairs above me as I head downstairs, two pairs of feet again, water running down the stairs now.

I'm bolting now. I hear the guy upstairs interrupt the men, but their voices are muffled, and then I just hear the footsteps again, faster now. Definitely a waste of time. I practically run out the door and around the corner now, shoving folks in the crowd. I look once behind me as I turn the corner and don't see them. That's good, but I doubt they've given up. I walk down the street and turn into an alley and keep walking. It's less crowded here, and the sun is blocked by the buildings around me. The cool shade makes the sweat that coats me turn icy and I shiver.

There's an archway in the middle of the alley, a throughway under a building back onto Broadway. I turn into it. I'm almost back at the door to Silverwoods now, but hopefully I've lost them. I glance out onto the street, looking for black suits. I don't see any at first, until I look back to my car. One of them is standing there, waiting. Smart. I have to go back to it sometime. The other one must still be tailing me. I need to move. I need to kill time. Where can I hide for a while?

I turn out into the crowd, head down, and look around. The Los Angeles Theatre stares back at me, neon lights over a baroque facade. *Gentlemen Prefer Blondes* is on the marquee. I smile. When in Hollywood . . .

I maneuver through the crowds, turned away from the guy at my car, and keeping my eyes peeled for the other one. People swim around me, fish in a stream, and I use them as cover until I hit the box office.

The kid manning it looks up at me confused. "The picture already started."

"I just wanna sit in the dark for a while." I put down enough for two tickets.

He shrugs and takes my money, tearing a ticket in half before waving me in.

The lobby matches the outside, with gilded flourishes on columns that probably don't need to be there. Whole thing feels like a Paris opera house more than a movie theater, but maybe that's what the movies are like here in LA. Downstairs there's a restaurant, so I walk up a long curved staircase and past a fountain on the second floor before finding the actual theater. I feel exposed, alone on a gleaming balcony. I wonder if this was a bad choice. I hear a door open below me, maybe onto the street, and a sudden shock of laughter. I rush into the theater.

The dark is good. There's a seat in the back corner, where I'll be practically invisible. I push past the angry people who have been watching for a while and sit down, trying to let my heart slow down, my body cool off. It's not so far into the movie. I've only missed the newsreels and maybe the first ten minutes, from what I can tell. So I sit, and I watch Jane Russell ogle and dance with the Olympians in their tiny workout shorts, and then Marilyn, all in pink, sing "Diamonds Are a Girl's Best Friend." The whole time I keep my eyes on the door, but no one else comes in. It's over an hour before the picture ends and I go back out onto the street.

It's possible they decided to hang around, depending on how desperate they are, how carefully they're monitoring *ONE* magazine. But when I creep back to my car, no one is waiting by it, and the car that had followed me into the lot is gone, too.

I take a deep breath before I start the car. That was close. Someone is watching *ONE* magazine, just like Mattie said. I'll have to be extra-careful dealing with them. I don't need to be picked up here, where I don't have anyone to bail me out.

The Dahlia Pharmacy is easy to spot, like Vera promised. It's got a big neon-green sign that says DAHLIA in large curving script, and PHARMACY below it in thin block letters. Inside, the place is divided, a lunch counter on the right, a drug counter on the left, with shelves in the back selling magazines, beauty products, candy, almost anything. Vera smiles at me from behind the pharmacy counter, a white lab coat today over her pencil skirt and blouse.

I walk over to her. The shelf behind her is lined with jars and bottles of medicines, and the counter itself is glass, and under it is an array of ads for soap, toothpaste, makeup. Lucille Ball uses Max Factor lipstick, Esther Williams uses Lustre-Creme shampoo, Ed Sullivan smokes Chesterfields. I wonder if I only notice all the endorsements after the gossip last night, or if it's just in LA that the stars and their shilling shine brightest.

"It's nearly time for lunch," Vera says as I look over the ads. "Come out and eat with me. There's a restaurant a few blocks down that serves a fillet that's to die for." She's already slipping off the lab coat and taking out a little cardboard stand with a clock on it: OUT TO LUNCH.

"That's kind of you, but really, I should focus on work."

"I insist," she says, smiling, then leans in close and whispers, "I'm breaking a lot of rules, at least keep me company at lunch."

I force a smile and nod.

"Just let me tell Jimmy." She walks across to the side of the pharmacy with the sandwiches and coffee. She leans over the counter to say something to the guy working there, and his eyes flicker up to me. I look back, wondering what she's telling him. Suddenly, he looks afraid, glancing away and nodding quickly. Vera pats him on the hand and walks back to me, taking my arm, and leading me outside.

Walking even two blocks makes a trickle of sweat run down my back. Or maybe that's Vera. She's up to something. I think of what Mattie said, how she can ask you for small favors until you don't recognize yourself anymore. With Mattie, it was turning her into the perfect Mattachine member: heels and dresses. What is she trying to turn me into?

She chats as we walk, apparently unaware of or unconcerned by my silence. She tells me about how there must be some kind of sore throat going around at the park because this morning a dozen mothers came in, asking her what to give their children for it. She tells me about the differences in the aspirins she can recommend to them, and how she managed to get several to also buy toothpaste. "I don't think it'll help with the sore throat, but it's not like it'll hurt the kids."

The restaurant is nicer than I expected, with dark wooden tables and cozy leather booths, real cloth napkins the waiter unfolds and drops in our laps. She orders the fillet with salad and a Coke and tells me to order the steak and onion rings, so I do, wondering about her car. She's spending a lot that she's not making. Hard for a woman to do—some banks might give her credit, but without a husband or a father also on the account, it would be an exception. She hasn't talked about her family. Maybe she comes from money. That would explain a lot.

"What are your parents like?"

She looks surprised by the question. "They're all right. Why do you ask?"

"Just wondering what kind of background you come from."

"We on a date, Andy?" she asks, a gleam in her eye. She looks down at the table. "Or are you trying to put together the grilled-cheese girl with the steak girl?"

"That. Your family is rich?"

She shrugs. "Let's not talk about money. It's so gauche." Which sounds like she comes from money.

"You told me this pharmacy paid better than the old one."

"That's talking about work. Everyone talks about work. I'd say it's all anyone talks about, really. Gets boring."

She's dodging the question, but I let her. After she gives me the address for the motorcycle gang member, I'll be gone.

"So did you see Martha?" she asks, after the waiter has brought over her Coke.

"I did."

"And?"

"She was in grease-stained denim overalls and a flannel shirt," I say, as I promised Mattie.

Vera laughs for a moment, loud, then shakes her head. "No, she wasn't. She told you to say that to me, didn't she? You two planned a little story." Vera waves her finger. "Naughty. Who's going to be the big help on this case? Me or her? Or do you think it really does have something to do with her little group?"

"I don't."

She smiles. "So what did she really look like?"

I shrug. "I'm not sure what she looked like before, but she wasn't in heels, if that's what you're asking. She looked good, happy."

Vera's face stays neutral, but she nods, acknowledging what I've said.

"Why'd you two break up, anyway?"

She shakes her head a little and sighs. "It's my fault. I don't date girls who . . ." She goes quiet as the waiter comes over with our food. It smells great and we start eating as soon as he leaves. She takes one of my onion rings and bites into it with a smile, then turns to her salad and fillet. "I don't date the kind of girls who I want to end up with. And so I try to turn them into the girls I want to end up with. But, of course, they never really were."

"Why not just date the kind of girl you want to end up with?"

"I've tried. Mattachine girls. They're nice. But they're boring. Like Marie and Ethel. I don't want to end up like them."

"What's wrong with Marie and Ethel?" I cut into my steak. It's delicious.

"They just . . ." She tilts her head, considering. "Mattachine is about attaining rights. I know last night didn't look that way, with all the gossip, but to me it's about one day being able to say 'my girlfriend' to someone and have them know I don't just mean 'friend.' And Mattachine can get that, I think. I'm not a fool. I know everyone is different. There are probably straight men who love to prance around in women's clothes—oddballs of all stripes are everywhere. The key is we can't be different. Not if we want to be accepted." She takes another onion ring. "Once we're just as human as everyone else, then society will let us act just as human, with all our weird little quirks. So until then, I order the salad when I want the onion rings because that's what a nice normal girl does." She sighs, takes another bite of her fillet, another sip of Coke, looking at me as if I should respond.

"So what does that have to do with who you date?"

"I guess I date girls I want to be like, and then get annoyed at them for not agreeing with me that conformity is the quickest way to equality." She smiles. "It's what you might call a character flaw."

"Sounds sad."

She shrugs. "I don't mean this to cause offense, but you don't strike me as the happiest person, either."

I chuckle and take another bite of my steak. The plate is pink with blood. "I'm happier than I used to be. And I used to be all about conforming. Didn't even have a life. Was a cop, no friends, just sometimes went to the clubs to . . ." I look up at her.

She smirks. "Pick someone up?"

I nod. "Never anything long-term though. I didn't see a life or future really. Now I do. Even if it doesn't really conform."

"That wasn't conforming, Andy. That was hiding." Her eyes flicker up, behind me. "Oh, it's Ramona, I should go say hi." She stands, instinctively folding her napkin and putting it by her plate. She takes a step toward the woman she spotted, but then pauses and leans close to me, both hands on the table. "Do me a favor? Ramona and I, we have this joke, about how I always date these terrible brutes. I make them all up, of course, but she doesn't know that. So if she looks at you, look mean. Hold up your steak knife, maybe."

"My knife?"

She nods, standing straight again, and walks over to the woman. She's in her forties maybe, matronly, expensive clothes. They talk in low voices. I try to listen, the restaurant isn't so loud. But all I hear is "new" and then Ramona glances over at me. I try to look brutish, holding the knife, but she doesn't laugh. She looks frightened. I don't think I overdid it, either.

They talk a moment more, Ramona nodding, but no longer meeting Vera's eyes, and then Vera walks back over, sits down, puts her napkin in her lap, and cuts into her fillet with a smile.

"What's going on?"

"What do you mean?" she says, raising her fork to her lips.

"I mean that's the third time you've walked over to someone, said something to them, and then they looked at me and got scared. What's the game here?"

She leans back, putting the fork and knife down, and locking eyes with me. "I've only done it twice."

"I saw the guy at the pharmacy."

She smirks, impressed. "Did you?"

"Three times now. You're using me to scare people. And I don't think it's just guys who paw at you."

"Mmmm." She nods, then reaches out and takes another onion ring. "That's true. Ramona would have thrown that off." She eats the onion ring, oil coating her lips and making them gleam. She dabs at her mouth with her napkin. "I could lie," she says finally. "I could make up some new story, tell you the pharmacy guy pawed at me, and this was his sister and I wanted to make sure it got back to him how violent and jealous you are, but I don't think you'd fall for that. Not at this point." She sips her Coke. "So let's just say it has nothing to do with you."

"I think it does."

"I think it doesn't. Not if you want that address. And besides, once you have it, you never see me again, right? What do you need to know for, really? Just a detective's curiosity?"

"I don't like being used."

She shrugs and picks up the knife and fork again, starts eating. "I promise not to use you again. Will that do?"

I sigh, not sure what other choice I have. She's right—she holds the only lead for my case, and whatever she's using me for, it won't matter after I get it. Then I'll be able to find Hank and Edward, and from them, Daphne. And then I'll go home.

"Isn't the food delicious?" she asks, as if nothing has changed.

"Yeah." I eat another bite of steak. It doesn't taste as good now.

We eat mostly in silence, or at least I do. She talks some more, this time going on about movies she likes—*Pickup on South Street*—and doesn't—*It Came from Outer Space*.

"If you were sticking around, I'd make you come see *Gentlemen Prefer Blondes* with me. I love Marilyn Monroe. That's my kind of girl."

I smirk, but don't mention that I just saw it. "She doesn't seem like someone you'd have to change to blend in."

"No, I guess not." She smiles, wistful. "Want to get dessert?"

"I'd rather just get that name and address."

She sighs and takes a slip of paper out of her pocketbook and hands it to me. "I wrote it down this morning."

I take the paper and look at the name and address—Russell Klein, down in Long Beach. Pretty far away to use a pharmacy here in Los Feliz. I hope it's not fake. "Thanks," I say, standing.

"I'm going to get some pie. Sure you don't want any?"

"I'm sure."

"Suit yourself. Nice meeting you, Andy. And thanks again, for all the help."

I'm not sure what she means, but I just nod, put on my hat, and leave. The sooner I can find Hank and Edward, the sooner I can be back home, away from whatever Vera is trying to wrap me up in.

I roll my car windows down but the drive is slow, the streets filling with cars packed with families and beach umbrellas, heading down to the shore. Long Beach is its own city, built around weekday auto manufacturing and weekend beach trips. Yellow-and-red signs in fun letters point the way to food, gas, swimsuits. Buildings rise up so close to the water people use them for shade on the beach. I hope for a breeze from the ocean as I get closer, but the air is hot and still. The palm trees outside look like they're wilting.

I don't know the address so I stop at a newsstand to buy another map, plucking it from among the magazine covers with the movie-star faces and scandals. The house isn't close to the beach, so I can pull away from the traffic and head west. Out here, the bustling city turns to busy suburbia, then turns to something else. The houses are farther apart, the yards browner. We're close to the industrial plants, and the air smells a little metallic. It's probably worse during the week.

The house is bigger than I expected for a member of a motorcycle gang. A long ranch-style building in white, a huge free-standing garage off to one side. But the only car I see is parked in the driveway, by the front door. I stop across the street and approach slowly, not sure what to expect.

I knock on the door, but no one answers. I can hear music coming from the garage, so I follow that. It's a three-car garage, but only one of the doors is open, and inside I can see it's not just a garage. There's a bar in here, a big painting on the wall. A military turntable from the war is on the bar, and it's playing music I don't recognize. It's a woman's voice singing in Spanish, I think, with flutes and strings and clapping. Her voice is almost operatic, but the music is too fast for opera. I'm entranced by it, walking closer, into the garage, the music surrounding me. It's strange for me not to recognize a song.

There's a motorcycle up on some bricks, like someone's working on it. Next to the turntable is a matchbook, black with a gray bird on it. I walk closer to confirm—THE SILVER JAY, SAN FRANCISCO. At least I know I'm in the right place.

I hear a noise behind me and turn fast. I wonder suddenly if this was stupid. If I should have brought a gun.

He's in his twenties, black hair and brown skin, in a tight white tee and jeans, a cigarette in his mouth and a sneer on his face. He's also holding a long chain like it's a whip, and he's ready to strike me.

"Who the fuck are you?"

SIX

I try to stay cool. He's angry, and that chain is twitching in his hand like the tail of a stalking cat, but he hasn't made to come at me yet. There's a cast on his left ankle. That must be why. I could probably take him, or at least run, if he doesn't get me in the head with that chain. It looks heavy enough one hit could knock me out. And he's holding it like he's hit people with it before.

I put my hands up. "My name is Andy. I'm looking for Hank."

"You a cop?"

"No," I say quickly.

"You smell like a cop."

I nod. "I was a cop, up in San Francisco. Till they caught me in a raid. A friend of Hank hired me to find him."

He snorts a laugh at that. "A gay private dick?"

"You're in a gay motorcycle gang," I fire back.

"Motorcycle *club*," he corrects. "We're not criminals." He smiles, takes the cigarette out of his mouth, and blows some smoke at me. "Except in the bedroom."

"Sorry. I don't really know the difference. I didn't mean anything."

"You're gay?" he says, skeptical. He takes another puff on the cigarette. "Prove it."

"How?"

The hand with the cigarette goes to his crotch. "Suck my dick."

"I have a boyfriend."

"So? I have two." He grabs his crotch again. "I ain't gonna believe it unless you show me." He starts to unzip his fly, and I stare at him, trying to figure out how serious he is. He looks amused, but the fly gets lower, revealing he's wearing nothing under the jeans. He's grinning, like it's a dare. But it's also the only test he's offering me.

"Look." I point at the matchbook. "The Silver Jay. I know the manager there. I helped him with some blackmail once, gave him some photos. Just call him, he'll confirm and then we won't have to—"

"What, you don't wanna?" he asks, amused. "You and your boyfriend don't play around?"

"Not really." I move away from the matchbook, still pointing at it. "Just check with Bert. I'll give you the money for the long distance." I slowly go for my wallet, take out a buck, and toss it on the bar next to the matchbook. He sticks the cigarette in his mouth and motions with the chain, snapping at my feet, so I back up, outside the garage. The chain makes a heavy jangling noise as he shuffles along the wall, leaning on it with his free hand, dragging the broken ankle behind him.

"Sit," he commands, like I'm a dog. I sit on the driveway pavement. I'm not going to start a fight.

He gets over to the bar and pockets the dollar, then shuffles behind it and pulls a phone out from somewhere and dials the number on the matchbook. The sun is low enough they're probably open by now. I just gotta hope Bert is in. And that he'll vouch for me.

"Hey, yeah. This is Javi. I was in there for a while a few weeks back. Me and my friends up from LA? In the jackets?" He pauses. "Yeah. You Bert? . . . Okay. I got some guy here, says he's a gay PI from San Francisco. Name is . . ." Javi looks over at me.

"Andy," I say from the ground.

"Andy. Says he gave you some photos back once." Javi takes a drag of his cigarette. "Yeah? What's he look like?" He stares at me, listening and nodding. "Okay. So he's queer, for real?" He watches me, and a smile creeps on his face. "Oh yeah? He likes it that way, huh?"

I glare. "I never did anything with Bert."

"Not what he's saying," Javi says with a grin. "What else does he like?" He nods, smoking again. "Yeah, he looks like the type." He laughs. "Thanks, Bert."

Javi hangs up the phone and sits down on a stool behind the bar. The chain drops from his hand with a thud, and he grinds out what's left of his cigarette on the bar, then pulls up a bottle and two glasses from under it.

"All right." He pours brown liquid into both glasses. "You can stand."

I pull myself up and brush my pants off, walking cautiously back in. He nudges one of the glasses my way and sips from the other.

"So, a queer private dick. Funny."

"Sometimes it is." I sip the drink. It's whiskey, so I sip it again. "Sorry for showing up unannounced. It's been hard to find your *club*," I say, not *gang*.

"Yeah, I don't love that you did. Can't say the other guys will like it, either."

"Other guys?"

"Us, the club. The Bacchanals." He points at a leather jacket hanging on a hook on the wall. There's the patch I'd been chasing. A purple glass. "But you can pronounce it how you want."

"*Bacchanals?* Back—" I stop, figuring it out. "Funny."

"Russ went to college. Says bacchanals were like big parties in the woods, these worshippers of the god of wine. They'd go out and go nuts, drunk, having orgies. So we named ourselves after them. Or at least after the parties."

"And Hank is one of you now? A Bacchanal?"

"He was gonna be. Came back with us from San Francisco. Joined up for a few weeks, then vanished, and took Tommy, our sergeant at arms, with him."

"Sergeant at arms?"

"A proper motorcycle club has a sergeant at arms. Maybe we're not a public, registered one, because, like I said, we aren't technically legal in some aspects, but we still operate right." He pushes his shoulders back, proud. "I'm the secretary."

I nod, taking this in. So they're an organization. That could be useful. "You take minutes?"

"That's what a secretary does. And I keep the records."

"Doesn't that make it less secret?"

"I use initials instead of full names," he says, annoyed. "The point is, we're legit. Same as any motorcycle club. Just secret. But we're not out there scaring old ladies or holding up gas stations."

I sip again. "That's sort of a relief, actually. I thought I was hunting a band of outlaws."

He laughs. "Well, no more outlaw than you, if Bert is to be believed."

I scowl. "He isn't."

He laughs. "I'm Javi, by the way." He extends a hand and we shake. His grip is tight. "So did some friend of Hank really ask you to find him?"

"Yeah. You know where he went?"

Javi shrugs. "Who's the friend? It's not the boyfriend, is it?"

"Edward? No. He's missing, too."

Javi tilts his head at this, curious. The record has ended, and he turns it back to the start. "He was here. Showed up a few days after we came back. Thought maybe he was taking Hank back to San Francisco or maybe wanted to play with us some more. But they just talked in the driveway. Low voices. Angry, I think. Then he left, Hank stayed. We didn't ask about it."

"A breakup?"

"Maybe. Maybe just a fight. I know they've been together a long time. Long rides like that, there's going to be bumps in the road. The key is you gotta keep taking new roads, otherwise you go around and around in circles, hitting the same potholes every time, seeing the same scenery."

"So Hank coming down here with you, that was new scenery?"

Javi shrugs, eyelids heavy, like the question makes him so bored he might fall asleep.

I stare up at the painting on the garage wall. It's of two men—cowboys, judging by the boots. Which is pretty much all there is to judge them by. One is sitting on the ground naked, aside from the boots, a cigarette in his mouth, staring at a fire. The other has on shorts so tight the fly is bursting open, and he's wringing out something. Clothes maybe. Some horses are in the background.

"Like it?" Javi asks, catching my eye. "George Quaintance. I'm not usually an art guy, but Russ saw it and liked it, and Russ usually takes what he likes."

"That's whose place this is, right?"

"Russ, yeah. He's the president. He and the rest of the guys are on a run to Salton Sea. I'm out of commission 'cause of the ankle. I could ride on the back but . . . gotta fix up Fernando over there." He points at the motorcycle on the bricks, then takes a pack of Lucky Strikes out of his shirt pocket and offers me one. I accept, and he uses the Silver Jay matches to light each of us up.

"You named your motorcycle Fernando?"

"When I'm riding a guy on the regular, it's polite to know his name," he says, smiling. "But I let him down. Some old white guy in an ugly orange Buick saw me driving and got that look people sometimes get when they see motorcycles. Ran me off the road."

I shake my head. "Sorry."

"That fucker should be the sorry one. I got this bike in Korea. They let me take it home when I was discharged, y'know? But no one sees a vet on his military ride over here. They see a brown guy on a motorcycle and think I need to get run over."

"You served?"

"We all served. Me, Tommy, and Stan in Korea. Russ and Will were in the Ninth Army. All of us kept our motorcycles." Javi grins. "I think Russ and Will were fucking when they were over there. I didn't know Tommy or Stan till we all got back though. But we all found each other at some dive bar or another, and we fucked and we found out we all rode so . . . why not start a club, right? Tommy's idea. He loved the image of it, matching jackets, riding together taking up the whole highway, like a cloud."

"How about Hank?"

"Oh, he's not a vet. He was just good in bed."

"But not Edward?"

"Edward was okay. Not really masculine the way we normally like them, though. And he liked to play at the hard stuff, not really do it, y'know? 'Oh, tie me up, spank me—but not too hard.'" Javi rolls his eyes and leans forward, a veil of smoke from his cigarette covering his face. "You look like you could handle the hard stuff."

I grin, not sure what to say to that. Seems like they have their own version of the Mattachine's "social rules." The music seems to get louder. "What's this song?"

He leans back, disappointed in me for changing the subject. "'Picaflor'—'hummingbird.' Yma Sumac."

I nod like I know what he just said. "I like it," I try, and sip more of the whiskey, taking another drag of the cigarette. I know he's amused by me, toying a little.

"So Hank is gone. But you might know where he is?"

Javi drinks again, slowly, eyes locked on mine. "What do I get for telling you?"

I smile. "You said he vanished with Tommy, another one of the club, right? Don't you want me to find them, then? So you know Tommy is okay?"

"Tommy will be fine," Javi says with a smile. "But I bet Russ would like to know where he is." Javi leans back. I watch him study the smoke from his cigarette. "All right. I don't know where they are. But I know Hank's family is around here, in LA. And I know his full name is Henry Nolton." Javi takes a long drag, leans in to blow the smoke over my face. "Junior."

"So if I find Henry Nolton, Sr.... You think he's with his family?"

"Best guess. Didn't sound like he had any old friends in the area. He and Edward met freshman year of college, apparently, and hooked up, and I guess just never let go. Edward really ran their lives, I think. Hank always would ask one of us what he was supposed to do next, no matter how many times we told him he could do whatever he wanted. Like a puppy waiting for orders. I think when he realized that, after a day or two with us back in San Francisco, that might be when he and Edward started fighting. I don't think he was happy with Edward, with the idea that he'd been doing whatever Edward wanted. He picked the bars, the guys they went home with. He was the one who made them move to San Francisco. Real control freak. Which can be fun sometimes but. This is why you shouldn't have just *one* boyfriend." Javi lets his eyes run up and down me, then sips his drink again.

I smirk. "You said Russ would want to find Tommy. They're a couple?"

"Yeah, but not in a greedy way. We all share. Just those two are each other's boyfriend."

Or were, I think. Before Tommy vanished with Hank. Maybe they got tired of sharing. Maybe Russ got jealous. No, I tell myself, I'm leaping to conclusions. They might just be playing house, or off on a day trip of their own.

"And your boyfriends are Will and Stan?" I guess.

He laughs. "Nah. My boyfriends don't ride. They like the jacket though, like the leather. Like bending me over the seat of my bike and—"

"Thanks," I say, over the dirty-talk intimidation. "I get it."

"Welcome to Long Beach," he says with a grin. "Hope you enjoy your stay."

I finish my drink and stand. "Thanks for the information. If I find Tommy, I'll come let you know."

"Sure," he says, like he doesn't care, but there's a flash of something behind his eyes. Worry? Relief? I'm not sure, the room is too filled with smoke. "And if Hank comes back, where can we find you?"

"I'm staying at a hotel over on Temple in LA. The one down the street from the Doc Kilzum sign."

He nods. "I know it. Good luck, Detective."

"Thanks. Nice meeting you, Javi."

He lifts his glass as if toasting me and downs what's left in one swallow. I leave, and behind me I can hear the shuffle of his cast on the concrete as he makes his way back to his motorcycle, to fix it up.

With a name, it's not too hard to get an address in LA. All you need is a phone book, which I find once I'm back in LA proper by going into a drugstore and asking to see theirs. Nolton is an unusual enough name there's only one Henry with it in the county, up in San Marino. Fancy neighborhood.

I glance at my watch. It's nearly four, which means I have plenty of day left to scout the place out and, if I'm lucky, catch Hank. If he's just hiding out there, maybe playing house with this other Bacchanal, Tommy, alive and well, then I'll approach him to ask about Edward and Daphne, if it feels safe. Maybe being able to drop Javi's name will help, too. If I'm lucky, I can start the drive home tomorrow morning.

The Nolton house isn't really a house. It's a mansion with a high gate and walls and trees to mark the rest of it. I walk by the gate slowly, glancing past it. There's a circular driveway with a fountain in the middle and a mansion beyond that; two stories, big archways, something you'd see in a postcard from an Italian vineyard more than Southern California. The building is too far to spot anyone inside, though I see a few cars parked in front. I don't have any other leads, so I get back in my car and wait down the street, watching the gate to see who comes out of it.

I keep the radio low, humming along to "Now and Then There's a Fool Such as I," feeling pretty foolish myself as the sun gets lower and lower, turning the sky orange. The air gets thicker, too, my neck and shoulders wet with humidity, even though I'm just sitting and watching. I wait nearly two hours before a car comes out, a gold Oldsmobile coupe, the driver blocked by the trees in front of the gate until they turn onto the road, and then I can just see the back of their head—a man. Beyond that, I can't tell. I turn on my engine and follow from a distance.

We drive ten minutes up to northern Pasadena, away from the nice suburban homes, and into something more pastoral. I think about pulling up next to him and getting a look at his face, but I worry about seeming aggressive. If it is Hank, and I'm going to be asking him for information, best to avoid that. He pulls off the parkway and turns a few more corners before pulling into the parking lot of a large blocky building. It's white stone, only three stories high, with some moderne lines around the doorway. The parking lot is to the side, but the walkway from the sidewalk is long, lined in palm trees, their leaves turning gold at the edges.

I pull slowly into the lot. It's got a few other cars in it, so hopefully it doesn't look too suspicious. The driver finally gets out—not Hank, not based on Myrtle's description. He's shorter, hair lighter . . . he looks like Edward. But why would Edward be at Hank's family home? It could be Tommy, I guess, if Hank has a type, but the way this guy is dressed, in a neat brown suit, doesn't scream motorcycle club. I wait until he's halfway down the walkway to the building before getting out and following him. Something is bothering me. If it is Edward, then something is very wrong. You don't tell your parents about your boyfriends if you're gay. You don't tell them you're gay at all. How would Hank's family know Edward well enough to let him stay at their place? And where are we now?

I follow him up the pathway, the sun low enough now that he and the palm trees cast long shadows, like the bars of a cage. For the first time all day, there's a breeze, and the palm leaves rustle. He goes inside, and I follow, stopping outside the door to read the small sign hung over it: NORTH PRIVATE CLINIC. The bad feeling I had grows more intense, a physical thrust in my stomach.

Inside isn't the creaky haunted old asylum I expect though. It's beautiful, in fact; black and white marble tiles in a large foyer. There's a white front desk with a nurse behind it, a few chairs, and white doors leading off on both sides. Standing fans are in every corner, blowing the air around, and it actually feels a little cooler. Several vases of flowers are placed around the room, too—on small tables in the corners and on the desk. Sweet pea and lilac, I think. Happy smells that mostly cover the faint whiff of floor polish and something else I can't identify, something unpleasant. They know better than to use dahlias I guess.

Edward, or whomever he was, is already gone. The nurse behind the desk looks up at me expectantly. She's in her twenties, too cheerful looking for a clinic.

"Hello. May I help you?"

"Uh, yes." I walk closer, thinking fast. How do I ask about someone whose name I don't know? "I'm looking for someone."

The door to my left opens. I hear it swing, but don't look. And then a new voice shoots through the lobby: "Evander?"

The voice isn't new, not really; it's just I only hear it a few times a year now. But I know it by heart without even looking. I put on a smile and turn slowly.

"Hi, Mom."

SEVEN

She looks exactly the same, but not, a double exposure of her from when I was a child and her now. She wears her hair the same way, in a bob to her neck, and her eyes are the same vibrant blue as mine. She's not a tall woman, though I didn't realize that until I was a teenager. She's got a round face and pointed chin, and even when she was scolding me, there was always a smile bubbling under the scowl. Now it's just a smile. There are new lines in her face, and her hair isn't quite the same shade of brown. I guess the salon couldn't get the dye the right color. And her nurse's outfit is nearly identical to all the other ones I've seen her in—white skirt, blouse, and hat.

She runs up and hugs me tight, her head buried in my chest, and I can feel the years I've been away in how she holds me. I hug her back, instinctively bending a little, trying to be as close as possible. It feels like the hug is too short and too long by the time she pulls back, hands still on my shoulders, studying me. We haven't seen each other in person in seven years.

"That's quite a tie."

I look down. A baby blue one today, with a few little white starbursts. Thankfully the shirt is white and the suit is a dark enough blue you might tell yourself it's navy. If I knew I'd be seeing her, I would have put on my Mattachine costume.

I laugh. "Yeah, I'm trying fashion."

She reaches up to touch my face and smiles. "You should have told me you were coming."

I feel an immense crushing guilt, all of LA falling down on top of me. I wasn't going to tell her at all.

"I wanted to surprise you," I lie.

She smiles, hugs me again. "And what a wonderful surprise it is! Seven years . . . you look older."

"Thanks." I laugh.

"No, I mean more mature." She squeezes my arm. "But I don't have food in the house for dinner tonight." She pulls off me and shakes her head. "We'll go out." She turns to the nurse at the desk. "Marge, this is my son, come to visit all the way from San Francisco!"

Marge smiles, lowering her eyelashes slightly. I know that look. Female suspects used to try it on me sometimes when I was on the force. We shake hands, and she keeps smiling. "I've heard so much about you. Your mom is so proud of you."

I smile, trying to shrug it off, but it just feels like more rubble from LA hitting me on the head. "She just pretends to be because I'm her only kid. It would look bad if she told you what I was really like."

Mom pats me on the shoulder, laughing, and Marge, frozen for a moment in confusion, then laughs, too.

"And funny," Marge says. "She didn't say you were funny."

"He normally isn't," Mom says, almost suspicious. "Well, I have to go turn in a few reports to Dr. North, but then I'll be right back out here and we'll go to . . ." She spins her finger in the air, as if a roulette wheel were really doing the choosing. "The Headliner. It's new, you'll like it."

"All right." I think about asking about Edward, but Mom would get suspicious. She kisses me on the cheek and walks out through the door opposite the one she came in, unlocking it to get through.

"You're just like she described," Marge says. "Are you really a detective?"

"I am. And it's a funny thing, but my detective eyes might be fooling me. Just a few steps ahead of me coming in, I swear I saw my friend Edward from San Francisco. But what are the chances of both of us being in LA, in this building, at the same time?"

I give her my best smile and she blushes slightly, then shrugs. "Stranger things have happened."

"So it was him? I'm not losing my mind?" I pause. Probably the wrong thing to say here.

She seems to think it was in bad taste, too, and sits back down, thinking. "I couldn't tell you if it was," she says finally. "We have a very strict privacy policy. I'm sorry!" She looks genuinely sorry, too, and I almost think about pushing it some more, but I can't, not now. Maybe there's a way to talk to Mom about it. This is going to be tricky. Of all the mental clinics in all of LA . . . though how many mental clinics are there in LA? I wonder. Maybe this was inevitable. And maybe—I swallow a sigh as I think it, LA crashing down on me again, a churning maelstrom of concrete and cement I'm never going to get out of—I can use it. Use my mother.

I smile at Marge as she tells me all about how wonderful my mother is, eager to fill the silence. Maybe the man I saw wasn't even Edward, and I'm just chasing wild geese. Though I think Marge would have just said no if it wasn't him. Probably. I'm not sure. Seeing Mom has got my head spinning.

Marge is telling me a funny story about Mom accidentally getting another nurse's birthday confused with her husband's when Mom comes back out. She's changed out of the nurse's uniform into a plain pale green dress, her hair pushed behind her ears.

"I thought since you're here, I'd change. Good thing I keep a dress in my locker just in case." She takes my arm in both her hands and spins me around to the front door.

"Bye, Marge!" she calls back behind us.

"Nice meeting you," I say to Marge as I'm steered out the door.

When it closes behind us, Mom says in a low voice, "Don't be too nice, she's desperate for a husband and I might have talked you up a little too much to her."

I laugh. Mom is kind, but she's also a little wicked. "She seemed perfectly nice," I say.

"She is. She's just not the shiniest penny, you know? Not someone who can compete with all the femmes fatales you must meet chasing cases." She smiles as we walk through the palm trees, which seem to be standing taller, saluting her. "But I guess you can take a break from those?"

The question lingers. Mom has a blind spot about my love life, but she's always been quick to figure out all the other little half-truths I've told her. It's part of why I don't visit.

"I'm here on a case, actually," I say finally.

She sighs and lets go of my arm. She's guessed it, but it still disappoints her.

"But I'm glad to see you," I say.

"I'm glad to see you, too." She takes my hand again and laces my fingers through hers. Her hands feel older than I remember, the skin on them rough but thinner, like newspaper. "It would be nice if it were more often. Once a year, maybe?"

"You can come up and visit, too," I say, almost instinctively, though my brain immediately points out the reasons she can't: where I live, where I work, Gene.

"In your little studio apartment? Where would I stay?"

"You can get a hotel, I'd pay."

She shakes her head. "What's the point of visiting you if I only see you a few hours a day?"

I swallow. She won't like that I'm staying at a hotel.

We're in the parking lot now, and she spots my car immediately. "That's yours?"

"How'd you know?"

"Only one I don't recognize. Also, it's ugly. Your father would have loved it."

I laugh, wondering how often maybe-Edward comes here.

"Okay, get in your ugly car and follow mine." She points at a bright yellow Mercury coupe. It is, I concede, a much-nicer-looking car. She hugs me around the waist again and then we head out. I follow her down a few small streets, through the nice suburban parts of Pasadena with the fancy houses shaded by wide-limbed trees, and then to the main drag of Colorado Boulevard, so lovely and anonymous it could be a movie set for any small city in America. She parks across from the old *Star-News* building, which is next to the restaurant she mentioned: the Headliner, named because of its neighbor, going by the paperboy on the menus.

Inside is an upscale diner, with red vinyl tablecloths and the smell of fried food. Mom orders the Swiss steak with a baked potato and a green salad, while I go back to a cheeseburger, and we both get Cokes. As we wait for the food, she asks me how I am, taking careful stock of my hands, skin, the circles under my eyes. Seven years of changes all at once, like she's making notes on my chart—the nurse in her comes out like this sometimes, and I was always sufficiently used to it to just let it happen again now.

"You're not getting enough sleep," she says finally. "And too much heat. Take cold showers. Your father always used to overheat in the summer. And this has been a hot one. Is it this hot up by you?"

I nod, sipping my Coke. "It must be tough on your patients."

"Oh, no more than anyone else, I think. They have windows, fans, usually."

"It did look fancy. It's new?"

"Well, it was a hospital until a few years ago. Now it's just the mental clinic."

"And"—I lean forward—"it's safe? I mean, you working with . . ."

She smiles, amused by the question. "It's sweet you worry. But of course it is. Sure, some of them have some moments, but none of them are violent or criminals. It's a private institution, people check themselves in voluntarily, or their families do it."

I nod, trying not to show how much I'm taking notes, and wondering how bad I should feel pumping her for information like this. But she's the best lead I have now.

I think about just laying everything out for her, asking honestly, but I don't think that would be fair to her, asking her to choose to betray her job or to disappoint her son. Instead, I just sip my Coke again, then say, "I'd love to see the inside of the place. Beyond the lobby, I mean. See how good they're treating you."

She beams. "Maybe I can give you a little tour, ask Dr. North to talk to you, just to ease your mind. He's a lovely man." She pats my hand. The waiter sets down our food, and Mom keeps looking at me, her eyes narrowing for a moment. "Will that make you feel better?"

I know she's onto me, so I just nod and eat. Of course she works Sunday and has Monday off, which means another day before I can get in there. Mom never minded working Sundays. We weren't very religious, just went to church on Christmas and Easter. Sometimes folks didn't love it, but she always told them, "Just because God's busy doesn't mean people don't need nurses." I always liked that response. Even if right now it means I'm one day further from going home. If I'd come one day later, maybe she would never have seen me. Another brick of the city falls on me as I think that.

"I haven't had time to make your bed up, of course. And your room isn't quite as you left it. I tried to make it a bit more of a guest room, for when your aunt Hattie comes to visit. Took down that baseball poster you had."

I nod, having forgotten about it. I'd never really cared much about baseball. Dad had, and it seemed like something I should care about so that no one would suspect. "That's fine."

"I still have your old high school medals up, though. You'll see. The room looks good."

I swallow a bite of my burger and put it down on the plate. There's no way out of this one.

"Mom, I'm at a hotel."

She leans back, eyes narrowing. "What?"

"I'm working a case," I say quickly. "I don't want that coming to your doorstep. I already checked in."

She rolls her eyes. "Evander, I lived with your father for thirty years, and most of those he had a job as an insurance investigator, which is dangerous, too."

"Not as dangerous—" She holds up a finger and I go silent, some long-buried instinct taking control.

"Maybe not as dangerous, but tell me, what kind of case is it?"

"I shouldn't tell you."

She keeps staring.

I sigh. "Missing persons."

"And has anyone threatened you?"

"Yes," I say, thinking of Javi and his chain.

"Did you talk your way out of it?"

"Yes," I repeat, already knowing I'm going to lose this one.

"And has anyone drawn a gun?"

"No," I concede. These were the questions she had for Dad, too, the few times his cases started looking deeper and darker than things vanishing off the back of a truck. He asked Mom to take me and stay with Aunt Hattie for a week. Only happened twice, but I remember Mom asking the same questions of Dad with the same look on her face: unimpressed, mildly annoyed. I think he had the same answers as mine, too.

"Then after dinner, you go get your things from the hotel, and I'll make your bed up. You can still find your way home, can't you? Remember the address?"

I roll my eyes. "Yes."

She studies me a moment, then leans forward again, elbows on the table. "If you're here, you're staying at home. Unless you didn't really want to see me?"

"Of course I wanted to see you, Mom," I say quickly. And I did, I realize. I do. I'm glad I'm seeing her. Even if I wasn't sure I wanted to. Even if I told myself to avoid it.

She smiles, believing me. The thing that's saved me all these years is that she never pushes. Sometimes she makes little comments or sighs a certain way, but I think if she ever suspected something was odd about my romantic life, she would just never ask, and it would eventually fade away. I guess that's what's happened. I'm about to turn thirty-seven, after all. I've never mentioned a girlfriend. Sometimes I wonder if she knows, but then I don't think she'd still call me on my birthday.

"Are you staying for your birthday?" she asks, as if reading my mind.

I pick my burger back up and start eating again, shaking my head. "I have some plans back home I've been told not to miss."

"Told by whom?"

There it is. That's why she still calls on my birthday. She's still holding out hope.

"Just friends, Mom."

She sighs and starts eating her food. "Well, maybe we can celebrate before you go, then. I can bake a cake. You still love coconut cake, I hope?"

"I've never had one as good as yours."

She smiles. "Good. Coconut cake. Tomorrow night. I have Mondays off, so I can spend the whole day cooking, and you can tell me all about your exciting detective life."

"I still have to work the case." I think I should be scouting out Hank's place some more. Maybe stop the guy I think is Edward, ask him some questions. That would be something, at least, until I can get a tour of the asylum from Mom.

"It's Monday," Mom says. "Crimes don't happen on Monday. Too early in the week."

I stare at her a moment to make sure she's joking before laughing. "I'll be home by dinner."

"Good."

The waiter comes and takes our empty plates away a few minutes later, and I pay, even though Mom tries to talk me out of it. Outside, the sun is finally really down, and it's only streetlamps and windows that light up the night, like sequins on one of Lee's dresses.

"I'll see you at home," Mom says, getting into her car, and for a moment the word makes me feel so lonely, because I miss home—real home, Lee's dresses, and the Ruby, and Gene's ice-cold hands lingering on mine.

"Sure," I say.

I get in the car and pull out my map to navigate back to the hotel. Los Angeles isn't really a city, not like San Francisco. It's too stretched out, dozens of small cities between long highways of dark. I make my way east to the Arroyo Seco Parkway and head south back to the hotel. The parkway is just a dozen years old and already the lights alongside it are half out, the asphalt stained with dark tire marks. By the time I get back to the hotel, the green light from Doc Kilzum seems almost comforting.

I pack my things up and check out, then throw my suitcase in the trunk of my car. I fish out some quarters. Better to call Gene from the pay phone than home. I count out the change and then close my car door, and turning to the street, I suddenly hear a roar of engines. Not car engines.

There are three of them, but it feels like more when they surround me. One pulls up onto the sidewalk, the other two stay on the street, on either side of my car, cutting me off from running. Riding on the back of one of the motorcycles is Javi, who points at me. The long chain is curled around his forearm.

"That's him."

The one on the sidewalk looks me up and down. He's forty, maybe, gray at his temples, dark hair swept back. He's got on a leather jacket over a white T-shirt and jeans. He keeps one foot on the ground. He glances back at Javi, gives him an unbelieving look.

"Really?"

"That's what the guy from the Silver Jay said," Javi says.

"We'll find out, I guess," the one in front of me says. He turns to look me over. "Pretty though." He doesn't smile when he says it, although his eyes spark. "Now, come on. We gotta talk."

I know an order when I hear one. I look left and right, but there's nowhere to run they couldn't grab me.

The one in front of me sees me analyzing all the ways out in my head and grins again.

"Buddy, there's no way out of this. Hop on."

I swallow, but he's right. There are three of them, plus Javi with his chain. I have no choice.

EIGHT

The one in front of me pats behind him on the seat of his motorcycle. "Come on, I won't bite unless you like it."

I slip my legs over the machine behind him, our bodies snug, the engine vibrating.

"Now wrap your arms around me, real tight. I can handle it." I feel like they're old words, a joke he's told before but he doesn't have it in him to make it funny right now. Something is off.

I do as he says. Before I even get comfortable, he pulls out. It feels like I'm a bullet just shot from a gun. Wind grabs at my face and hair, shoots under my jacket, yanks my tie so hard I feel like I'm being strangled. No wonder they wear the leather jackets. It's been so hot, but we go so fast the air gets cold, wraps around my skin with a pleasant chill, then keeps moving until it's rough like sandpaper. It feels like we're on the road for an hour, but we just end up back at the house I'd first found Javi at. They slow down, and each pulls his motorcycle into the garage. Javi's is still up on bricks. The place looks mostly the same. A few more beer bottles out, a worn white tee thrown over one of the barstools.

I get off the motorcycle, my legs weak. I didn't realize how hard I'd been gripping the bike with them. The man I'd been riding behind looks me over and smirks.

"Come on, sit down." He pulls out a stool next to the bar. "First time is always terrifying. That's what makes it fun."

I sit, letting my blood slow down a little, until I remember I didn't exactly come by choice. "What do you want?"

"I'm Russ. You met Javi, and that's Will." Russ nods at a guy about his age, but with a lot more gray in his otherwise black hair. It's crept up so it's really just the top center that has black now, but his hair is sharply parted and combed to the side, the black shadowing over, making him almost lopsided. He's big, his muscles tight against his T-shirt, and he looks tired. "And that's Stan." He's younger, with curly reddish hair and a faint scar on his chin, freckles on his arms and nose. Much thinner than the others. They're all dressed identically, like in uniforms, the white tee, the jeans, the black leather jacket with the Bacchanal patch.

I nod. "Good to meet you, maybe. Though I don't love being taken somewhere without a choice."

Russ smirks and goes behind the bar, pulls out some beers, pops the caps, starts handing them out—one for me, too. I drink it down.

"Javi says you're a gay PI."

I nod.

"That true?"

"Yes."

"And you're looking for Hank? Any luck?"

"Maybe some. I'm not sure yet."

Russ stares at me, drinking his beer.

"Just tell him," Javi says, sitting on the stool next to mine. "The tough-guy thing doesn't work when everyone is being a tough guy. Nothing gets done."

Russ sighs, and he looks at the ground. I suddenly see how sad he is. "Yeah." He kicks the ground and looks back up at me. The smirk is gone, the machismo. "Hank vanished with my boyfriend, Tommy."

"I know. I haven't seen Tommy, if that's what you want to know."

"No." Russ shakes his head. "We found Tommy. He's dead."

I feel my eyebrows shoot up. "Murdered?" I wonder if Hank

has turned from Mattachine to motorcycle to murderer all in a few weeks.

"Yes," says Russ at the same time as Will says, "No."

I look between them. Russ is glaring at Will, angry, hands clenching into fists.

"He was a junkie," Will says. "I'm sorry, Russ, but he was, and he overdosed. The police said so."

"The coroner already saw him?" I ask.

"Yeah," Javi says, glancing between the two older men. "They told his family first. His mother called today, knew Tommy lived here."

Russ sighs. "She thought I was his landlord."

"I'm sorry," I say.

Russ nods and downs the rest of his beer before taking out another. Everyone else finds ways to look at the floor or walls. I stare at the cowboys again.

Russ drinks a whole other bottle of beer and then puts it down on the bar with surprising gentleness. "Over in Korea, he got injured pretty bad. Lost a finger, arm was broken in a lot of places. Whole thing looks like patchwork, all the scars over it." I look over at Russ, and when our eyes meet, he flinches, like telling the story to someone is harder than just saying it to empty space. He looks down. "They gave him painkillers. I don't know if it was the wrong kind, or too many, or if Tommy is just the kind of guy who gets hooked on stuff, but when they sent him back, he needed it. Said the pain came back otherwise. I don't know. First time we met, next morning, I found him with a needle in his arm in the kitchen. He knew how to score the good stuff. But I liked him. So I decided I'd try to help him out, get him to quit. Took a while, almost a year, but we . . ." Russ pauses, searching. "We figured out a system. And he was clean."

"That you know," Will says.

"He was clean!" Russ roars, picking the bottle up again and smashing it on the bar. Everyone is silent as Russ stares at each of them in turn, finishing with me. He seems to remember I don't know him and shakes his head. "He was clean. I know it. He was killed. He left his jacket." He points, desperate, at a leather jacket on a hook in the corner. It has the same purple patch as the others. A Muir cap hangs over it. "He loved that jacket. The patches were his idea, he designed them. He never went anywhere without it." Russ looks around for confirmation, but none of the others will meet his eyes. "He wouldn't have left without it." His voice is softer, pleading.

Javi lights a cigarette in the silence, the smoke drifting up to the roof of the garage.

"So you think someone forced him to take the drugs?" I ask Russ.

He shakes his head. "I don't know. His mother said they didn't even do a real autopsy. Just found him in an alley in the bad part of town, an empty needle next to him, and they assumed. She told them he'd had trouble with drugs, that probably cinched it. Tommy didn't exactly hide it. Everyone knew about his problems."

I nod. A junkie, ex or not, found with an empty needle made for an open-and-shut case. "What kind of drugs was he into?"

"Morphine," Russ says quickly. "I don't know if that's what they gave him in the hospital, but . . . it was morphine."

"Okay. So you think he was too clean to shoot up again. But you hadn't seen him in how long?"

"Just over a week," Russ says softly. "Not enough time for him to fall back into it."

In my experience, there's no timeline for how fast a junkie can get back into drugs, but I don't say that. "What do you want me to do?"

"You're a detective, right? Prove he was killed. Find who did it."

"And what will you do?"

"Visit justice on the guilty party." Russ's expression turns haughty. "I know what you're thinking—the motorcycle, the jacket. But I'm a lawyer. I know how to make someone's life hell without killing them. I know how to wrap them up in all kinds of trouble they *will* get caught for."

I try not to look too surprised by the lawyer thing.

"Russ," Stan says. "Please, just . . . we just lost Tommy. We don't want to lose you, too. To anger. Y'know?"

"If the detective here can't find anything, will you accept it was an overdose?" Javi asks.

I can feel the vibrations between the men. The smoke from Javi's cigarette is white lines sectioning them off, like the bars of a cell. Everyone's silent.

Finally, Russ nods. He looks up at me. "Get it done." He walks out of the garage.

I look at the rest of the club, all of them deflated in different ways. Even Will, the one who'd been arguing with Russ, seems sad about the outcome.

He sees me looking and shakes his head. "There was no ending to this we liked. He's hurting."

"You'll take the case?" Javi asks, the only one who seems to realize I haven't agreed to anything yet. I take a deep breath. It smells like tobacco and sweat. This won't get me home any earlier.

"I'll take it. I'm already looking for Hank, so maybe he can tell me what happened."

"He's probably sleeping it off somewhere," Will says. "Tommy always needed more of the stuff, same as any dopehead. But Hank was mostly clean. Never saw him doing more than a little reefer. So if Tommy introduced him to the stuff, if he was careful, he's fine."

"He might be hooked now, too," Stan says, shaking his head sadly. "Sometimes it just takes one try."

"Yes, drugs are bad," Javi says, rolling his eyes. "Let's let the detective come up with the theories, though."

"When was the last time anyone saw Tommy?" I ask. "And Hank?"

The three of them look at one another, trying to remember.

"Between one and two weeks ago," Will says. "I think Javi had just gotten run off the road, so we were taking turns visiting him in the hospital. Russ was at work late, so he wasn't here, but Stan and I"—Will looks to Stan, who nods, confirming—"we went off to see Javi."

"I brought him a teddy bear." Stan grins. "The nurses thought that was hilarious."

"That was . . ." Javi's eyes trace the smoke. "Two Wednesdays ago."

"You remember the day I gave you little Axel?" Stan grins.

"It was the day before they let me leave." Javi smirks slightly. "So, yes."

"You remember what time?" I ask, trying to get them back on track.

"Visiting hours are four until seven," Javi recites. "They usually showed up late though and stayed long enough the nurses got annoyed."

"So you just left them here?" I ask Will, trying to get them back on track. "Tommy and Hank? Around four?"

Will nods. "Tommy was showing Hank something with his

bike. Hank didn't have one yet, he was trying to figure out what kind to buy. They were here. Four sounds right."

"And when you got back, was anything amiss?" I ask. "Signs of struggle or anything?"

Javi barks a laugh and gestures at the garage. He's right, it's a mess.

"Anything strange though?" I ask.

Will shakes his head. "Tommy's bike was gone, so I just thought they'd gone for a ride. Russ is right that it's strange Tommy left his jacket, but it was so hot I didn't think anything of it. Russ was back by then, but he didn't mention seeing them. You can ask him, but . . ." Will's eyes drift to the main house. He's right, Russ is too emotional right now. I think about maybe asking them about Hank and Edward, seeing if the others know anything Javi didn't mention, but it's quiet in a way that I know my questioning would change for the worse. Like smoking around a puddle of gasoline.

"Tomorrow," I say. They nod quietly. "Can someone give me a lift back to my car?"

Will chuckles half-heartedly. "Forgot about that. Sure, I'll take you."

I nod goodbye to Stan and Javi, unsure if I should say anything else. They're clients now, but I don't think they're going to invite me to join their knitting circle anytime soon.

Will gets on his bike and waits for me to join him. I sit behind him, tuck my tie into my shirt, and then he takes my arms and adjusts them around his waist. "Careful now. You steady?"

"Yeah." I wait for some sexual innuendo or joke. But he just nods and then we take off.

The wind rips too loudly in my ears to even try having a conversation with him. He drives a little slower than Russ did on the way here and takes the turns more gently, like he's being careful with me. When we stop in front of the hotel, bathed in the green light of Doc Kilzum, I carefully lift my leg off and stand for a moment, thighs shaking, but he stays on the motorcycle, idling.

"You seemed to think it wasn't murder."

Will shrugs. "I've seen what dope can do to people. And I don't think Tommy was as clean as Russ thinks."

"What makes you say that?"

Will stares at me a moment, and I realize he doesn't trust me. None of them do, except Russ maybe. I was hired to placate him, not really solve anything. "Just . . . his eyes sometimes. He'd have this glazed, sort of far-off look like he was high. Not so high he was in danger or anything, but . . ." Will shakes his head. "Maybe I should have said something to Russ. Gone through Tommy's things and taken the drugs away, but . . ."

"How'd Tommy and Russ get together?"

Will laughs. "Lust at first sight. Russ likes those young pretty boys, and Tommy likes them a little older, but manly, muscled."

"But he never went for you?" I ask, and realize it sounds a little like a come-on as I do.

Will's gaze never leaves me, but it shifts, evaluating. "I don't have a type really," he says finally, taking out a pack of cigarettes from his jacket pocket. He offers me one, and I take it. The matches are in his pocket, too, and he strikes one, lighting my cigarette first, then his. I take a deep inhale, letting the nicotine steady my legs. He leans back a little, looks up to watch the smoke that's left his lips. "If I were going to pair off with someone, not just sex, but someone for keeps, I think he'd have to be made of stronger stuff than Tommy. I don't mean to sound conceited or anything, but I like a steady life, and that means having a steady partner to ride with. Strong, inquisitive, gets the job done." He smiles so slightly

I can't tell if he's being funny. Then he sighs and looks at his cigarette, barely smoked. "Anyway, come by tomorrow, and Javi can help you out some more, answer more questions, maybe direct you to Russ, if he's at work. I better take off. I have an early shift."

"You a doctor?"

He throws the cigarette down and crushes it with his boot, then looks up at me, smiling, a little amused. "No. I'm a cop. Like you were."

And before I can think of a response, he's gone, the loud rip of his engine tearing open the night and leaving it naked.

I'm holding the cigarette without smoking it long enough it singes my fingers, and I throw it down next to his, stomping it out. Then I get in my car. I stay seated behind the wheel for a while without moving. My hands are stiff. Another gay cop. I thought I was the only one in the world. That was some kind of arrogance.

I pull into my childhood driveway a little while later. Dad and I used to have paper airplane races here, coming up with more complicated folds and additions, trying to see who could fly farther. I get out of the car and stare at the fixed porch beam. Through the window I can see Mom in the living room, and she waves, smiling. I have a life I can't tell her about.

Inside, the house isn't nearly as changed as outside. The sofa has a different fabric, and the pillows have changed, but it's still in the same place. Still the same pale yellow wallpaper with the daisies. And it smells the same, too, like vanilla and soap. Mom has the record player on, and even the music is the same—Ethel Waters singing "Am I Blue?" One of Mom's favorites when I was a kid. She smiles and takes my hands, dancing with me a little.

"I never liked that this was a sad song, but sounded so happy," I say.

"You loved it when you were little," she says, still dancing with me. "You would stand on my feet and we'd dance like this."

"That was before I understood it."

"Sometimes you have to make the sad things seem happy." She lets go of my hands and walks over to the record player, opening a cabinet next to it. It's filled with records, maybe more than I have. "I wanted to show you . . ." She takes out a small record in a paper sleeve that looks sort of like a postcard. I flinch, recognizing it. During the war, some of the Pepsi canteens let you record messages as records and mail them to people you loved. I made one for Mom. "I know you hid it last time you were here."

"Mom—"

"Don't even try to deny it, Detective," she says, her voice playful. She takes it out of the sleeve and puts in on the player.

"I just—"

"I realized it was missing the day after you left. Only took me a few hours to find. Not as clever as you thought, hm?"

She turns the player on.

"Hey, Mom, it's me." My voice is broken by the cracks and pops of the record and pauses that could also be the record or just my past, not sure what to say. "I thought this was kind of neat. Add me to the record collection, right?" I laugh. "Maybe I should sing? I can sing a little of your favorite, 'Am I Blue?'" And then, horrifically, I start to sing. "'Am I blue, am I blue. Ain't these tears in these eyes telling you. How can you ask me am I blue. Why, wouldn't you be, too. If each plan with your man done fell through.'" Just the chorus, which is a relief. I remember the funny look from the guy in the recording booth when I got to the "with your man" part, but he didn't say anything. "I'll be home soon, I promise, okay. I'm staying safe. I miss you. I love you. Don't be blue."

They weren't long records, though maybe it could have been longer if I'd prepared something, instead of just stepping into the booth because it felt like a fun idea, and recording one for her because I didn't know whom else to record one for.

"It's my favorite record, I listen to it every night." She told me that last time, too. Every night. That's why I hid it. Made me feel cold, picturing her in front of the record player every night, hearing my voice, this same stupid message. Not embarrassment, not exactly. Something close to it, maybe. Shame, but only because it seemed so lonely. Was I the one making her lonely?

"I wish you wouldn't do that, Mom." I turn the record player off. "I can call you, if you want."

She puts her hands behind her back, smiling. "Well, now I have you here, at least for a little while. Come on, I put fresh sheets on the bed, and it's late. Took you a while getting here."

She walks out of the living room and I grab my bag, following her, though it's not like she needs to lead me anywhere. My room is in the same place it was when I was a kid, upstairs and just down the hall from her and Dad's.

"Yeah, sorry," I say, not sure how to spin it. "Someone showed up as I was leaving, case related. I should . . ." I realize I never got a chance to call Gene. "You mind if I make a long-distance call? I can pay you back."

We're upstairs now, in front of the door to my room. "Andy, you don't need to pay to use the phone."

"I don't want to be any trouble."

She puts her hand on my face for a moment and looks a little sad. "You won't be. The phone is in the same place it's always been. I'm going to get ready for bed." I glance at my watch. It's nearly ten. She sees me and laughs. "I don't keep detective's hours."

"I just don't want to keep you up."

"Oh, don't worry, I can sleep through anything. You remember how your father snored."

I nod. He sounded like a truck barreling over a pothole.

She stretches up to kiss me on the cheek. "Good night, sweetheart. I'm so glad you're home."

"Me, too."

She goes into her bedroom down the hall and closes the door. There's a private bath in there, while mine is back downstairs. Also where the phone is. First I put my bag in my room, which hasn't changed too much. The posters are gone, but the walls are still baby-boy blue, the dented nightstand still has the lamp shaped like a monkey holding the shade with its tail. My desk is opposite, too small looking now, books on the shelves above them. And my two medals—high school bronze and silver in cross-country from junior and senior years at county meets. I never really liked it, but sometimes running was the only way to feel alone in high school, and that's when I usually felt safest. They're on the shelf, open, face out, but still in the cases they were presented in. And clean. Mom must dust in here regularly. On a corner of the desk is a framed photo of me, Mom, and Dad, me in my graduation robes. I stare at it a moment. We're all smiling, but I can see now how my smile doesn't fit right, how it's forced. I was afraid of what the world would do to me.

I put the photo back down. The world's done plenty, and I'm still here. But this isn't home anymore, either. It's like being on a movie set of my old life. I half expect some child actor to walk in any moment, dressed like me.

I unpack my stuff into my old bureau, then head downstairs, to the living room, where the phone is. It's red, with a comically long cord, and sits on a small table by the door so Mom could talk on it in the kitchen, too.

I pick it up and dial the Ruby. Gene picks up and I can hear a blast of music and laughter before he speaks. "This is the Ruby."

"It's me."

"Andy?"

"Yeah." I smile, hearing his voice. I miss him enough I feel like a can someone has squeezed all the soda out of, and now there's just that noise of the metal crackling and bending.

"You wrap up the case?" he asks, voice loud.

"Not exactly. Kind of took on a second one. But they're related. Still looking for the same people, they'll help me out."

"You really don't want to come back for your birthday, huh?"

"Gene—" I hear a creak on the stairs. I thought Mom went to bed. "I'll be home soon, I promise."

"Okay," he says, but he sounds disappointed. I get it.

"I have to go."

"I love you," he says, voice loud.

"I love you," I say back, trying to keep my voice loud enough he can hear it and low enough no one else can. I hang up and go look at the stairs. No one is on them. I'm alone.

NINE

I wake up to the smell of waffles. I glance at my watch—nine. I didn't pack any pajamas, I've just been sleeping in my jockeys—but I don't want to go downstairs like that. If I throw on a clean shirt before I've showered, though, Mom'll give me an earful. I riffle through the drawers and find an old pair of blue-and-white-striped pajamas and slip them on. They smell like mothballs and they're too tight and too short, but they'll do for now, I guess.

Downstairs, Mom is dressed, hair set, a yellow-and-white plaid apron over a floral dress. Patti Page is on the radio, singing "I Went to Your Wedding," and Mom is humming along as she fills the waffle iron with fresh batter. It's the same one we had when I was a kid, a ceramic top with bluebirds on it. The mixing bowl, at least, is new. Pink. There's a plate of waffles, tall as my hand, already on the kitchen table, along with a bottle of syrup, a butter dish, and two empty plates laid out with forks, knives, and yellow napkins.

"Morning. You've been busy."

"You sleep too late."

"Detective's hours." I go to the cabinet the glasses are normally in. But they're not. The plates are here now, ones I've never before seen with a pattern of daisies around the rim. "Water glass?"

She points. "I switched things up a little. And there's a pitcher of fresh orange juice in the fridge, if you'd like."

"Thanks." I haven't had a home-cooked breakfast since my stay at Lavender House, over a year ago. And I haven't had one cooked by my mom in a lot longer than that.

"You sleep all right?" she asks, as we cut into our waffles at the table. They taste sweet as childhood.

"Yeah, great." The bed felt too small, but I was out pretty quickly.

"And today you're going to . . . ?" She lets it hang.

Visit the bikers and learn more about Tommy. Stake out Hank's family home. See if I can find out anything about the clinic that employs you. "Work on the case," I say.

She nods, frowning a little. She wanted to know more. "Well, I'll have dinner on the table at seven. Will that work for your little pre-birthday soiree?"

"Sure." She smiles and I know if I miss it, her heart will shatter.

"Good. And anyone you want to invite?"

I look at her, puzzled. "I don't know anyone around here aside from you."

"No old friends? You're not still in touch with what was his name, Billy . . . Harrigan?"

I shake my head. Billy and I were never close, as much as I had wanted to be.

"Well, all right. Just us then." She says it very neutrally. I'm not sure what tone she's trying to hide.

"You want me to invite someone down from San Francisco? It'll take a while for them to show up."

She smiles a little at that. "No, no, you're right. I guess I'm just sad that you don't really have any roots here anymore."

"Sure I do. Just last night when I pulled in, I remembered airplane races with Dad. And I saw Mr. Garcia. He's still got his shop."

She narrows her eyes. "And still closes at eight."

She's right, damn. I shrug. "Maybe I saw him closing up, or on the street."

She holds my eyes a moment, then nods. "Well, I'm glad you still remember the old neighborhood. You can always come back. Be close to home."

I shake my head. She's brought it up before, but not in a while. "Mom, I can't do that."

"But you're not in the police anymore. You can move your job. Set up down here, maybe work for a movie studio, they need detectives."

"But I have friends, and—" I stop myself from saying a boyfriend. "A life. I can't move all that."

She sighs, but nods, her mouth folded into a line. "You're right. I'm sorry."

"I miss you, too." It only feels like a lie once I've heard it.

She gets up and starts putting things away, and I rush the rest of my waffle into my mouth before hopping in the shower, getting dressed, and pecking her on the cheek goodbye.

First I drive by Hank's family estate, just to see if there's any activity. It's around ten when the gold coupe emerges again. And again, I follow him, this time to a liquor store a mile or so away. The guy I think is Edward gets out. He's got on a blue polo shirt, slacks. He looks like a college kid, not moneyed or swishy or anything, really. He's a nice smile and a faint memory, but I get the impression that's intentional.

I get out of my car and follow him into the store. He's examining the red wines. He adjusts a few of the bottles so they're all facing exactly forward. He looks relaxed as he does it. Happy. I decide to take a chance.

"Edward," I say, not shouting, but loudly enough he'll hear it and look over if it is his name. He does. I get closer.

"I'm sorry"—he smiles, looks me over. Evaluating, but polite—"have we met?"

"I'm from San Francisco," I tell him, careful. I'm not sure how to play this.

He smiles at that, but it feels flimsy, cellophane. "What a coincidence. But, again, I'm so sorry, I must have forgotten. How do we know each other?"

It's him, then. I was hoping it wasn't for some reason. "The meetings," I say softly. "You know. At Myrtle's?"

His eyes go wide, and his smile grows, eyes running me up and down in a different way. "Oh, of course. I'm so sorry. What a small world it is." He stares at me a second, and then his smile falters for a moment before coming back, plastic again. He looks at the shelf and takes down a bottle of red. "Do you know this one? I know Italy, 1906, is a good year, but I'm not sure about this label." His voice is light, educated. Hank was the one from money, the motorcycle club told me, but Edward must blend right in.

"Myrtle has been worried you've been missing, actually," I interrupt. "You and Hank and Daphne."

He puts the wine back on the shelf, staring at me again. "Well, Hank and I are just fine." He doesn't blink as he says it. "Daphne I don't know anything about though. Is she missing, too?"

I nod. "Didn't you give her a ride home once? Do you remember where she lived?"

He shrugs, still baffled by all of this. "She was in Sea Cliff somewhere, I think."

"Maybe Hank would remember? He around? We can all go for a drink." I give Edward my best, most welcoming smile. The one I usually save for Gene.

He tilts his head at me, curious. "Both of us?"

"You know, a triangle is the strongest shape." It's an old pickup line my ex and I used during the war sometimes. It works on him. I can see it in the way he licks his lips.

But then he shakes his head. "We're staying with his family, it's . . . complicated."

"Oh?" I ask, voice still pleasant. "How do you manage that?"

"They think we're just old pals. College roommates who stayed roommates after graduation." He takes a bottle of wine off the shelf. "But I should really get going, Mr., ah—"

"Andy. I'd really love to see you two. Seems a shame to bump into each other and not take advantage. Where is Hank, anyway? Didn't want to go wine shopping?"

He flushes slightly, like he's embarrassed. "He didn't want to leave the pool. But I'm sorry, I just don't see how it would work, as I said." He offers an apologetic shrug. "Good to see you again."

He takes the bottle of wine to the counter and buys it, then nods at me once as he leaves. He doesn't look worried, and he spoke like they're back together. Maybe they are, and Hank is just waiting by the pool for a fresh bottle of wine. That doesn't explain what happened to Tommy though. Did they go out on the town and after Tommy overdosed, Hank ran back to his family and Edward? Did Hank have something to do with it? I have to talk to Hank, not Edward. I think about following Edward back, but that would be too aggressive. I already overplayed my hand; he got cagey pretty fast. I punch the steering wheel back in my car. I messed that up. I'm not sure what I could have done differently, but Edward was hiding something. And what was he doing at Mom's clinic? Maybe I'll know more after my tour.

I drive down to Long Beach, to the Bacchanals' garage. As expected for a Monday, everyone is at work, except Javi, still dragging around a cast and a trail of smoke. His unfamiliar music is playing again, rattles and high voices. He glances over from the bar as I pull in. The smoke from his cigarette is thick and white as sea-foam, churning over his face as if his body were underwater. I get out and walk up to him. The smell of smoke is stronger than ever, woodier.

"Hold still," he says, as I walk into the garage. I pause. He blows out another thick stream of smoke, his eyes studying the curls and tendrils of it. "All right," he says, which I take as permission to enter. "My grandfather used to say you could tell the future in smoke from hand-rolled cigarettes. Taught me how to do it when I was six."

"You're reading my future?"

"I want to know if hiring you was as stupid an idea as I think it is."

I smirk. "I thought it was yours. Get me on it, calm down Russ."

He shrugs. "That was the idea, but after seeing how he was last night, I don't know if he'll believe you when you tell him it was just another junkie overdose."

"Maybe it wasn't." I walk closer to the bar. "The smoke tell you that?"

He shakes his head, then snubs out the cigarette on the bar and grabs a wrench, limping back over to his motorcycle, still up on the bricks. "Don't get me wrong," he says, carefully getting down on his back. "I liked Tommy. I just know what he was. We all did. Except Russ maybe."

"What he was?"

"Headed for an early grave."

I let that one sit, and the music swells, the singer's voice stretching high and then plummeting down again.

"What makes you say that?" I ask, leaning on the bar and watching him work under the bike. His shirt rides up, showing off a flat stomach.

"It was just something you could see in him. If we drove along a cliff, his eyes would flash as he looked over the edge, like he wanted to jump. I don't know what happened to him in Korea. I saw some pretty nasty shit myself, but it did something to him. He wanted to suck death's dick and then bend over for him. The morphine was one way of doing that, but even off it, he drove too fast, too reckless, took stupid risks. I like fun and risks as much as the next guy with a bike, but he once played chicken on the highway with a freight truck because he thought the driver looked at him funny out the window."

I whistle slowly. "So you think this was just a long ride toward death?"

He looks over at me. "Pretty set of words for it, but yeah. Tommy was never going to make it, no matter how much Russ wanted him to. No matter how much Russ did for him." Javi sneers slightly and turns back to the motorcycle, twists something, then sighs. "Can you hand me . . ." He looks over at the bar and points at another wrench. "That one?"

I grab it and bring it over to him, kneeling down, close to him as I hand it over.

"Why do you think Russ loves Tommy so much?"

Javi laughs as he takes the wrench. "He had a great ass. Sometimes that's enough, y'know?"

"Really? He was that upset last night over a nice ass?"

Javi sighs. He's getting annoyed. He turns back to the underside of his bike. "I don't know. Will says Russ likes fixing people."

"Is that what Russ would say?"

"He'd probably say he likes helping people."

It feels like a fist to the stomach, but Javi's eyes are too much on his motor to catch my flinch.

"I guess that can feel like love," I say.

"Anything can feel like love." Javi doesn't look away from the engine. "Especially if sex is involved."

"But Tommy ran out on Russ. Vanished with Hank. So maybe the love wasn't mutual?"

"I don't know. Tommy and I didn't talk about our feelings much. But I think he liked Russ well enough. He just did this sometimes. Morphine, cliffs, trucks on the freeway, strange new men—it was all the same."

"So he'd run off with other guys before?"

"Sure, there was this guitar player in Mexico. We went down there for the weekend, met him in a bar, and Tommy took off with him. We came home without him, he turned up a few days later. I bet he got high back then, too. We're lucky he died close enough to home someone knew whose body it was. Or maybe it would have been better for Russ if he'd . . ." Javi stops, licking his lips, and scoots out from under the bike. He leans on it, turns the motor on. It purrs and a look of relief falls over him. Last time I saw a look like that, I was a cop giving a mother back her kidnapped baby. I let him enjoy it for a moment.

"So why is Russ so convinced Tommy was clean?" I ask.

Javi turns the motor off and looks at the bike, seeming to remember he can't drive it yet. "I don't know, ask him," he says, voice hard.

"That's a good idea. Where does he work?"

"Los Feliz. He's got a little law office. McCall and Associates, but it's just him and a secretary. I'll give you the address." Los Feliz, by the Dahlia. That explains why it's Russ's pharmacy.

Javi limps over to the bar and grabs an empty matchbook and pencil, jotting down the address. Then he pulls himself onto a stool and pours himself a full glass of whiskey.

"I'm sorry you got it fixed and can't drive again yet," I offer.

He looks over at me, his mouth open to shoot barbs, but he closes it and nods instead. "Thanks." He takes a long drink. I walk out of the garage.

"Hey," I say, stopping outside. The sun beats down on me and my shadow spreads out like a puddle at my feet. "Did you tell Will I used to be a cop, like him?"

Javi smirks. "The white hair is kinda sexy, right?"

I keep my face still. "I just never met another gay cop." That's the truth. "I'm curious about him."

"Well, he's here almost every afternoon. He's mostly on desk duty now. Gave some back talk to his boss, apparently."

I nod, though I find it hard to picture. Will had seemed the most even-tempered of all of the Bacchanals.

"He doesn't have a boyfriend, if that's what you're wondering." Javi smiles.

"I do," I remind him.

"Yeah, but just the one?"

I roll my eyes and get in my car, headed to Russ's law firm. I'd love to get into Will's mind, talk about the job, but that's not going to help me finish the job sooner. Get home sooner.

I drive through Los Feliz slowly. Russ's office is on the same drag as the Dahlia Pharmacy, pale stone buildings like a wall against the too bright blue sky. I make sure I don't see Vera's fancy car parked anywhere nearby before pulling up. I glance in, and she's not behind the counter; there's some other lab coat. Good. I don't want to see her, even in passing, if I can. I feel like she'd draw me into something again.

I'm walking by an alley next to the Dahlia when I spot another familiar face though—the guy who was behind the sandwich counter when she took me out for lunch. Jimmy, I think. She'd whispered something in his ear and his eyes had gone wide, staring at me. Wide like they do now as I glance at him, smoking a cigarette in the alley.

"Hey," he says quickly, pleading. The cigarette is on the ground as he walks close.

"Hi."

"You here for it?" He looks around, nervous. "I don't have it on me but I can get it. Just tell Vera I'll give it to her next shift, okay?" He's speaking too fast.

"I don't know what you mean."

"Just next shift, I promise, you don't gotta rough me up or nothing."

He's close now, eyes huge.

"What do you need to get Vera?"

He blinks. Takes a step back. "I have to get back to work."

He scurries into the pharmacy, glancing back once at the door. He's confused. I'm confused. Some part of Vera's little plot. I don't want anything to do with it. I keep walking to Russ's office.

It's above a dry cleaner's that's been painted a happy teal and has black-and-white-checkered tile. There's a list of signs inside, next to a staircase: McCall & Associates is the second floor. Upstairs, the door opens on a small carpeted office with a desk and some chairs. A cheerful-looking woman of about sixty looks up at me, smiling.

"Welcome to McCall and Associates, how may I help you?"

"I need to see Russ. He free?"

"Let me check. Your name?"

"Andy," I say, then try to remember if Russ ever heard it. "Tell him we met last night."

She seems a little confused by that, but stands and goes through a door behind her. I look around the room. It's shabby, the carpet worn, the venetian blinds dusty, but everything is decent quality. It doesn't seem like a cheap and dirty law firm. Just small.

She comes out a moment later, leaving the door open. "He'll see you now."

The office is nicer than the waiting room, the blinds pulled up, a portrait on the wall of an old woman, shelves of books. His desk is piled high with papers. And he looks professional, too, in a brown suit and tie, a pair of horn-rimmed glasses on. He glances up.

"Close the door please." He sounds and looks tired. Eyes red, with deep circles under them. I shut the door and sit down in a chair opposite his desk. "What did you find out?"

I raise my eyebrows, surprised. "It's only been a few hours," I remind him.

He frowns. "So why are you here?"

"I need information."

"What kind?"

"Well, if you can get a copy of the coroner's report, that would be helpful. I want—"

He holds up a finger and then picks up the receiver of a white phone on his desk and dials. "Yes, hi, it's Russ. Can you connect me to Will? . . . Thanks."

I nod. Makes sense, Will is a cop, probably no issue for him. Strange how fearless Russ is, calling the police, though. He must deal with them a lot. Him and Will, just hiding in plain sight.

"Will, it's me. The detective wants a copy of Tommy's coroner's report. Can you get it, or should I do the paperwork?" Russ pauses. "Great, thanks. See you later.

"He can get it to you, just drop by Long Beach PD. Ask for him."

"That's it? Just waltz right in?"

"Well, don't shout you're there for the fairy biker club when you walk up to the desk." He shakes his head. "Weren't you a cop? Don't you know how this works?"

I shrug. "When I was a cop, I didn't really have other gay friends."

He blinks, taking that in, then nods. "I see. Safe, sure." He leans back in his chair. "Is that all you need?"

"No. I want to search Tommy's place—your place. He might have left something."

His mouth scrunches up for a moment, considering. "Sure, come by tonight after work. Six."

I'm about to say yes when I remember Mom, the coconut cake that's probably in the oven by now, and shake my head. "Can't tonight. Tomorrow."

He sighs. "What else do you have?"

"The case that brought me here—looking for the guy Tommy vanished with," I remind him. It's a lie, but his impatience is grating on me. "He's the last person to see Tommy alive, right?"

Russ nods, still annoyed. "Fine. Tomorrow."

"And I want to hear about Tommy from you."

He sighs. "You want to eat while we do this? I have work." He gestures at the papers on his desk, then stands. "So let's at least make this useful."

I stand. "Sure. Just not that pharmacy, all right?"

"The one with the Mattachine girl behind the counter? No."

He breezes past me as though he didn't just say something odd. Maybe to him, he didn't. "You know her?" I ask as he opens the door. "From those meetings?" Vera had just called him a patient, didn't say he'd been a member.

"I went to one once, a year ago. Thought . . . I don't know what I thought. It would be funny, maybe." He nods at the secretary as we leave and says, "Lunch." In the stairwell, he whispers, "I thought maybe it would be fun to take one of those buttoned-up good-boy types home and make him a bad boy." He grins. "Tommy thought it would be fun, too. . . ." The grin vanishes. Strange thing for Vera to omit, but maybe she didn't remember. Or maybe she just felt like withholding all the information for some other reason. It doesn't matter.

Out on the street, we walk away from the Dahlia and into a greasy spoon with a blue Formica counter and white Formica floors. He leads me to a small table in the back, the guy behind the counter handing him a menu as we pass.

"The BLT is good," he says as we sit. He hands me the menu, doesn't even look at it.

"Sure. Can we talk now?" I look around.

He nods. "Just not loudly. But I've taken clients here. It's pretty safe." He holds up his hand and waves at the guy behind the counter. "Two BLTs, two Cokes." The guy nods and Russ turns back to me. "So what do you want to know?"

I nod. "The day Tommy and Hank vanished, the last people who saw them were Will and Stan, before they went to visit Javi in the hospital. When they got back, Hank and Tommy were gone, along with Tommy's bike, but you were home. This is two Wednesdays ago. Do you remember seeing them, or were they gone by the time you showed up?"

Russ raises his eyebrows, a little impressed for once. "A timeline, right. I should have . . ." He shakes his head. "They were gone. I got home around six, same as always."

I nod. "And did you get the sense they might run off together? That Tommy was . . . looking to have an adventure?" I try, not sure how to phrase it politely.

Russ doesn't look offended. "You could never tell with Tommy what would catch his fancy, what he'd chase. Sometimes he just got so bored...." The guy at the counter rings a bell and points at Russ, who stands and brings back our food.

"Anyway, no, I didn't know he'd run off for a while. He didn't usually leave a note when he did."

"How about his bike? He always took that?"

Russ looks at me like I've lost my mind. "Of course. And it's not missing. His mom said they found it near the body."

"So if Hank was with him, he had no way home?"

"It's LA—walk, take a trolley, hitchhike, call a cab. Easy enough to get anywhere you want." He pauses. "And he always took his jacket before, too. Never left that. That's how I know something is wrong."

I take a swig of Coke and we eat in silence a moment before I ask the big question: "How are you so sure Tommy was clean?" I don't say none of his other friends seemed to think so. Russ doesn't need me to say it, he knows it.

"I just am," he says, not meeting my eye.

"You can't give me more than that? I'm taking this case because you believe something that the evidence isn't showing. I just want to understand why you believe it."

He looks up, and his expression isn't angry, or defensive. It's sad. Guilty, maybe. The lines in his face are deep and soft, his skin pale. He hasn't slept; he spent the night crying.

"We had a system," he says softly. "And it worked."

"What kind of system?"

He looks away again, takes a large bite of his sandwich, chews, swallows, then washes it down with the Coke before he answers. "If he was feeling the itch, he would come to me, and I would make it go away."

I stare at him. He doesn't want to say something. "How?"

He frowns. "How do you think?" He looks around the diner. "You want me to say it aloud?"

Sex? "Really?" I've never met a junkie whose cravings could be eased by an orgasm. "You must be very good at that then."

He smirks. "Wanna find out?"

"I'm all right, thanks." I invited that one. "That's it though? That was the system?"

"I would"—he leans forward, voice soft—"tie him down, y'know? Helpless. Occupy him until the craving passed."

"Sure." If Tommy was in as bad a way as everyone says, and even Russ says he had cravings, then being tied up and fucked for a few hours isn't going to get rid of them.

We finish eating and pay the bill, and then he gives me a handshake. "I have to get back to work. But I'm counting on you to find the guy who did this."

"And if it was him?"

"It wasn't." His jaw clenches. "And that's not what we hired you to do."

I almost point out that no one has paid me, but he seems angry at my suggestion, so I just say, "I'll find out the truth," which seems to placate him. Outside he nods at me once before walking back to his office.

I head to my car, not looking in the window of the Dahlia so I don't meet anyone's eyes. I take out my map and find the Long Beach Police Department. I don't know how long it would take Will to get a copy of the report, but I should check in before I head back up to San Marino and spend some more time watching Hank's place.

It's about forty minutes back to Long Beach. The heat is worse than ever today, the sun an interrogator's spotlight, so that every bit of you not in shadow feels as if it were going to get peeled away. But walking into the Long Beach station gives me a chill. I haven't been inside a police station since the day I was fired. I know down here it's not like they'll know me, but I can still feel eyes on me as I walk in, and I worry there's something too revealing. My clothes, my walk, my smile. And at the same time, the noise of the place, the chatter and laughter—it feels like my past. Something I almost forgot, or a reflection of it. Familiar, safe, a place to hide, like a fortress a kid makes out of pillows.

I have a sudden memory of Lou, my old partner. Our desks faced each other, pushed close like they were kissing, and he liked to wad up little pieces of paper and toss them at me.

"You're quiet, but you got good instincts," he told me the first time I caught one without looking up. He laughed. He always had a toothpick on him, liked chewing them. Then he called out to the other guys, "You see that?" And he tossed another crumpled ball of paper. Again, I caught it without looking up.

"You should play ball, Mills," one of them said.

"You should throw it back at Lou," said another. I looked up. Lou locked eyes with me and grinned, spread his hands wide, toothpick in his mouth, and raised his eyebrows, daring me. This is how they talked, the guys, these weird little games, ways to outdo one another. But if I threw the ball, would I do it right? Would my wrist be too limp, would my expression if I hit or missed give something away? You have to be careful. If I missed and they called me a fairy, what sort of face should I make in response? Defensive, laugh it off? I was doing the math when the chief walked through, and everyone went quiet and settled back at their desks.

"What are you planning on doing with that paper, Mills?"

"Just going to put it in the trash, Chief."

The officer behind the reception desk of the Long Beach Police smiles pleasantly enough at me. He doesn't care how I throw a piece of paper. At least not right now. "I'm looking for Will. Name is Andy." I pause, wondering if I need to explain myself. Not sure how revealing I'm a PI will go over, so I just let the name hang. The officer nods and shouts, "Will! Some guy is here to see you!"

A few of the guys in the bullpen chuckle, and Will stands up from a desk in the back. He's in uniform, and it looks good on him. He comes to the door and nods at me. Physically, he doesn't look tense. He looks relaxed. He even smiles at me in a way I would never have smiled at another man when I was on the job.

"I need a smoke," he says, putting on a pair of aviator sunglasses, while walking outside. I follow. We walk around the side of the building, where it's shady, not that it helps with the heat much. There's a curved palm tree in front of us, a few yellow leaves around its base like stab wounds in the grass.

Will doesn't say anything, but he takes out a pack of cigarettes and offers me one, which I take, and then, just like last night, lights us both. Then he lifts up his shirt, untucking it to show a flat, hairy stomach, and a few folded pieces of paper tucked in his waistband. He hands them to me. They're a little damp.

"I couldn't make copies of the photos," he says through lips clenched around the cigarette. He starts tucking his shirt back in. "But you don't need to see those anyway. Sad, seeing him like that."

I look at the pages. His handwriting is gentler than I thought it would be, curvier.

"Anything interesting?" I ask, reading them over.

He shakes his head, smoke trailing his lips. "Everyone saw it as open-and-shut."

Maybe too open-and-shut, I think—they didn't test his blood

or the needle. But with how they found him, part of me gets it. Just another junkie in an alley.

"The decomposition is kind of strange." I point at the page. Will leans in over me, radiating heat and the smell of his cigarette and sweat. "They found him Thursday, that's eight days after he left with Hank, right?"

Will nods.

"So it says he'd been dead a while already—estimated his death between three and ten days earlier."

"So maybe he and Hank were holed up somewhere for a week before he overdosed." Will shrugs.

"Or maybe he died that night."

Will tilts his head, considering, but I can tell it's not enough to make him think it's anything other than what it looks like.

"Then where's Hank?" I ask. "If Tommy felt the itch and got high that night, or even a week later, why did Hank leave him in the alley?"

"He got scared, took off. He wasn't in the war, never seen someone die before."

"Maybe." It's reasonable enough. But if Tommy was really as clean as Russ thinks, then it would have to take something to drive him to get that high again. Something Hank would have seen. Or been part of. Maybe it was Russ, more jealous than he lets on, and he came home, broke Tommy and Hank up, maybe killed Hank. Or Edward, Hank's ex, showing up again and deciding if he couldn't have Hank, then a whole motorcycle gang wasn't going to. Either way Hank ends up dead, Tommy sees it, runs. That would make him want to get high, no matter how sober he'd been.

Will is still leaning in close, the cigarette floating between his waist and mouth, smoke cutting into the daylight around us like lace.

"You know, I was a cop," I tell him.

He takes the cigarette from his lips and smiles at me. "Yeah."

"I never met another cop"—I glance around—"like us."

"No? Maybe you didn't know."

"How'd you get into it?"

"After the army, they let me keep my bike, so I came here. Usually I'm out on patrol on it. The desk is temporary. It's boring, I miss just driving around all day, sometimes chasing assholes who ran red lights for fun, but days like this . . ." He wipes his forehead with the back of his hand. "Better than out in this heat, maybe."

"But you're not . . . scared?"

"What? That they'll find me out, beat me up?" He blows smoke out of his mouth in a thick column. "Not really. I mean, I know it's possible, but I don't mind the idea. I've been in scrapes before. Weren't you in the war?"

I nod, take a hit of the cigarette. It's got a deep sweetness to it. "Navy. I was in a minesweeper."

He tastes that for a moment, rolls it around in his mouth. "That's it, then. You were always looking for things to blow up, firing cannons, torpedoes. I was more up close than that. Not saying I'm braver. You're clearly . . ." His eyes look me up and down. "I bet you've seen things, too."

"Yeah," I say, trying not to think too much about it.

"So, maybe now, you joined up here or something, you wouldn't be so worried."

"Maybe."

He leans back on the wall, shifting to the side a little so if I leaned back now, our shoulders would meet. I can smell his sweat, the hot-fabric scent of his uniform, smoke. I wonder if it's that simple—that he just doesn't mind getting found out because he saw so much worse overseas—or if there's something more fundamentally different between us.

I wonder for a moment what it would be like to be him. How my life would be different. I don't know.

"How about the guilt?" I ask. "The way those guys in there are shutting down clubs, beating up folks?"

He's quiet, so I watch him out of the corner of my eye. His face relaxes for a moment, and I realize he's really thinking about it, and maybe a little sad to be doing it.

"It's rough. I don't like it. But what I try to do is go along on the raids and just be the procedural guy, like yell at other officers not to beat anyone up, we don't want a complaint, stuff like that. Most of the guys respect me. Think I'm by the book. I guess when I'm on the job, I am." He pauses and takes another drag. "I don't talk about this stuff usually. The other guys in the club just think it's a job. Maybe it is. But it's hard, too. One thing I've been trying to do, since I'm on the desk, is I find out about the raids early sometimes. And then I warn the bartenders. Then everyone is set, the raids are calmer. I feel like I can sort of help from the inside. But I also hate it sometimes."

"That's . . . good of you. I was always too scared to do that." I take another hit off the cigarette. The heat feels like a punishment, and for once, I don't mind it.

"I get that," he says. "It's hard. I don't know if I like my job. I think about quitting on the bad days."

"You seem a lot more fearless than I was."

He smiles. "You just think that because you're out now. You were brave to stay a cop. Every day." He takes a drag on his cigarette.

I wonder if I was. If I've ever really been brave.

"You look like you're thinking real hard about something," he says, and I turn around to look him in the eye, realizing he's even closer now, our faces almost touching. I see my reflection in his sunglasses and wonder if this is what he's seeing, too. If he thinks he's seeing someone like him.

I step to the side, lean against the wall next to him, and smoke. "Just wondering about your life, I guess."

He smiles and pulls his hand through his black-and-white hair. "It can be rough, but I actually like it. Gets lonely, though."

I swallow. "Even with the club?"

"They're friends. And sometimes . . . yeah, I mean, I know you've probably heard how we met. But there's a difference. Like what Russ and Tommy had." He shakes his head. "Poor Russ."

"Javi says he has two boyfriends," I say softly. "Maybe he can lend you one."

Will laughs loudly and claps me on the shoulder, his fingers lingering a second too long. "I'll be sure to tell him you suggested it when I ask." He takes another drag off his cigarette, shakes his head. "It's just . . . I'm getting older. Turned forty this year. Starting to look out at the future, you know? Never had something that went on a while, but I think I'd like that. Someone to ride into the sunset with."

I nod, throw my cigarette down. I know what's happening. I know I should say I have a boyfriend.

"You'll find it," I say instead. "Thanks for these." I hold up the papers and fold them up, put them in my pocket.

"Good luck with your case," he says, still leaning against the wall, and gives me a smile I can't read behind the sunglasses, but that makes something swell inside me. A desire to hug him goodbye, even though I know I'll probably see him again soon.

I nod and get in my car, peeling out of the lot fast as I can.

I start to cool down as I drive up to San Marino. Maybe the heat is finally abating. It's just about two thirty when I park the car down the street from the gate to Hank's family mansion. I can sit here for hours, waiting.

One eye on the gate, I take out the copy of the coroner's report from my pocket. The car suddenly smells like sweat and I feel a strange twinge of embarrassment. I put it out of my mind and go over the notes again, but nothing new stands out. I go over theories in my head for the next few hours, watching the gate, but can come to no conclusions about Tommy's death. Hank is key. If he's alive, dead, saw something, I need to know. All I can do for now is wait.

I'm thinking of just heading home early, picturing Mom, and the coconut cake, and wondering if she meant I needed to be home at seven or just that's when dinner was going to be, so I had to be home earlier. But that's when a car finally comes out the gate.

Again, they turn away and I can't see faces, but it's a black town car this time, and I see the back of three heads in the back seat. I follow them, not far, they could have walked, to a swanky restaurant with a red awning. I can see through the giant window from my car: white tablecloths, waiters in suits, the whole deal. Three heads in a town car—maybe this is the whole family, and I'm finally going to see Hank.

A man gets out of the driver's seat. He's in full livery, a chauffeur, and he opens the curbside door. First an older man gets out, tall and broad, like Myrtle described Hank, but what hair he has left is gray. Then he helps a woman about the same age out of the car. She's wearing a red dress and hat. Fashionable, expensive. After them comes a young girl, with a dark ponytail and long dress, who looks so much like the woman she must be their daughter. Finally, from the front passenger seat, comes a young man.

He turns as he gets out, surveying the street. It's Edward. So where is Hank?

TEN

They go inside and are seated immediately, and conveniently in the window. Wine is brought. They toast. They drink. The woman laughs. The girl steals a sip of her mother's wine. This would make so much more sense if it were Hank with them, having a family dinner, like I'm going to tonight. I don't understand this combination of people, not when they're all smiling, acting as if everything is normal.

They order and chat and seem all very happy. I'm even more confused now. Edward makes everyone laugh, and Hank's father claps him on the back. He had said that he and Hank were staying with Hank's parents but not that he was pals with them. When six thirty rolls around, they're on dessert and their second bottle of wine, so I don't think they're going to be doing much else tonight. And besides, Mom would be really upset if I was late. I drive away wondering where Hank is, and how Edward has made himself such a part of the family.

I pull the car into the driveway just before seven. I can smell the coconut cake in the oven when I open the door. Mom is in the kitchen, same dress, same apron, like she hasn't moved all day, even though I know she must have gone to the store. She smiles when I walk in.

"Just in time. I was worried you'd forget."

"Never."

"Not the cake, anyway." She smiles.

I smirk. "Can I help with anything?"

"Put on some music."

I walk out of the kitchen into the dining room, which is really just another side of the living room. The table is already set.

In the living room, I flip through her record cabinet and pick out an old Glenn Miller 45 and put it on. The orchestra swells to fill the house, and I look out the window at the little curved porch and the repaired railing.

"When did you repaint the house?" I ask, calling into the kitchen.

"Oh, I think three years back. Maybe four? The paint was fading and I thought it might be fun to try something new. I was wondering if you'd say you liked it."

"I like it," I lie. "You fixed the railing, too."

She laughs, walking into the dining room and setting a bowl of salad on the table. "You wanted me to keep it broken?"

I laugh. "No, just . . . I don't know. I felt sad when I saw it was different."

She sighs. "Andy, I can't keep a broken rail just because you broke it. I have friends over, we have drinks out there. What if Mrs. Lansky leans on it and it collapsed?"

"No, no, you're right."

She goes back into the kitchen. She returns with a pitcher of lemonade and sits down at the table. I sit, too, and she starts dishing salad out onto our plates.

"It's just a simple garden salad," Mom says apologetically. "Nothing fancy."

"I don't usually eat fancy salads. Or any kind of salad."

She tsks me, frowning. "You don't eat well?"

"I don't have a real kitchen. There's this place down the street from the office, they do eggs okay."

She sighs. "No one is keeping track of what you eat? Cooking you meals?"

I shovel some lettuce in my mouth. This is veering much closer to questions about my love life than Mom usually gets.

After swallowing, I say, "No."

"Really?" Her voice is amused. I look up at her. Her eyebrow is arched the same way mine does when I'm skeptical. "No one?"

"Just me."

She frowns now. She's upset. "I don't know why you're lying to me. I heard you last night, on the phone."

I feel the color drain from my face as I try to remember what I said. What she knows. "Mom—"

"If you're saying 'I love you' to someone, I feel like you should be able to tell me about it." Mom shakes her head. "What did I do that you'd keep it secret?"

"Well . . ." I stare at her, willing a lie to appear in my head. But all I can see is her disappointed face, and how much worse it might get if I told her the truth.

"Gene," Mom says. "That was the name."

I swallow. I can't move.

"Is she some kind of floozy? Are you embarrassed of her? Or of me?"

Her. I blink. Gene. It's a woman's name, too. *Her.* The lie practically tells itself.

"I'm not embarrassed of either of you," I say quickly, filling the silence. "I just—with my work, I never know—" I'm sputtering like a busted faucet.

"She one of those femmes fatales?" Mom asks, unimpressed with this excuse. "Daughter of a rich man, murdered her last husband, you don't want anyone to know?"

I stare at her a moment too long before a laugh shoots out of me, awkward, a bad shot, would have knocked over the lemonade.

Mom sighs.

"I wanted you to meet before—" I shake my head. "I guess I just didn't know how to say it." That much is true. "I don't know. Since Dad died, I worry that—"

"You think I'm lonely?" Mom chuckles. "I had a date with a lovely widower a few weeks ago, actually. I've gone on several dates, actually."

This is also news to me. It makes my face warm, but I don't know why. I don't know how to feel about it at all. Or about Gene, and her knowing about her/him, and the lie I'm going to have to tell.

I have no idea what's going on at all. I'm tossed around, seasick with feeling. I look down at my salad and spear a tomato.

Mom sighs. "I guess we're both keeping secrets."

I feel like mine is bigger, but I just nod.

"What's this widower like?" I ask, protective instincts clawing their way to the top of my emotions.

"Oh, he's all right," Mom says between bites. "Honestly, none of the men I've dated even hold a candle to your father. I don't mean he was such a perfect man. But he made me laugh. No one else really makes me laugh." She pauses. "How about Gene? What's she like?"

I shovel more salad in, giving me time to think. The best lies are close to the truth, but a woman can't be a bartender in California. And I don't think Mom would approve anyway.

"She's a nurse." Gene would have been a doctor, after all, if someone hadn't sent those photos to his medical school. And he's my nurse, at least.

Mom laughs. "Oh dear. Is that why you didn't want to tell me? Don't like us having the same profession?"

I hadn't even thought of that. It also makes me blush. I'm blushing a lot. This is a terrible conversation.

My salad is gone. "Want me to clear away the plates?"

"She doesn't make you eat well? What kind of nurse is she?"

"Trauma." True enough. "She works at a free hospital for underserved communities." One way of putting it.

Mom nods, impressed by that. I hate this. I hate lying.

For a moment I think about saying everything: Gene is a man, he's the manager of and tends bar at the gay club my office and home are above, and he is kind and funny, and his hands are always cold with ice. He makes me try weird drinks, reads the Narnia books to me, and he takes care of me every time someone mistakes me for a punching bag. And I love him.

But instead I say, "Gene's really great."

Mom hands me her empty salad plate, and I bring the two plates into the kitchen, putting them in the sink. She follows me in, opening the oven and taking several dishes out and bringing them into the dining room: meat loaf, scalloped potatoes, spinach casserole. All my favorites from when I was a kid. Mom dishes out the food, and I pour myself and her some lemonade.

"Well, I'd love to meet her," Mom says. "Maybe you can bring her down?"

"Sure." An easy promise for me to make with no intention of keeping it. We both start eating. Everything tastes amazing. Buttery, warm.

"Do you have a photo of her?"

I laugh. "You think I brought a framed photo down with me?"

She tsks again. "Of course not. But something small in your wallet?"

I do have a photo of me and Gene in my wallet. From a photo

booth at the beach. No one looks twice at two men getting in one of those together; they think it's just tomfoolery, and no one sees the photos except you, if you're quick to grab them when they print out. So you can have a photo of you with your arms around each other, maybe looking into each other's eyes—stuff that people might write off as just two pals, but you know it's not. I have a whole strip with me.

I shake my head. "If someone wanted to hurt me, and they went through my stuff, they could find her photo, threaten her. Safer."

"Your father always had a photo of me in his wallet."

"It's not the same, Mom."

She shrugs. "I suppose. But I'm glad she's a nurse. How did you meet? You got hurt on the job and she stitched you up?"

I smile. "Exactly." No lie there, at least.

She sighs. "Are you sure you don't want to do something safer? If you love this girl, and you're thinking about marrying her and starting a family—"

"Whoa, Mom, slow down," I say quickly. The green *ONE* magazine cover flashes into my memory: *HOMOSEXUAL MARRIAGE?* "I don't know if we're there yet."

She looks a little disappointed, but nods. "Ah, well. All right. But you're not getting any younger, you know."

"I feel it in my knees every time I walk downstairs."

She laughs.

"And besides, you're working at a psychiatric clinic. Your job isn't exactly safe."

"Oh, it's perfectly safe." She shakes her head. "You'll see tomorrow. I'll show you. These men couldn't hurt a fly."

"Men? Just men?"

She nods and opens her mouth as if to say something, then

closes it again. "I'll have Dr. North explain it to you. I called in today while you were out, and he said he'd be happy to show you around and reassure you."

"All right," I say, wary. She's been working a while, though, and hasn't told me about any patients attacking her or anything.

"Between the two of us, I think I'm the one more allowed to worry about the other," Mom says. "But if you trust me to be careful, I'll trust you to do the same."

I smile. That was like our family motto growing up. Mom said it to Dad, Dad said it to me, I said it to Mom. "Deal," I say.

We turn the conversation away from the topic of danger and dangerous topics and over to new songs we heard on the radio, and her new Doris Day album, which she excitedly puts on, turning it to "Ain't We Got Fun," and dancing back to the table, then holding out her hand and pulling me up, dancing with me in the living room. She trips over a chair leg, but I catch her, and we laugh. She puts her hand on my face and smiles. "Oh, I miss having you around," she says, hugging me. "I love you, son."

"Love you, too, Mom." I hold her tight.

The coconut cake is somehow even better than my memory of it. Mom even sticks a candle on top and makes me blow it out, but thankfully doesn't sing "Happy Birthday."

"I can give you your present now, if you want. Or I can mail it so you can open it back home."

"This is present enough." I take a second slice of cake. "I haven't had this since I was a kid."

"I'll write up the recipe for Gene."

For a moment, I forget the lie and think she's talking about Gene and imagine them meeting for real, imagine them friends, exchanging recipes, joking about the trouble I get into, the scars of mine they've stitched up. I imagine telling her everything right now and her taking it all in, shocked at first, but then seeing how happy I am, how I'm starting to actually like who I am for the first time in . . . forever, maybe. And I imagine her taking my hand and saying, "I'm so glad you're happy, and I love you."

I open my mouth, all of it ready to pour out, wanting this imagined reality to be true.

I shove some cake in it, instead. Tonight I'm eating my favorite cake, and she's changing the record over, and outside the porch may be fixed, but it's my porch, and part of me is still leaping off it, still flying.

After we clean up, she gives me some privacy when I call Gene, which I'm grateful for. Says she doesn't want to embarrass me and goes upstairs, getting ready for bed. Maybe Mom would react perfectly, but she probably wouldn't. Why make both our lives worse with the truth? If she couldn't accept me, she wouldn't have anyone left.

Gene picks up on the first ring. It's Monday, much quieter at the Ruby.

"Hey."

"Hi," he says, and it's like we're actually hearing each other for the first time in days.

For a moment, I remember Will, his scent, but it fades like smoke in the wind. Gene I can picture every part of—his hands, the smell of him like warm stone, the taste of him, the smoothness of his skin. Smoke doesn't compare to that.

"So how's the case going? Or, cases, I guess?"

"I'm making some headway. It's strange though. I found Edward, but he's staying with Hank's family, and I haven't seen Hank at all."

"That's kind of weird. But you said they've been together forever, right? College? So maybe they just know him as a good friend of their son's."

"Maybe," I say, wondering how they'd pull that off. "But I want to lay eyes on Hank to be sure. They had a fight, I'm not sure what's going on." I wait a moment, not sure how to say the next part. "The other thing is"—I pause again—"I'm staying with my mom."

There's silence for a moment, then a chuckle. "Okay."

"I was trailing the guy I think is Edward, he went into this psychiatric clinic, and . . . there she was."

"Coincidence? Sounds like fate really wanted you two to see each other. How's it going?"

"She made me my favorite cake."

"That coconut you told me about? Try to get the recipe."

"Already did." I wonder if I should tell him everything. I glance up the stairs. No one is there. "She gave it to me for you, actually."

There's a long beat. I can hear the band onstage. "Me?"

"She heard me talking to you last night. But she, uh"—I lower my voice—"she thought of Gene Tierney, y'know?"

Another pause. "She thinks I'm a woman?"

"Yeah."

The band swells up in the background.

"That okay? I wasn't sure what to say."

"No, no, it's fine," Gene says quickly. "Kind of weird, but I'll probably never meet her, I guess, right?"

He sounds disappointed, and surprised by it. I feel the same. "Yeah. I don't love that either, you know."

"I know."

"But if I told her—"

"I know, Andy. My parents don't talk to me at all anymore. I wouldn't want you to go through that."

"I wish I could."

"Me, too." I can picture his face, the sad little smile, the way he'd lace his fingers through mine. "I miss you so much."

"I miss you, too. So hurry up and finish the case."

"I will," I promise. "I found one of them, right? So it's just a matter of getting him alone and figuring out where the other one is, and getting an address for Daphne."

"How about the other case you took on?"

I sigh. "I don't know. This kid overdosed, and everyone believes it except his boyfriend. There's nothing pointing at murder. So it might not even really be a case. Which is fine, since no one has even offered to pay me."

Gene laughs. "You didn't give them your going rate?"

"They're a motorcycle club and they'd kidnapped me at the time, so I didn't feel like hashing out prices."

"Kidnapped? Andy."

"It's fine, they're actually all pretty nice guys." I think of Will again, the smile on his face, my reflection in his sunglasses. "I mean, they're a little wild. Leather jackets, innuendo. But they actually sort of remind me of this girl I met at *ONE* magazine. She said they were trying to build this community center. That's what they feel like. A community. Same as Mattachine, I guess."

"Well, the Ruby is your community, so don't go putting on a leather jacket."

"You don't want me to get a motorcycle, take you for a ride?"

He chuckles, low and soft. "Well, maybe. But knowing you, we'd crash."

"Probably true."

"Wait, have you ridden on their motorcycles?"

"Yes." I suddenly feel a little guilty.

"Oh." There's a long pause and over the phone I hear ice pouring into a glass. "I think I'm jealous."

"It's not like that," I say, maybe a little too quickly, thinking about Will in front of me on his bike. "It was just when they were kidnapping me."

"Repeating that word doesn't make me like it better."

"And bringing me back. It's all worked out now, don't worry."

"Are they fast?"

"The bikers? Some of them."

He laughs. "The motorcycles, Andy."

I shake my head. "Yeah, those, too." I smile. I feel so much more myself, talking to him. Like I haven't been lost in this insane mirage of a city, not sure if what I'm seeing is memories or just some illusion someone is projecting on a screen. "I should go to bed. Tomorrow Mom is giving me a tour of the psychiatric clinic."

"A normal family outing."

I laugh. "I love you."

"I love you, too. Hurry back."

I hang up, but before I go upstairs and get into bed, I go out on the porch and light a cigarette and smoke, staring at the railing, daring myself to jump off it.

ELEVEN

I put on my gray suit and a plain blue tie in the morning. Mom is dressed in her uniform. We look a perfect mother and son. Myrtle and the other Mattachines would be so proud of me.

I take my car, following Mom, so I can leave before her. I have an appointment to search Russ's house, after all. The long walkway through the palm trees is almost white in the early-morning sun. Mom's heels seem to echo off it. Inside, the lobby is the same, though a different woman is behind the desk.

"Morning, Bonnie," my mother says. The woman is young, in her twenties, beautiful, and blond.

"Good morning, Mary."

"This is my son, Andy. I'm giving him a little tour today. He wants to make sure I'm not in danger."

Bonnie chuckles. "You clear it with Dr. North?"

Mom nods. "Called him yesterday. He said to give him a tour like he might be putting family here and then bring him by the office to reassure him."

Bonnie laughs again. "Well, have fun. And welcome, Andy. Your mom is perfectly safe here."

"Thanks. Just curious to see where she works."

Bonnie nods and motions at the door to the left, where Mom had emerged from yesterday. Mom leads me through it.

I'm not sure what I expected. Rows of beds, people tied to them, maybe. Or a narrow hallway with doors with small windows in them looking into padded cells. But it's almost the same as the lobby—large windows, white walls, white carpet.

The room is open, with several beige sofas around, a few blue blankets thrown over them. There's a table, and some men are sitting around it doing a puzzle. They all look up when we come in. They're different ages, ranging from kids who should still be in school to men who look like they have grandkids. Their eyes linger on me a little too long, and there's something familiar in the way they stare. Maybe they think I'm a new inmate.

"See, nothing dangerous at all," Mom says. "Hello, gentlemen."

They all respond hello with varying degrees of enthusiasm, calling her Mrs. Mills. She walks past them, to where this lounge area tapers into a hallway. I follow her. Now there are doors on either side, but no windows in them. Some are open, and they seem to be bedrooms—simple beds, dressers, wardrobes. The whole place seems more like a hotel. The only thing that feels like a hospital is the smell—that sharp caustic smell of cleaning supplies. It's everywhere, something different underneath it that I can't place but makes my stomach roil.

Another nurse passes us in the hall, carrying a little tray with little paper cups of pills. She and Mom exchange hellos as we keep walking.

"So your job is to medicate?" I ask.

"Partially. And to be there if they need something, monitor them, make sure they're doing well. The usual nurse stuff."

"Doing well with what? Their puzzle?"

"Andy, don't be silly. Their mental state."

We come to another large open space, this one a cafeteria. It looks more like a fancy restaurant, though. White tablecloths, a bar where the patients are serving themselves on one side of the room. There's a murmur of conversation here, the patients—all men, all ages, all but one or two white—cluster in groups, chatting and laughing. I also spot a few orderlies—large men in plain outfits, standing in the corners of the room like bouncers.

"Not too close now, Mr. Johnson," Mom says to one of the patients as we walk by. He shuffles away from the man he was leaning toward. They were laughing.

"Close?" I ask her in a low voice. "He sick?"

She takes a moment to think about it. "I think it'll be best to let Dr. North explain." She stops in the middle of the room and looks around. "But as you can see, it's perfectly safe. These men are all gentlemen."

"Yeah? Then what are the orderlies for?" I look to the large men in the corners.

"Oh, they're such sweet young boys. They're mostly here in case a patient is having trouble walking after their treatments, though I admit sometimes if someone doesn't want to take their medication, the orderlies assist in administering it."

"All right," I say, trying to parse that. Treatments that make walking difficult and medications people don't want to take. I suppose that would be any mental hospital. "But they don't ever try to hurt you to not take them? Threaten you so you give them keys to escape?"

She laughs and pats my arm. "No, no. They're all nice young men, and many are here willingly, for themselves, or because their families committed them to our care. Come on, I'll show you the yard."

She starts walking again. All in all I've counted just over twenty patients, and a handful of nurses to oversee them. The place is immaculate, filled with air and light. It must be expensive. I can see why, if you had to check yourself in somewhere, you'd pick here.

Mom leads me to a beautiful lawn out back, with a track and

tennis court. No one is using it at the moment, but I could see it being a nice place to exercise. "Isn't it beautiful?" Mom asks. There's a huge chain-link fence around the area, almost two stories high. "Pity we can't have a garden, but just a lovely space. It's so nice to work here."

I nod. "I still don't understand what you're treating though." As I say it, I feel something in the back of my skull like an ice cube. Some thought that I can't articulate, something wrong, a haunted house. I shiver slightly.

"Let's go talk to Dr. North."

I follow her back inside, retracing our steps, through the lobby to the other wing of the hospital. The white walls remain, but the floor is tiled here, not carpeted. And here, finally, are those doors with the small windows on them. I look through them as we walk, but the lights are out in all of them and all I can see is my reflection. Mom takes me up a staircase. Now the walls are wooden. There are offices. A room marked LOUNGE, one that says NURSES' LOCKER ROOM. Staff stuff. We walk down the hall here until we must be nearly right over the lobby. The door here is labeled DR. NORTH, and Mom knocks and waits for a voice to call come in.

The office is as large and open as the patient spaces downstairs. The carpet is beige, but the walls are paneled wood. Is stretches the whole length of the building, small windows looking out at the row of palm trees, large ones looking out at the lawn. There's a desk, bookshelves built into the wall, a few armchairs, a divan. It all looks expensive. On the walls are a few photos of the man who currently sits behind the desk, with various people, some I recognize—movie stars, mostly—some I don't.

He stands as we enter. Dr. North. I thought he'd be older, but he looks to be in his early forties, silver streaking his ashy-brown hair, a pair of thick black glasses. He's short, but fit, with strong-looking shoulders.

"Mary, how are you?"

"I'm well, Doctor, thank you for asking." Mom smiles.

He takes her hand, laying his other hand over hers affectionately.

"This is your son?" He extends his hand to me. I shake it.

"Yes, this is Andy."

"Nice to meet you, Doctor. I admit, I'm surprised you're willing to. I told my mother I was a little worried about her working here and she said she could give me a tour to set my mind at ease, but I didn't realize I'd be meeting the man who runs the place."

He laughs and motions for me to sit in one of the armchairs. I do.

"Well, I am the chief psychiatrist. But honestly, your mother runs the place—she oversees all the nurses."

"Oh, don't be silly," Mom says, laying a hand on my shoulder and squeezing. "You're the boss. And I'd better get to work. Wait in the lobby before you go, and I'll come say goodbye."

"Thanks, Mom."

She leaves, closing the door gently behind her. Dr. North is sitting in the armchair opposite mine, legs crossed, studying me. So I study him back. He's got that pretentious air most doctors do, but otherwise there's nothing telling about him. He's in a white coat over a gray suit, black tie. Everything looks expensive. His smile is professional.

"I understand your concern, of course," he says after a moment. "Looking out for your mother is a good thing to do. Though she has been working here a while."

"I didn't realize what kind of a place it was from her letters."

That is true. She'd been coy about it, I can see that now. "She told me it was a new clinic but didn't mention it was all-male patients. Or the psychiatric aspect."

"Ah, yes, well, it's a sensitive subject. I can understand why your mother might ask me to explain the sort of treatments we do here."

"All right, so explain. I'm a private eye, I was a cop, I deal with sensitive subjects all the time, so you can count on my discretion."

He nods. "Dangerous profession, I don't envy you." He uncrosses his legs and then crosses them on the other side. "But to get to it, our institution handles the treatment of deviant sexuality."

It hits like an icy tidal wave and I have to use every muscle to keep my face and body still. That's what the feeling was. It all makes sense now—the men none of the nurses are afraid of, Mom making the guys laughing scoot apart, the look the patients gave me as I came in. It was familiar because I've given it to men myself: desire. I look behind me, a terrible thought suddenly in my mind—that Mom had figured me out, and all this was a trap to make me the next patient.

But she's gone, the door is closed. I swallow and turn back to Dr. North, trying to keep my expression placid.

"I see. So homosexuals?"

"We don't like throwing that word around too much in here," he says with a faint smile. "Some men have deviant desires or have had deviant experiences. That doesn't make them a whole new type of person. It just means they need a little help getting back on track."

I nod. My stomach is roiling. Why was Edward in here, then? Did he get put in here and was then "cured" and now he has to check in? Do they do outpatient work? He certainly didn't seem cured when we talked. And he said Hank was fine—but I haven't seen Hank. He could be the one in here. Does Edward not know what kind of place his boyfriend is in?

"If you don't mind my asking, how does that work?"

Dr. North smiles. "I don't mind at all. Deviant sexualities are often discussed in the papers these days—the State Department, Kinsey. Everyone always wants to know why, but no one ever asks about how to change." He looks at his watch. "It's time for me to administer a treatment. Would you like to see? It's not for the faint of heart, I should warn you."

Everything in my body is screaming no. "Sure, as long as you don't think less of me if I run out of there."

He laughs. "Not at all. It's disturbing and might even seem nonsensical at first, but let me show you." He stands and reaches for the doctor's bag on his desk. It's a beautiful thing, monogrammed brown leather, old looking but well taken care of, worn-out on the handles a little, like he's always carrying it. I follow him out of the office, back downstairs, to the rooms with the little windows. "Now I want you to know, you might be disturbed by the images you'll see, especially knowing your mother might have seen them as well. But I assure you this is a proven medical technique. The images are of no harm to your mother, or even you, though you might find them distasteful. The nurses, I'm told, find most of them somewhat funny."

I'm not sure what to say to that, so I stay silent. He leads me into one of the rooms with the small windows. The floor here is tile, and a hard-looking chair is in the center of the room, a wide tin bucket next to it. At the back of the room, behind the chair, is a tall table with a slide projector, and next to it a more comfortable-looking chair and desk. Dr. North motions me over, inviting me to sit. I do, and he perches next to his case on the desk.

"What we do, you see, is show the patient images which arouse their deviance—ranging from muscle-magazine shots to more explicit images." He puts his hands up immediately in defense. "I know, I know, you don't like the idea of your mother seeing such things, but rest assured, she doesn't need to be in here except at the very beginning, when we show the less ribald images, and the end, when the images have been shut off. I'm sure she's gotten a glance at the more explicit things now and then, but as I said, I'm told the nurses generally find them funny." He smiles, trying to make it all sound so palatable.

I tilt my head up at him. His sitting higher makes it feel like I'm a child in school. "How does that cure the deviance, though?"

"Ah." He takes a syringe out of his case. "Good question. Just as we turn the images on, I inject the patient with apomorphine."

"Morphine?" I ask, shocked.

"No, no, similar names, I know, they're derived from the same source. But apomorphine doesn't dull pain or have addictive properties. In small doses, it causes nausea, vomiting." He nods at the bucket next to the chair. "The idea is that the patient will learn to associate these images, which currently arouse them, with nausea and unpleasantness, instead of, well, sex."

I'm feeling pretty nauseous myself. "I see."

"It's very popular in England. Here, this sort of therapy is more often done by attaching electrodes to the patient's testicles and shocking them when they begin to show signs of arousal. However, I find that overly crude and invasive. Our methods are better than that. Humane. We treat good men, who either want to get better for themselves, or for their families. There's no need to be so rough with them."

"Sure." Again, I'm at a loss for words.

"Of course, there's more to it than just this. Some patients also are administered daily pills by the nurses, which decrease the sex impulse, make arousal impossible. And having them all in an environment with other men, but sleeping separately, and being monitored by women like your mother who tell them when they're being inappropriately friendly, or when they're walking a little too effeminately also helps them learn to live like normal people." He leans in, smiling. "And I hire some younger, attractive nurses, too, to give them something healthy to look at."

"Clever." I can't respond with more than one word at a time. My brain is stalled out on the highway. This is where my mother works.

The door opens and the nurse Mom passed in the hall walks in, followed by one of the men I saw from the lounge. He's older, maybe in his sixties, with streaks of steel-colored hair over a mostly bald scalp, and a pair of large round glasses. He's thin, delicate looking. His face has a look of half-hearted resolve. His eyes glance back once, at the door, as if he wants to make a break for it, and I want so badly for him to try. But instead he marches into the room, chin up. The nurse waits in the doorframe behind him.

"We have an observer today, Mr. Johnson," Dr. North says, standing. "So let's get started. Do you feel a need for the straps?"

Mr. Johnson glances at the doctor's bag on the desk, then shakes his head. Straps to keep him in the chair, I'm guessing.

"Then sit down please." Dr. North turns to the door. "Thank you, Nancy, that'll be all."

The nurse nods, smiling pleasantly at him, before leaving.

Mr. Johnson sits in the chair facing the wall as Dr. North walks around him, surveying, but speaking to me.

"Mr. Johnson has been staying with us for two months now. We used to administer the treatments every day except Sunday, but now he's doing very well and only needs them every other day." Dr. North claps Mr. Johnson on the shoulder, and he flinches, almost jumping. Dr. North lifts his hand, then pats the shoulder reassuringly. "You've been doing very well. Just one more month and you might be cured."

"I hope so," Mr. Johnson says weakly.

I wonder what brought him here. His family finding him with a man? A confession? Maybe he's a member of Mattachine, and a doctor came in and told them how curable his condition was, how he could be normal. I wonder if Dr. North has spoken at Mattachine meetings.

"Well, let's get started." Dr. North goes to his bag and pulls a syringe out of it, already filled. Then he bends over Mr. Johnson and injects just a little into the man's arm. Mr. Johnson doesn't flinch this time. Dr. North turns on the slide projector, which for now just shines an empty white space on the wall. Then he turns out the lights.

"Here we go," Dr. North says to me in a low voice. He turns to the first slide.

It's not especially racy, just an image from one of those physique magazines: a handsome young man in a pair of jockeys, flexing. Dr. North leaves the image up and goes to look at Mr. Johnson.

"Eyes open now, Mr. Johnson. I don't want to have to ask one of the orderlies to hold them open for you, right? We're past that."

Mr. Johnson nods. I can't see his face from where I'm sitting, and I'm glad.

Dr. North waits about a minute before clicking to the next

slide. Another like this first, but this time the man is just in a posing strap and is angled slightly to his side, so the naked curve of his ass is visible.

Mr. Johnson retches, leaning over to vomit into the bucket. It's brief, and neither he nor Dr. North comments on it. Mr. Johnson sits up again, and Dr. North clicks to the next slide. Men kissing now. Fully clothed. Mr. Johnson stares at it. The silhouette of his head against the image of the two men kissing is unmoving. Just darkness in the shape of a human head, a burnt hole in the image. The next slide has men kissing shirtless. He vomits again. On the next slide, too: two men naked, staring at each other.

I focus on the silhouette of his head instead of anything else. It bends to the left as he vomits again and again, and the images in front of him grow increasingly more explicit—naked men with erections kissing, giving each other blow jobs, penetrating each other. Dr. North has a larger gay pornography collection than any of the gay people I know. Sometimes he only leaves an image up for a minute, sometimes much longer. He walks to the corner to look at Mr. Johnson sometimes, check that his eyes are open.

The smell of the vomit gets stronger, and without saying anything, Dr. North takes out a handkerchief from his bag and offers it to me. He pulls out one for himself and uses it to cover his nose and mouth, and I do the same. It smells of mint.

Mr. Johnson's breakfast is long since gone, but he keeps retching, doubling over in the chair, his body trying to force everything out of it. He convulses in quick spurts, bent over like an insect, arms in sharp corners. He's so thin, I'm worried he might break. The images keep coming. I don't know how long it goes on. I can't see my watch in the dark. It feels like hours. Like days. Watching this poor man be tortured. Again and again I tell myself to just sit, and say nothing, and not react. My brain feels so quiet, like an animal hiding in the corner of a cage. My heart is a war drum. I want to break him out. I want to smash the slide projector and the doctor's bag and the doctor and take poor Mr. Johnson out of this place.

I don't.

I sit and watch and breathe in the mint of the handkerchief. I have never felt so powerless.

When the last slide clicks through to an empty beam of white, Dr. North turns the lights on again. He's smiling from ear to ear.

"You did very well, Mr. Johnson. I think you're well on your way to being healthy."

He doesn't look healthy. A long trail of vomit goes down his chin and chest, and splatters of it are on his clothes. He looks dazed, vacant. If anything was left in the man when he came in, it's gone now.

The door opens, and the same nurse who brought Mr. Johnson in waits again in the doorway. She's smiling.

"Nancy, Mr. Johnson did very good work. Take him back to his room and let him lie down for a while."

"You're not going to let him shower off?" I ask as Nancy escorts Mr. Johnson out. He follows like a sleepwalker.

"It's better if we let him sit in his own filth for a while, so it lingers," Dr. North says. "Don't want to just wash this experience away. We want it to stick. He'll rest for about an hour before we let him bathe."

"That is . . ."

"I know," he concedes, frowning slightly. "It is unsightly and might seem disgusting, especially for the poor nurses. But our methods are humane, progressive, and the women who work here are professionals. I'm sure your mother has seen worse than a man with vomit on his chin."

I nod. "I'm sure she has." Especially if she's ever seen one of these treatments.

"I hope now your mind is at ease. Your mother is very safe."

I stand, my legs stiff. I have to play a part. "Yes, thank you, Doctor." I extend my hand and somehow shake his without flinching. "I can see all that now."

He smiles, pleased to have shared his medical knowledge with someone. He's proud of himself. Proud of all this that he's created. He leaves the room and I follow. Outside, the smell of cleaning products is stronger than ever. A janitor waits by the door for us to leave, then goes inside. I wonder if it's just him cleaning all the vomit from every room.

Dr. North says good morning to the janitor and then taps his bag. "On to the next one, Mr. Mills. Lovely meeting you."

"You, too."

He marches down the hall to another door, another treatment room. A nurse is waiting outside with a patient—he looks thirteen years old. I clench my fists as they walk into the room together.

Most of me just wants to leave. To find the nearest door and flee. But if Edward was coming here, I want to know why. So I wander, searching. From what I've seen there are two wings—the one with the cafeteria and bedrooms and patient lounges, and the one with the staff lounges and locker rooms, the "treatment" rooms, and the offices. They're connected by the lobby, and Mom had to use a key to get from the lobby to each wing, so if I leave this one, I probably can't get back in. So I look around here first. There's a back door that leads out to the lawn—unlocked, interestingly. I wonder if the nurses and the doctor come out here for smoke breaks. There are half a dozen treatment rooms, all with the same setup as the one I was just in, three on the first floor, three on the second. Also on the second floor are a locked room labeled STORAGE and what looks like an actual infirmary, with some beds, curtains, and a nurse by a desk with containers of gauze, alcohol, and other first-aid-kit stuff. No one is in it currently aside from the nurse, who eyes me suspiciously, but if I were a patient here and couldn't escape, I'd probably try hurting myself at least once, and this is where they'd bandage me up.

"Was Hank brought here?" I try asking the nurse.

"Who are you?"

"Family. Mary's son. I met one of the patients, Hank, and I was looking for him."

"He's not here," she says, still wary. Almost a confirmation, but not quite. "You should find your mother. It's not good to just wander around. Someone might think you're a patient trying to escape."

"Do they try to do that?" I ask, making my face surprised. "Dr. North said everyone is here by choice."

She stands and walks over to me in the doorway. She's one of the pretty nurses, maybe twenty-five, with a dark bob that reminds me of Elsie's. She looks me up and down, evaluating. "I did hear Mary's son was visiting. Worried about his mother working at a place like this."

I nod. "I'm protective."

She leans against the wall, looking at me with a smile. "That's sweet."

"So do patients really try to escape? That sounds dangerous. I've only seen a few orderlies, and while I wouldn't doubt my mom could put up a fight, some of these guys look pretty tough."

She laughs at that. "You know what we do here, right? What kind of patients we have?"

"Well, sure." I nod. "But that doesn't mean—"

"They're all harmless as pussycats." She puts her hand on my forearm. "It is sweet you worry, though. I'm Jean, by the way."

I almost laugh at that. "Andy. Nice to meet you." I shake her hand. "But then, how do they try to escape?"

"Over the fence out back, usually. They try climbing it. Mostly at night. But most fall before they make it to the top or realize there's some razor wire up there and cut themselves and then come crying here." She sweeps the room with her hand. "The infirmary."

"Huh." I do my best puzzled face. "Well, I guess some of them are bound to have a change of heart."

"Some never really wanted to be here. Their parents have them committed, or if they've been caught acting on their impulses and the family can afford it, a judge will agree to let them be treated here instead of prison or a psych ward. We're the most humane option for these poor men."

I nod, every fiber in me wanting to scream at the word *humane*, but just going along with it. I want the earth to open and swallow this building in one gulp.

A year back, I wonder if I would have come here willingly, if I knew it was a choice.

No. I don't think so. But I'm not sure, and that makes the pit of my stomach shiver, as if Dr. North has injected me with something.

"Well, I'm glad you're all helping them get better." I force a smile. "And I'm glad my mom is safe working here."

"Very. But you really shouldn't be wandering alone. Should I walk you to the lobby? We can ask them to find your mother there."

"Oh, no, I know the way. I was just being nosy and wondering about that guy Hank I met. He seemed so . . . normal."

She nods. "Yeah, he does. Tall and muscular like that. But his family put him here for a good reason, so sometimes they can really fool you."

I mirror her, nodding, to hide my shock. His family put him here. Then what were they doing with Edward?

"Sure, why don't you show me to the lobby," I say.

We walk back to the lobby, and she chats at me, telling me how wonderful my mother is, how sweet I am to worry. I'm not paying much attention though, I'm too baffled. Does Edward know what kind of place his boyfriend is in? Something doesn't feel right. Could just be where I am, though. Hard to imagine anything feeling right in here.

Jean leaves me in the lobby with the receptionist, who tells her where to find my mother, and Jean walks there. Mom is smiling as they enter, but when she looks at me, I can feel her evaluating. I suddenly wonder if she suspects. If this has all been some test from her.

"Nice meeting you, Andy," Jean says, leaving.

"You, too."

I turn to my mother. I want to say a million things. I want to scream and ask her how she could work in a place like this, how she could be so cruel. But instead I just sigh.

"Isn't Dr. North such a lovely man?" She leads me to a corner of the room. "Has his quirks—he loves that bag of his like a child—but he's one of the nicest men I've worked with." We stop and she looks at me. I haven't said anything and I know I should, but nothing will come out of my mouth. "So? I'm safe, you can see that, right?"

"Yeah." I don't meet her eyes. "You're safe."

"What is it, then?"

"I just . . . I watched one of those treatments."

"Oh," she says, surprised. "I didn't think he would . . . I'm sorry. I know they can be intense."

"It felt like watching a man get tortured," I say softly.

I look up. Her face is blank, unreadable. "It's just a medical treatment, Andy. These men need help."

"Do they?" I ask carefully. "They're just living their lives. They're not hurting anyone."

Her face flickers, wavers, like she's never considered that before. "Well, they want to change. They want to be normal."

"Not the ones here against their will."

She frowns. Now she's getting annoyed. She really cares about this work, I guess. Wants to defend it. "Andy, this is my job. This is the best option for these men, the kindest. Trust I know what I'm doing."

"I do." I can't keep the disappointment out of my voice. "You know what you're doing."

There's a long pause, just the sounds of the whirring fans, the smell of flowers trying desperately to cover the layers of odors from cleaning supplies and stomach bile. Once you know what it is, though, the smell is always there. You can't not smell it. It haunts this place.

"I'll see you at home," she says, and stands on her toes. I lean down to let her kiss me on the cheek. Then I turn and go.

Outside, the air is hot and thick and smells of car exhaust and baking concrete. It's the freshest air I've ever tasted.

I stop at the first pay phone I see and gather all the change I have in my pocket.

He picks up after two rings. "Hello, this is the Ruby."

"Hi." My voice breaks a little as I say it.

"Andy?" Gene gasps. "You okay?"

"I'm fine, I'm okay," I say quickly, then take a deep breath. "I just . . . saw something awful. And I wanted to hear your voice." I trace the telephone cord between two of my fingers. "I miss you."

"I miss you, too. What did you see?"

"Are you sure you want to know? It's pretty bad."

"Okay . . . yes. Tell me."

So I do. I describe it as briefly as I can. The treatment.

"I've seen apomorphine given when someone has taken too many sleeping pills," he says. "Or drank too much. It's pretty gross. But given for that . . ."

"I haven't told you why I was there," I say softly.

"The case?"

"Yes." I pause. Pull the curl of the telephone cord straight. "But also that's where my mother works."

"Oh, Andy . . ." He sighs. "What are you going to do about it?"

"I don't know." I lean against the glass wall of the booth, wrapping the cord around my fingers now. "I could barely look at her. What can I do?"

"Finish the case, come home."

"Who is that?" I hear Elsie in the background. "Is that him?"

"He's having a rough time. His mom works someplace . . . unkind to queer people."

"Andy," she shouts, her voice close to the phone now. I imagine her leaning over the bar, almost cheek to cheek with Gene. "I'm your mother now. And I say finish the case and come home."

"That's what I just told him," Gene says.

I chuckle weakly. "You two should tour."

"We just want you safe and home," Gene says. "We miss you."

"I know."

We're all quiet for a moment.

"Sorry about your mom, Andy," Elsie says, softer now. "If you want my take on it, now that I'm a mom, if she knew about you, she'd quit that job in a second. She just hasn't had her eyes opened, you know? But if you sat down and said to her, 'Hey, I'm queer, and I'm happy'—well, in your case, happy for you—'and I don't want to be cured because I'm not sick,' then I can't imagine any mom who loves you not quitting that place."

"I can," Gene says, a little hardness in his voice.

There's a pause, then: "Sorry, you're right," from Elsie. "Who knows? My parents, it's not like I've ever told them, but back in New York I had some notoriety. Especially after I divorced my husband and started palling around with that showgirl. But they never asked, and I never told, and we lived in a state of pretty happy indifference. I mean, I exasperated them. They didn't like what they called my 'antics,' but . . ." She sighs, a little sad now. "Point is, I don't know. But like I said, it doesn't matter. I'll be your mom now. Yours, too, Gene."

"I think I'm older than you," I say.

"It's a metaphor!"

"I know," I say. "I love you both."

"Then hurry back. I gotta go audition some new guy now. Gene, get him to come home."

Gene chuckles and his voice comes on stronger, closer to the phone, so close I can almost imagine his head on my shoulder. "Come home."

And I want to so badly it feels like an ache. Like my muscles being pulled back north, stretched as far as they can go. "I will. I think for now I need—" What do I need? I need to search Tommy's apartment, find proof he was using again, or not. But someone needs to help Hank, and there's one person who might be able to. "I'm going to go see if the boyfriend knows what kind of place Hank is in, see if he can get him out."

"Be careful. And with your mom, too. If she found out and—" Gene takes a deep breath. "My parents just disowned me. But if they had known about a place like that, I don't know what they would have done."

"There's no way I'd end up there." They'd have to kidnap me, take me by force. "I'll be careful, I promise."

"I love you."

"I love you, too."

I hang up, the operator asking me for more change, which I slot in before driving back to Hank's family mansion. Edward lied about Hank being by the pool. He visited the clinic. But he must not know what's being done to Hank. If he really loves Hank, or ever did, he'd want Hank out of there. I have to tell him.

TWELVE

I watch the Nolton mansion for a few hours, trying to come up with a way in. I could buzz and lie, or I can climb the fence, if needed. I drive around it looking for a back way, and there is one, but it's locked, too. I decide scaling is best. Parents who would send their kid off to a place like that are dangerous, though. I'm not going to break in while they're there. So I wait, I watch. I don't even turn on the radio. When a car finally emerges, it's close to three. The town car again. This time just two heads in the back seat, both women, and I spot Hank's father driving. No Edward. How is he living with them? How do they know about Hank, but not Edward? And why invite your son's boyfriend to stay with you when you put your son in a place like the North Clinic?

I get out of my car and find a shady spot where the wall around the mansion is rough and not too high. After a few false starts, I manage to vault it.

I land in some bushes on the other side and crouch low, looking around for anyone who might have spotted me. But there's no one. I'm in a dark area of the estate, trees and lawn, but not much else. I'm behind the main house and I can see a pool and pool house, and someone lying in a lounge chair. A portable record player is in the grass behind the chairs, and Frankie Laine is singing "Tonight You Belong to Me," the volume almost a lullaby from here.

I approach carefully. It's Edward in the chair. He's on the opposite side of the pool from me, wearing some skimpy red swim trunks and a pair of sunglasses. The bottle of wine he bought stands on the stone tile next to his chair, one empty glass next to it.

"Hi again," I say across the water.

He looks up, startled. "You again. Persistent. Did a maid let you in?"

"Climbed the wall. I needed to talk to you, and you'd said it was complicated, so I didn't want anyone to know I was here."

He considers that for a moment. I can see him weighing calling for help or entertaining me. He stands and wades into the pool, walking until it covers his waist, then over to my side, the sound of the water being pushed lapping over the music.

"Dip your feet in," he says when he's just below me, looking up with an inviting smile. "The water is nice when it's so hot."

I sit down next to the edge of the pool and dip my hand in. It is nice. I would love to jump in.

"You want to borrow a suit? Or just strip down? Hank's parents are gone. The help are all trying to relax while they're out."

He looks up at me, then glances down at the water, studying his reflection.

"Without Hank?"

He shrugs.

"I found him, you know. That place." I wait, read his face. He keeps staring at his reflection, which ripples against the bright blue. "You know what they do there?"

He stares at his reflection awhile before looking back up. "I know it's embarrassing that someone should need that, but it's a mental clinic. Really it's like a nice hotel, from what I've seen. I visit every few days. He's asleep a lot. But they say he's getting better, and he'll be home soon. And then we can go back to San Francisco." Edward leans against the side of the pool kicking his feet out so they float on the water. An easy, practiced motion. He's comfortable here.

"Better?" I can't keep the edge out of my voice. "They're torturing him."

He screws his face in confusion and turns to look at me, but his feet stay floating. "What?"

"They're trying to cure his homosexuality." Can he really not know?

He shakes his head, eyes unreadable behind the glasses, and kicks the water once, making the sound of an unplugged drain. "It's for exhaustion. That's what his parents told me. They're a little ridiculous, I think, but they're not wrong. He's been acting crazy lately. He needs some time to relax."

"Crazy? Running off with the motorcycle gang, you mean?"

He stares at me, a faint smirk on his lips. "You really have been playing detective. Who are you really? You're not from Mattachine."

"I'm Andy. I work above the Ruby, I'm a PI."

He turns to stare at his feet and kicks the water, a little fountain of froth. "I've heard of you," he says, his voice carefully neutral. "And Myrtle cares so much about little old me you came down here?"

"That's about it."

"And now what? You've found me. You've found Hank. Daphne isn't with us."

He's right. I know where they are. I know Mattachine has nothing to do with this, and that the case is over. It just doesn't feel over.

"I just wanted to make sure you knew about Hank." My voice sounds strained. "About what they're doing to him in there."

"Giving him some nice good alone time?"

"Trying to pull the gay out of him through his stomach. They give him drugs, make him vomit."

Edward flinches and turns away. I don't know if he knows what I mean or not.

"How can you be all right with it? Don't you miss him?"

"I told you, I visit him nearly every day." He pulls himself out of the pool, water running off him like a falling veil. His body is smooth and wet, his swimsuit clings. He steps close to me. "As for what I miss, you can help me with that."

I shake my head. "While he's locked up, in his parents' house? How are you even living here?"

"Like I said, they think I'm an old school chum. His best friend."

"So they take you out for dinner, let you use their pool?"

He grins, proud of himself. "Yes. They love me like another son. His mother says so all the time. And frankly, after all I've done for Hank, I think I deserve a little relaxation, too. We can both have a vacation." He gestures at the pool. "The water really is lovely."

"All you've done for him?" I don't like this.

He walks back around the pool to where he was sunbathing, and I follow. He's got a towel on the chair and he starts to dry off as he speaks, listing things. "I got him through college. He wasn't much for studying. I was the one with a real paying job after college, too."

"The movies?"

He smiles. "Not in them, I don't really want that kind of life, but it was fun being around it. Learning so much. But all the while Hank was just fooling around. Tried his hand at photography, but didn't want to work for a photographer, learn more about it. Just bought an expensive camera, took some photos.

Got bored. Painting, too. Screenwriting—I got him a meeting with the Epstein brothers, he forgot about it. When I tried tightening the purse strings, he went to Mommy and Daddy. So I decided we needed a change of scenery. He finally got a job in San Francisco, you know. Studio assistant for a photographer. Was finally learning. But then some bikers come along and he's chasing some dream of himself again."

"Sounds rough." I fish out my cigarettes and offer him one. Keep him talking. It doesn't sound rough at all. It sounds like a bad relationship between a wanderer and a control freak. But he's proud of what he's done—seems like he's been wanting to tell all this to someone for ages. All he's done for Hank. All his martyrdom. And now Hank in that place. I know what that looks like but I don't want to believe it.

"Why stay with him?"

He smiles a little, looking off, then takes a cigarette. I light us both.

"Because I love him," he says finally. "I know I'm complaining, but he's just so damned charming. Born to all this"—he opens his arms taking in the whole estate—"but he's not a snob or anything. He loves everyone he meets, and he's so happy all the time. Like a puppy, you know? Who doesn't love a puppy?"

"That's sweet," I say, wondering if it is.

He sits down, lies back in the chair, dangling the cigarette between his fingers, then lifting it to his lips. "But sometimes, you know, he gets ideas. So I thought a little rest, a little time for reflection, would be good for him."

Edward thought. I try not to show anything on my face, but inside I feel cold. The pool would freeze me now. "You said his parents put him in there."

He nods quickly. "Well, sure, but, I mean, I could probably ask them to let him out. Say I'd go back to looking out for him, like I've always done. But I just . . . wanted a break. Is that so wrong?"

A break. I feel myself inhale sharply like I've been slugged. "It is when he's getting pumped full of drugs, then shown porn so he vomits when he thinks of naked men, and you're out here lounging by the pool."

Edward shakes his head. "Don't be ridiculous. That's not what they're doing." His voice has enough confidence I genuinely don't know if he believes it. I want him to. I don't want to think he could knowingly put Hank in a place like that. That anyone could. But there were dozens of men there. Dozens of people had put people in that place.

He takes a drag off the cigarette while I stare at him. "This is good for him. Let him think about the sort of man he wants to be. A good member of society, of Mattachine, my boyfriend? Or some biker with no home? I've always been his true north, so why not let him realize that for once?"

The smell of the cigarette smoke makes the chlorine of the pool smell even stronger somehow. Smoke and bleach. It reminds me of the clinic and I throw my cigarette down, stomping it out.

"You want to have some fun?" he asks. "No one ever goes in the pool house."

I shake my head. I don't know what he is, willfully blind or some kind of evil. "I just wanted you to know, that place they have him locked up, it's not a good place. You should try to get him out." My voice sounds weak.

He shakes his head. "Not yet." It hangs there. The music plays softly. The pool laps against the edges in the breeze.

Over it suddenly, I hear a car pulling into the driveway on the other side of the house. Edward sits up as if a gun were fired. He turns to me.

"Go," he says quickly. For the first time, he seems worried.

I smile. "Don't want me to meet the Noltons?"

He seems to realize he's given a little away, and his smile slides back on, so smoothly I can't see the seams. "I imagine you'll find them very dull, but they're sweet, in their way. Stay if you want."

I put my hands in my pockets. "Sure."

He frowns slightly, but turns as he hears a gate open, footsteps. I didn't get a full lay of the land, but there's a gate leading from this lawn with the pool, and a flower garden and a white table, to what I assume is the front of the house.

"Eddie?" comes a young voice. The girl the Noltons ate with. "You out here?"

"Yes," Edward shouts back. He stands and takes a polo shirt from one of the other chairs and quickly slips it on. "A friend came to visit."

The girl comes bounding around an artful round of trees, followed closely by the older woman. Hank's mother, I assume. They both look surprised to see me.

"Oh?" the older woman asks. "Company? I didn't realize you'd invited anyone."

"I didn't invite him," Edward says, going over to her, his voice apologetic.

"I was just walking by and decided to drop in," I say. "Sorry. Old friend of Hank and Edward's. I bumped into Edward the other day buying wine, and then when I was walking by today, I just thought I'd buzz in, say hello, and he let me in. I'm sorry for intruding."

"Nonsense," the woman says, waving me off. "Any friend of

Eddie's is welcome. I'm Marianne Nolton, and this is my daughter, Virginia."

"Ginny," the girl corrects, studying me. She's older than I took her for, early twenties, not teens. It's the way she dresses that's confusing me, with capris, a Peter Pan collar shirt, and her dark hair up in a ponytail. "Do you work at a movie studio? Is that how you know Eddie?"

"Nice to meet you, Mrs. Nolton, Miss Nolton," I say, nodding and shaking Marianne's hand. "I'm Andy Mills."

"Andy does work at the studio," Edward says. "But just in accounting. I'm afraid he doesn't have many stories." If he weren't talking about me, I wouldn't even guess he was lying.

I shrug at Ginny. "Sorry."

She sighs, a little dramatically. "That's all right. Eddie has the best stories."

"She wants to work in the movies," Marianne says, her tone filled with that condescending humor parents use when talking about something they know their child wants to do and never ever will.

"I'm going to be a senior at Scripps College in the fall," she says, more to her mother than me. "And after I graduate, I'll apply to work at Paramount. Or maybe MGM."

Marianne snorts a little laugh. "Of course."

Ginny frowns and crosses her arms and looks at Edward, pleading. "They hire girls out of college all the time, right?"

Edward, though, is focused entirely on Marianne. "I thought you'd be gone longer."

"We were driving and realized it was such a nice day, why go out? So we came back and Louisa is going to serve tea out here." She turns to me. "Would you care to join us, Mr. Mills?

My mother was English, you see, and so we have a custom of a teatime respite."

"It would be my pleasure," I say quickly, before Edward can say no. I smile at him, but his face doesn't slip. I turn back to Marianne. "Is Hank with you?"

She colors, slightly, a faint blush just at her throat and the rounds of her cheeks. "No, no. Edward, you didn't tell him? Hank is away right now."

"Vacation," Ginny says glumly. "Without us. I don't think it's fair."

"He needed some relaxation," Marianne says, patting Ginny's arm. "And sometimes it can be so hard to relax around family."

Two maids in full uniform walk out, carrying a large tray laden with finger sandwiches and a pot of tea, plates, cups, napkins, and utensils. They were prepared—I wonder how often the family goes out and comes back for tea.

They're followed by the man I saw out to dinner with them all, in a polo shirt and slacks. He smiles and claps Edward on the back as the maids take the tray over to the table by the flower garden.

"Oh, Louisa, can we get some lemonade, too?" Edward calls out. "Mr. Nolton prefers cool beverages outdoors during the day."

The maid nods, as if one of her employers had just given her an order, and walks back to the house.

"Who's this?" the man asks, nodding at me.

"Andy Mills, dear," Marianne says. "An old friend of Edward's who just happened to be stopping by and will be joining us. He works at one of the studios, too."

"But just as an accountant." Ginny pauses, considering. "You never get to meet any stars?"

I shake my head. "I just know how much we pay them."

She rolls her eyes. "Everyone knows that. It's in the trades."

I laugh, and she smiles at me, and then her eyes flit over to Edward. He doesn't look over.

"Andy, this is my husband, Henry."

I extend my hand and shake with Henry. His grip is firm but his hands are soft. They move to sit at the table, and I follow, finding myself next to Marianne when Ginny goes to sit next to Edward. Everyone waits for a moment before the maid emerges again, with a pitcher of lemonade and glasses. She puts plates and napkins in front of each of us. I watch her to see if she seems particularly cold or angry toward Edward, but her expression is just bored.

"So Hank is on vacation alone?" I ask, turning to Marianne. "Where?"

"Oh." She blushes again.

Henry laughs. "Vacation? Is that what we're saying? He's—"

"Henry," Marianne says, her voice low, glancing at Ginny.

"We don't need to talk about that," Edward says, all smiles. "We'd all just get jealous of the relaxing time he must be having, while the rest of us are here."

Marianne and Henry both nod, smiling at that response.

"Well, it's very kind of you to put Edward up, even when Hank isn't here," I say to Henry.

He picks up a finger sandwich from the tray and takes a bite, nodding. "Of course, of course. You know, Eddie is a good boy, took very good care of our Hank, no matter how lost he was. He's even the one who—" Henry stops himself, eyes on Ginny. "He's part of the family."

"Another son," Marianne says quickly, smiling at Edward. "We adore Eddie."

"You're too kind," he says to them. "But, it's true. Since my own parents passed, Henry and Marianne are the closest I have." He turns to me, his smile a little cocky. "We're family."

"Oh, you sweet boy," Marianne says, reaching up and stroking his hair affectionately.

Everyone eats as though everything were completely normal. Maybe for them it is. Edward picks up a cucumber sandwich and tells a story about the time he had cucumber sandwiches with Gene Tierney, and Ginny and Marianne listen, rapt, while Henry enjoys some of the lemonade, ignoring the tea. Edward has them eating out of the palm of his hand. Family, indeed.

The food is good, but I'm not hungry. The bad feeling is back, the idea that this is somehow what Edward arranged. He was the one who knew about the motorcycle gang, about being here. Motorcycle clubs are fun to bring to bed, I guess, but not to be in. I think of Mattie suddenly, telling me how Mattachine doesn't accomplish anything. How blending in doesn't earn anyone rights, how I called her brave. Edward wants to blend in, at least outwardly. How angry would he be if Hank didn't want that anymore? If Hank left him over it?

Everything smells wrong on this lawn, in these bushes, like the vomit scent is still stuck in my nostrils. Maybe it is. When tea is over, I thank them all and excuse myself, walking out the front gate this time. They all wave at me from the driveway, one big happy family. Except Edward has taken Hank's spot. Was that always the plan? I wonder. Get close to Hank, so ten years down the line he could take his spot? No, that's too long a plan. This was in response to something. Hank leaving him. I'm almost sure of it. When I get back in the car, it somehow smells like the cleaning supplies at the clinic, and I gag a little. I can't believe Edward would do this to his boyfriend of ten years. I can't believe anyone would do it to anyone.

I drive away. I've told Edward about Hank, where he is. That's what I wanted to do. I'm done here, right? Aside from Tommy. Maybe I'll find some drugs at his place tonight. Maybe I can wrap everything up, kiss Mom on the cheek without thinking about what she does now, and run back to San Francisco, where everything won't feel so queasy.

It's not six yet, but I drive back down to Long Beach. There's nowhere else for me to go now. Edward is either lying or delusional about Hank's situation, but neither of them are missing meetings because of some vast conspiracy or anything to do with the Mattachine Society. I have a neighborhood in which to look for Daphne, but her being gone doesn't mean anything either. Just some other sad story, probably.

It's close to five when I pull in front of the garage. The lights are on, the doors wide open, but I don't see Javi anywhere. I get out of the car and hear music playing, but it's not Yma Sumac. It's "Put the Blame on Mame," from *Gilda*. In the garage, I find Will, smoking as he polishes his motorcycle. His shirt is off, slung over a chair, his hair swept back with sweat. He's even more muscular without the shirt, definition cut into his skin and body hair. Grease stains are smudged just above his hips. He doesn't see me. He's singing along in a soft baritone.

"Hi."

He glances up. He's still attractive, no doubt, but without the sunglasses, the uniform, I feel less of a pull to him. I wonder if it was really attraction to just some familiarity. Some yearning for whom I used to be, or should have been. Which is strange, because I'm happier now, aren't I?

"Hi." He smiles. He makes no move to put on his shirt. I go behind the bar and take out the jug of whiskey Javi had poured me a glass from and pour myself another.

Will laughs. "Just helping yourself to our liquor now?"

"I've been working on your case and no one has even offered to pay me yet. So I think that means you think of me as a member. Where's Javi?"

"Doctor's appointment. Stan took him. What are you doing here?"

"Russ is going to let me poke around his place, look at Tommy's stuff. I'm early but I had a long day and nowhere else I wanted to go."

He sits down opposite me at the bar. "You wanted to come here?"

"It's probably the closest thing I have to a home here, right now. I miss San Francisco."

He doesn't say anything to that, just nods. "Pour me one, too?"

I do, handing it across the bar. His fingers graze mine, intentionally I think. But it only makes me think of Gene when he hands me a drink, the cold water on his skin. I smile, thinking about it.

"I should tell you. I have a boyfriend."

He doesn't react, just sips his drink. "I know. Javi mentioned it. Said you weren't any fun."

I laugh. "Maybe not to him."

"How about to me?" He smiles.

I laugh. "Look, you're a very handsome guy, but—"

"Okay. I get it. You don't have to do the whole speech."

"You said you wanted someone to ride into the sunset with. I'm going back to San Francisco. I was never going to be around long enough to ride off with you anyway."

He nods. "Yeah, I know. I think . . . I want one thing in my heart, and another in my pants, y'know?"

"Well, I hope you can reconcile them," I say, smiling. "You seem like a good guy."

"Really? I thought the ex-cop would hate that I was still one."

I sip my drink. "No, you're better at it than I was. I didn't tell anyone about raids, just avoided the places I knew they'd hit. I didn't have queer friends, just guys I screwed in the bathrooms. My friend Elsie, she met me right after I got fired, and she said I wasn't alive or didn't have a real life. Half of this, half of that. She was right. But you . . . you've got it all together. I wish I had been like that."

"You seem like you're like that now."

I open my mouth to object, but nothing comes out. He's right. I have a life now. I'm not the guy who wouldn't warn the bars anymore. I would call each and every one if I could.

"Maybe," I say finally.

"Maybe? You're down here looking for some missing guys you don't even know."

"Not missing anymore." One trapped, one I don't know what.

I realize it suddenly: I'm not the kind of guy to leave Hank trapped in a place like that.

"You found them? What are you hanging around for, then?"

"Tommy. I promised to find out what happened to him. And—" I down the rest of my glass, for courage. "Hank, he's in a psych clinic. They're trying to cure his homosexuality. Torture it out of him."

Will sucks in through his teeth.

"I think we should get him out. You and the guys up for helping me?"

"Hank is one of us. We were going to give him his jacket soon. Yeah, I think everyone would help. Do you have a plan?"

"Not yet. I'll think of something though." I bark a laugh. I'm going to storm my mother's psychiatric clinic with a biker club. It's an insane idea.

"You okay?"

"I don't know." I pour myself a fresh glass. "I just came up with this idea, so let's not tell anyone about it until I have it figured out, okay?"

He raises his eyebrows. "Okay," he says, dubious. "But we are going to rescue him, right?"

"Yes," I say, positive of it. "But we can't be reckless. You're a cop, you get it."

"Yeah." He nods. "And these guys, aside from me, none of them have even held a gun since they got back from overseas. They're not exactly criminals outside the bedroom. Just play at it a little."

"I know. You're all a bunch of softies, really."

He laughs. "Not every part of us." He wiggles his eyebrows.

"Yeah, yeah." I laugh. "Well, first let me figure out Tommy. Try to get Russ's head clear. Then I'll try to figure a plan. Get Hank back to you guys, back home."

"Did you find his ex?"

"Yes. Living with Hank's parents."

Will lets out a low whistle. "While Hank is locked up? What's that about?"

"I don't know. I think maybe—" I shake my head, just contemplating it. "They were together a long time. Sometimes that sort of thing can go sour. Someone running the other off the road. Hank wanted to leave him. What if . . . Edward decided to punish him for it? Tell Hank's parents he found Hank with a man or something?"

"That would be fucked-up."

I nod. "It would. I hate to think it. Maybe he's just visiting Hank to try to make his days better. I don't know. Edward came here, right? They argued?"

"Yeah. It wasn't pretty. I mean, it wasn't like they were punching each other, but their faces—" Will shakes his head. "And afterward, Hank drank a lot and begged us all to take turns on him. He wanted to get out of himself, I think. He was better by the morning, though."

"And his parents never came by here or anything, and he never went to see them?"

"Not that he ever mentioned."

I sip my drink. "So the only one who would have even known he was in town was Edward. He has to have been the one to tell the parents, to get him committed. . . ." I pause, something bitter on my tongue. "How *did* they get him committed?"

"What?"

"Hank's a big guy, right? And he didn't seem like he wanted to cure his being gay, right?"

Will laughs. "No."

"So even if Edward told his parents—how'd they bring him in?"

Will shrugs. "I don't know."

"Me neither." I swirl my drink in the glass. "I don't like that."

"Well, I'm just a beat cop. You're the detective. Figure it out."

I glance up at him. He's leaned over the bar on his elbows, staring at me, faint smile on his lips, the dark center of his hair like a cloud against the moon. His eyes are a brown that's almost gold, flecked with olive green.

A car pulls into the driveway, veering around mine and parking next to the house. Russ gets out, his suit more disheveled than yesterday. "You find anything on Tommy?" he asks me. No hi, not even for Will.

"Not yet. I'm hoping searching your place will help."

He sighs. "You're not going to find anything. He was clean."

I nod at Will, who downs what's left in his glass and goes back to his bike. I walk up to Russ, who's unlocking the front door.

"No looking in my case files. Those are confidential."

"I won't."

He seems agitated, angrier than he has the past few days. I wonder again if he could somehow have gotten rid of Tommy. Maybe he even sent Hank away—they all knew his last name, that his family was in town. It wouldn't have to be Edward, bitter over the breakup. It could be Russ, angry at Hank for moving in on Russ's boyfriend. It's easier to believe Russ, big as he is, could have knocked Hank out, dragged him to the asylum. Maybe Tommy got in the way, and Russ lashed out. Tommy took off and relapsed. This rage could be covering guilt.

He turns on the lights inside. It's a long house, but not big. And definitely not clean. A little foyer opens onto a carpeted living room, a few couches on either side and a small TV. The couches look beat-up, dented from folks sleeping on them—or at least lying down—and stained here and there. The carpet, too. There's a coffee table and some bookshelves, and these are covered in law books, case files. I pointedly ignore them, like he asked.

Russ busies himself in the kitchen, which looks like it regularly feeds the whole club. It's a mess of dirty dishes and half-filled glasses covered in watermarks. They may keep their motorcycles clean, but not anything else. Russ cleans as he prepares to cook. A cutting board gets washed along with a knife, then both used to chop a tomato. A pot gets scrubbed and put on the stove. I check the fridge—mostly beer—and the freezer. No drugs hidden in the back. Nothing strange at all.

"I'm telling you, he was clean," Russ says, smirking at me. He looks more relaxed now, cooking. "We had a system. You won't find anything."

There's only one bedroom, and I feel a little strange poking through it while one of its residents is in the kitchen, but I have his permission. It's a little neater in here, the bed made, corners tucked, most clothes folded and put away. The laundry basket is overflowing, and I go through it to the bottom, but still no sign of drugs. There are two bathrooms, and I search those carefully, the water tank in the toilet, every bottle in the medicine cabinets—though there's nothing more than antacid and aspirin. Everything is clean. Russ is right—if Tommy was using, he wasn't doing it here.

I head back into the kitchen. The table has been cleared off now; he's washing dishes while something boils on the stove. I wonder if it wasn't so much a mess as it was just not cleaned yet. If this is the system—he cooks every night, and some or all of the club comes and eats and then they get drunk and go to bed, and it's not until he has time the next day that he cleans up. And he's the only one. Always cleaning up after all of them.

"So you find anything?"

"No," I confess. "If Tommy was still doing drugs, he wasn't doing them here."

"He wasn't doing them at all. That's my point. Where else was he doing them? We're all always together. Work? You think he can get high at a motor plant without losing a hand?"

I shake my head. He's right. But something else is bothering me. Something was missing.

"And their lockers there get checked every week," Russ continues. "He can't hide a stash there. I'm telling you, no way he was still using."

"That doesn't mean he didn't go out and buy some the night he died. Hadn't done it in a while, misjudged the dose."

"No." Russ turns pink in the face. "He would have come to me. We had a system."

I nod. A system.

And then it hits me—aspirin, antacid. No allergy medicine. If Vera wasn't selling him allergy medicine, how did she have his address?

THIRTEEN

I watch him scrubbing a plate down under the water.

"How do you know Vera?"

"Who?" He doesn't look up, but his shoulders hunch a little.

"The Mattachine girl from the pharmacy. You said you knew her."

"Oh yeah, sure. Like I said, I knew her from that meeting I went to."

I think of the kid from the pharmacy, scared, promising me he'd get the stuff. The man in the diner, the lady at the fancy restaurant. I was being used to scare them. They owed her money I'd bet. That explains the car, the expensive lunch. There's one obvious thing she could have been providing them, that would require some intimidation, that would be illegal—drugs. She has access to a whole bunch of them. And she had Russ's address.

"You have allergies?"

He turns to me, forehead scrunching in confusion. "What?"

"Allergies? You have them?"

"No."

"Vera said she gave you allergy medication. She's how I found your address. Said you were a customer."

He tosses the plate down in the sink, hard. The water keeps running. "That fucking bitch."

"She used me, I think. Scared some customers. But she must have had someone to do that before. She can't just count on random guys to stop by and do her favors."

Russ turns the faucet off, the squeak of it closing echoing in the kitchen. His head drops.

"Tell me about this system you had with Tommy."

"It worked," he says, voice quiet but confident. He turns to face me. He looks sad now. "It really worked. I roughed some people up for Vera now and then, and she gave us the pills for free. Low dose of morphine. When he was feeling like he needed them, I would give him one, maybe two if it was really bad. We'd fuck, we'd drink, we'd do anything else to take the rest of the edge off."

"But you gave him the morphine."

"Low-dose pills!" he says loudly. "They found a needle next to him. I would never do that! Not enough control." His head drops again. "We had a system."

"You did. But he wasn't clean."

"No," he says softly.

I sigh and pull out one of the chairs around the kitchen table, offering it to him. He sits, and I take another, opposite him.

"It worked though," he says softly. "He hadn't done anything more than a pill or two in almost a year."

I smile, sadly. "Sometimes these systems work until they don't."

"But he didn't even come to me." Russ wipes his eyes, sniffs slightly. "He would have come to me if he needed it."

I nod. "You knew him best," I say softly. "But do you really think he wouldn't have been embarrassed? Maybe he was tired of you controlling the purse strings?" Which makes me wonder if he knew who controlled Russ's supply. "Did he know Vera was the dealer?"

Russ nods. "He always waited outside when I went in to get the drugs and the addresses of who to visit, to remind them of payments due."

"How often was that?"

"Once a week. I didn't want to have a lot of pills on hand at once. Just four every week. He usually didn't even need that, but I would flush them down the drain in front of him and then go get more, so he knew it was limited."

Tommy has been gone two weeks, and Russ hadn't refilled. No wonder Vera enlisted me as her new enforcer.

"Do you think if he went to her, asked for more, she could have given it to him?"

He looks up at me, eyes wide. He'd never even considered it. "You think she killed him?"

"No," I say carefully, "but she might have given him the means to kill himself."

Russ shakes his head again. "I'm telling you, he didn't." Russ stands so quickly the chair falls back behind him with a clatter. He's turning pink again. He bends down, close, and I can tell he wants to lift me out of my chair by the collar, but he doesn't. There's a belief in his eyes so hot that for a moment I believe it, too: Tommy was murdered. "Find out who killed him. That's what I hired you to do."

I nod, but stay quiet. His belief doesn't make it true. But it does make me want to find out for sure. He pulls back, looking a little ashamed, and I wonder again if he's truly distraught or guilty for something he did. He might believe Tommy was murdered because he had something to do with it and wants to be caught. I'd known guys like that when I was a cop. Husbands so desperate for me to find their wife's killer—really desperate, pleading, and all along it was them. They always cried with relief when I cuffed them.

"I found Hank," I say carefully.

He looks at me, curious. "Does he know what happened to Tommy?"

I shake my head. "I haven't spoken to him. He's locked up."

"Jail? Will can get you in to talk to him."

"No, worse than jail. It's a clinic for treating homosexuality."

He squints at that, confused. "What?"

"They torture guys while making them look at gay porn. Make it so every time they see a guy who might interest them, they feel sick instead."

He turns off the stove. "Let's go get him."

I stand and put my arm on his shoulder. I can feel his rage in his muscles, tight, the taut string of a bow. It feels like my anger. He didn't put Hank in the clinic. "We will. Not yet. We need to be careful."

"Careful?" he sneers. "We're gonna burn the place down, Andy."

"You're a lawyer. You said you could handle this stuff legally."

He pauses at that, and for a moment I can see his mind at work, eyes somewhere else. "We could do that, too." He grins. "Yeah, okay . . . let me think about that."

Outside, another car pulls into the driveway and honks. I'm in the space.

"That'll be Stan, bringing Javi back." He looks at the stove and frowns, turning it back on.

"I'll head out. You know when the pharmacy closes?"

"Seven. You won't make it. Stay and have dinner."

I shake my head. "Thanks, but I said I'd find out what happened to Tommy, one way or the other."

He nods, face a little sad.

I head out and wave at Stan and Javi, who is hopping out of the car with crutches now.

"You park like a tourist," Javi says flatly.

"I'm heading out."

"What?" Will says, standing in the open garage door. "You don't want to eat with us?"

"Doctor says I can get the cast off in a month," Javi says. "We should celebrate."

"He also said you need to stop dragging it around," Stan says, exasperated. "It was not a good checkup."

I smirk. "I need to talk to someone." I think about telling them about Russ and Tommy, the "system," but it doesn't matter. Tommy is gone now, no need to tell them about any of that. I get in my car and pull away, watching them walk inside. Will turns to wave at me.

The sun is setting and turning the sky the deep orange of an egg yolk as I drive. The few other cars on the road look like they're on fire. When I get to the Dahlia Pharmacy, the bright green light is turned off, leaving it a dull green-gray. The lights inside are still on, though. I go to the door, and I can see Vera, pouring powders into capsules behind the counter. I knock and she glances up. She's surprised to see me, but smirks and walks over to open the door.

"You here to ask me to dinner?" she asks, opening the door only a little, not inviting me inside. She smiles, sly, but not inviting.

"Why, you have more clients you need me to shake down?"

Her smile doesn't falter. "If you're willing . . ."

"I'm not. But I promise not to tell the cops about your side hustle if you answer a few questions."

She sighs, opening the door wider and letting me in. She closes it behind me, and when I turn, she's carefully pulling the window curtains closed, a gun in her hand and pointed at me.

"I really don't like being threatened," she says.

"You probably shouldn't be a drug dealer, then."

She scoffs. The last window is covered and she walks toward me. Her finger isn't on the trigger. She's not serious about it, just making a point.

I sit down on one of the stools by the lunch counter, hands up so she can see them.

"I'm a drug dealer anyway. Uppers, downers, whatever people rich enough to have compliant doctors want. I just know how to forge a prescription or two, and which doctors are absentminded enough that they won't notice their name being used for patients they don't remember."

"So you write fake prescriptions, sell the drugs for more than they're worth, and then mark them as sold and keep the profit?"

"Exactly." She smiles. "I'm an enterprising woman. You have to be when you don't plan on having a husband, which clearly I never will. The world is made to live off a man's income, not a woman's. And even if one day Mattachine manages to get us equal rights, recognition, how much longer before we're paid enough to live equally? The men in Mattachine don't even think about it. They'll be rich. But me? I deserve more. So I make it."

I shrug. She's not wrong and I'm not going to fight her on it. "You going to shoot me?" I nod at the gun.

She sighs and puts it in her lab coat pocket. "No. But don't threaten me again."

"Fine. But I have questions."

She sits down next to me, looking me up and down. "This is the case? Missing people?"

"And one new dead one."

She turns pale at that. "You can't think I have anything to do with it?"

"Dead guy is Tommy—Russ's boyfriend, the one he was buying the low-dose morphine for."

She sighs, shakes her head. Weariness seems to grab her body, pulling her to lean against the counter, her eyes turning toward her wall of pills. "The system. Russ was sure it was working. I felt bad for both of them, honestly."

"But you kept selling them drugs."

She looks at me like I'm insane. "Or else what? They get it off some dealer on the street? Don't tell me they wouldn't."

"Did Tommy come to see you alone?"

She shakes her head, confused. "No. Russ always was the one who collected the pills. We went over the dosage and amount every time. He was very careful. So was I. If Tommy died because of me, I know Russ would have gone to the cops. Or killed me."

"Tommy overdosed. They found him next to a needle in an alley."

"I figured, when you said he was dead. But I didn't sell him anything. I swear. I want to keep my clients alive. And I never gave out liquid morphine. You need to be a doctor to administer that, so they have their own supplies."

She looks me in the eyes and I believe her. What she wants is money, and she wasn't about to lose Russ's enforcement if she could help it. Her desperate little tricks to slot me into the role prove how much she needs him, and she knows it.

"I would be better at this if I weren't a sap about it." She sighs. "Let people buy things on credit, down payments, inflated interest. The thing is, I'm not really a bad girl. I just like nice things—fast cars, good food—and I don't want to have to sleep with a man to get it."

"You seem to be doing all right at it."

"I suppose." She stands. "Is that all you wanted? To know if I killed Tommy?"

"Yeah." I lift myself off my chair. Something is bothering me. Liquid morphine is rarely prescribed. Harder to find on the street. Why not stick to pills if that's what you usually take?" "So anyone can get a prescription with the right doctor, you said?"

"Sure. That's how it works. I mean, a good doctor won't give just anyone a prescription, but this is Hollywood."

"Yeah, you told me sometimes you would get prescriptions for young kids from studios but you knew they were really for big stars, right?"

"Sure. All the studios have doctors to handle all their stars' issues—pills are just the start."

I nod, thinking of the photos on Dr. North's walls. "Is North one of those doctors?"

She thinks for a moment. "It's familiar." She goes behind the pharmacy counter and ducks under it, taking out a large metal case and flipping through. "Yes, yes, he must have moved or something because I haven't gotten one from him in ages, but before that he was sending all sorts of kids my way with all sorts of prescriptions. Stuff for the clap, morphine, pep pills. All to patients who clearly didn't need them." She looks up. "You think he wrote a prescription for Tommy and he got it somewhere else?"

I shake my head. "No, not that." Hollywood is in the background of everything in this town. Photos on the walls, gossip at parties. Edward used to work for the studio as a fixer; Dr. North was a studio doctor. It doesn't answer the question though—how did they get Hank into the clinic? "Just a thought," I say finally. "You know anything about apomorphine?"

She looks at me baffled. "What? No. No one wants a prescription for that stuff."

"I know, I've seen it. But what can you tell me about it?"

She shrugs. "Small doses make you sick, large doses kill you."

Kill you? Dr. North didn't mention that. "Would it look like morphine? If there was a dead body of a morphine addict in an alley, and an empty needle next to him so you didn't bother to look into it much, could it have been apomorphine?"

"There'd be a few differences. Pupils would be big, not small, blood clotting would start different places, probably. What are you getting at?"

I take out Will's handwritten copy of Tommy's report and show it to her. "Is this morphine overdose, or apomorphine?"

She takes it and starts to read. "He was dead a while, so . . ." She keeps reading. "It's hard to say. I'm sorry. It was just too long after death."

"But theoretically, it could be either?"

"If they didn't test anything in his blood or the syringe?" She nods. "Outwardly, those two overdoses look very similar."

I picture it. Edward and Dr. North coming for Hank, knocking him out with something. But Tommy is still there, in the bathroom or somewhere, and he comes back, sees the kidnapping and tries to stop it. They fight. Dr. North reaches into that doctor's bag of his, pulls out the syringe, stabs Tommy. They look at him, his body, the arm—maybe Edward even knew Tommy was a junkie from their time together. They drop his body and bike in an alley somewhere. Take Hank to the clinic.

It's possible. With drugs, Hank might go down easy. The only question is why. Edward had said Hank needed alone time, to consider his life, but had claimed not to know about the treatments, the torture. Would he really knowingly use the clinic to punish Hank? Maybe. Maybe he's that cruel, or that angry. Hank had left him after ten years, not even for a particular man, but for a whole motorcycle club of them. Had blown up both their lives. But why Dr. North? Edward may have known him from the movie business, but not enough the good doctor would risk his reputation by kidnapping.

I stare at Vera, who's still looking at me confused.

"What?" she asks.

"Thanks. You've been helpful. I don't love the drug dealing, but my advice to you would be to get the money up front. Either you're hard enough for this life, or you're not. You can't be both."

"No? You sure about that?" She says it like something is funny.

"Good meeting you, Vera." I head out and get back in my car. It's time to go see Mom.

FOURTEEN

It's past eight when I get back to my mom's place. I don't know what I'm supposed to say to her. How I'm supposed to look at her. But I know I need to understand what the connection is between Edward and Dr. North, and she's the best source of information I have. The sun is down, but the lights in the house are all on, casting a buttery light out onto the porch and lawn. I see Mom in the window, looking out at me, head tilted. Part of me wants to drive away. But she might have answers for me to finally put together the picture I've painted in my head.

I get out of the car. The night is still oppressively hot, the darkness like the press of bodies at the Ruby. Inside, though, it's chilly. A large block of ice is set up in front of a fan in the living room. Kay Starr is singing "Half a Photograph" from the record player. Mom has sat back down. She's in a housecoat, frowning.

"I thought you'd be home for dinner."

"Sorry. I didn't remember us planning to eat together."

"Well, we didn't plan it." She sighs. "I just thought since you were here . . ."

"I'm still working a case, Mom."

She nods. "I know."

It's silent for a moment; a conversation we know we're going to have but neither of us wants to start sits between us, heavy, sucking the air. The fan whirs on, and cool air blasts my face. I take off my hat and coat, hang them on the stand by the door.

"I'll fix you a plate," Mom says, standing. "You didn't eat, did you?"

"No, didn't really feel hungry today."

I follow her into the kitchen, where she takes some of yesterday's meat loaf out of the fridge and turns on the oven. "I didn't know he'd show you a treatment. I'm sorry about that."

"He was showing off."

She laughs. "Probably."

I search for words, ways to beg her to quit, tell her how horrifying it all was to see without revealing that I could be in there myself, without asking if she'd institutionalize her own son. I don't want to know the answer. Then I remember what I have to do.

"He worked for the studios, right?"

She nods, putting the meat loaf in the oven, pouring me a glass of lemonade and setting it on the kitchen table. I sit and sip. It's strange how these busy little movements, her feeding me, how they soothe me into things: She pours lemonade, I sit and drink. She hands me food, I eat. And it feels normal on my skin, but inside I'm still spinning.

"He was a fancy studio doctor. Did you see all the photos in his office? He treated June Allyson, Barbara Stanwyck. I knew him then, you know, he worked out of the hospital a lot. I met Mrs. Allyson once, she was so kind."

She sits down opposite me, watching the oven until my meat loaf is warm.

"Why did he leave?"

"I think he wanted to open his own clinic, and he just finally got enough money together to do it."

"And he'd always been interested in"—I search for the words—"this kind of medicine?"

She shrugs. "Like I said, I didn't know him that well, but I guess he must have been. He's very proud of the work we do there. We all are."

I nod, like that means something, but it doesn't. "Were there any rumors about him?"

She tilts her head at me. "Rumors?"

"That he'd been fired, or that he had to leave the hospital because of scandal—anything like that?"

For a moment, her eyes flash on a memory. I recognize the look. But she shakes her head. "He's a good doctor, Andy, and he treats me and all the nurses very well."

"There was something. I can see it. Tell me."

She frowns. "You're too much like your father sometimes."

"You could spot a lie as well as he could."

She smiles at that, chin up, a little proud. "Maybe."

"So what was it? A rumor?"

"Yes. Just that. And it was a long time ago. Eleven or twelve years, I think, just before Pearl Harbor. You were still living here." She smiles and looks at me, and in her eyes I see a me from further back than that, me as a kid, or a baby. "But that has nothing to do with him as a boss, or how safe I am at work."

"Tell me, and maybe I'll agree." I lean back, ready to listen.

"It was just a rumor, like I said." She shakes her head. "But there was a young woman, an actress, not a big name or anything. Grace Burbank. Only done one bit part, but the studio had taken her under their wing. She was going to be a star, everyone said so. She had been treated by Dr. North for a while for insomnia, but then one day she came in. She was bleeding. It was pretty clearly"—Mom pauses and lowers her voice—"an abortion. That sort of thing would ruin her reputation of course. She wasn't married. But it had been botched. Poor thing died."

"And Dr. North performed the abortion?"

Mom shakes her head. "No, no, that wasn't something he would do. But the rumor was since he was so close with Miss

Burbank that maybe the baby . . ." Mom stands as she lets that hang there and takes out a plate of meat loaf, pouring some gravy over it and putting it down in front of me with knife, fork, and napkin before sitting again. "So you see, that wouldn't make me unsafe at work."

"No? He's never made a pass at you?"

She laughs at that. "Andy, he's practically your age. Don't be silly."

"How about him making a pass at the other nurses? What would happen if a nurse told you that he forced himself on her?"

She shakes her head. "He's not that sort of a man, Andy. And it was just nurses' gossip about the baby."

I look down at the meat loaf. I haven't eaten since breakfast, and I don't want to, but I know my body needs it. I cut off a piece and chew.

She smiles, a little nervous. "Was it terrible, the treatment? I know what it is, of course, but you seemed so shaken, I thought—" She stops herself, sucking her lips in. I can hear my heart pounding so loudly I don't know how she can't hear it. "And now all these questions. That is, I thought maybe you were angry with me for some reason."

I take a long drink of the lemonade. It's cold and I can feel it trickle down my throat all the way to my belly. I put the glass down and it clinks on the small yellow table. The three of us used to eat here in the morning when I was a kid. Mom made pancakes or eggs and toast. The table is old, rough, dented with all our meals.

"I guess," I say slowly, "I'm not mad exactly. Sad."

She nods. "It's very sad for all those men."

"No," I say quickly. "I'm sad that they have to go through those treatments. Or think they have to."

Her eyebrows crawl together in confusion. "What do you mean?"

"I mean I don't care who people go to bed with, Mom. I know some homosexuals. Good people. It's sad that they should feel they have to torture themselves to try to be normal."

She looks at me a moment and I think of a million ways she could react—agreeing with me, or looking guilty, or telling me how wrong I am. I don't expect what she actually does though: She laughs. Throws her head back to bark a laugh in a way that reminds me of something—me, I realize immediately. She's laughing the way I laugh.

"Andy, what else do you want them to do?"

I blush for some reason, feel my face get hot. "Just live their lives. Be happy."

She shakes her head, still smiling. "If your father could see what a softy you are, we'd have a good laugh about it."

"Mom—"

"It's not bad, Andy. I'm glad you can care about so many different kinds of people. Especially after seeing so many terrible things people can do."

"It's because I've seen those terrible things. Being queer isn't hurting anyone."

"Well, it's hurting them. Their wives. The government."

I roll my eyes. "Only because society doesn't let them just be themselves."

A soft, condescending smile blooms on her face like a dahlia. "If these people were forced into the clinic, I'd say it was all a bit severe, but they go there because they want to be normal. They know it's hard work. And this really is the best place for them—other places use much more severe methods."

"They go there because the world won't accept them." I

remember it suddenly, like a physical feeling, being a cop, knowing what the men around me thought, what they'd do—what they did—when they found out. Like being bricked into a wall, stone so tight on your skin, if you shift, it scrapes you, draws blood. "I just don't think you should work at a place like that. Why not work at a real hospital, where they're helping hurt people?"

She sighs. "Because this pays much better and I only have to work nights if someone calls out sick."

"They're not all there willingly," I say quietly, poking my fork into the meat loaf like a sulking child.

"What?"

"Hank Nolton. He's not there willingly, is he?"

She sits up, face folding like paper into something new: evaluating, severe. "This is about your case," she says finally. "There's no way you would have found Mr. Nolton."

"Why not?"

"He . . . is kept separate. The second floor has a lot of men who try to leave, so their rooms are locked when they need to be, an orderly watching. So, yes, he doesn't want to be there. But his family does. For treatment."

"Torture." It slips out before I can think about it.

She's glaring now. "Did someone hire you to interfere with his treatment?"

"No." It's true. I'm going to do it without anyone paying me. "But, yes, I was hired to look for him. People were worried."

"Well, you can tell them he's just had to get some help." She folds her arms.

"He doesn't want to be there. You said if they didn't want to be there—"

"I've met his mother, Andy. She wants him there. How could

any mother not want what's best for her son? Want his life to be safer, better? Mr. Nolton is going to emerge from his treatment with a good life, both for his family and for him. No matter how much he thinks he doesn't want to do the actual work."

My meat loaf is barely a quarter eaten. I stand. "I'm going to bed."

She glares, and I can see her tongue running over her teeth inside her closed mouth. "I don't know what you're getting so upset about."

"Don't you?" I expect it to hang there, heavy with meaning, but she just shakes her head. I open my mouth, not sure what I'm going to say. The phone rings. Mom walks over to answer it, stopping whatever was about to start, a movie cutting to a blank white screen because they forgot to load the next reel.

"Hello, Mills residence . . . Oh, hi, Marge . . . She did? That's terrible, is she all right? . . . Oh, I see." Mom glances over at me, shrugs apologetically. "Of course, of course, I can come in. No, no, it's fine, I'll just have a cup of Nescafé before I leave, that'll perk me up. . . . Sure, okay, see you soon."

She hangs up the phone and sighs. "One of the night nurses broke an ankle coming into work. They need me to cover. Sorry." She walks upstairs and I sit there, wondering if our conversation left any trace on her at all, a fingerprint, a speck of dust. I almost told her everything. The only thing she thinks about me now is I'm a "softy."

I shake my head and put what's left of my meat loaf in the trash. It doesn't matter. Silence is what we live in, Mom and me. Three phone calls a year. Letters that never say anything. It swaddles us so tight that if I tried to scream, it would sound like a muffled sigh.

I find the powdered coffee and boil some water and make it,

handing her the mug when she comes back downstairs in her nurse's uniform.

"Oh, thank you, sweetheart." She drinks deeply. "I should get off very early tomorrow, and I'll need to sleep, so I don't think I can make you breakfast."

"No problem, I can make something for myself. You want me to take you and pick you up so you don't have to worry about driving?"

"Oh, that's all right. I don't want you getting up early. Are you going to bed now?"

I shake my head. "I have some more work to do."

"This late?" She sips, finishing the cup and handing it to me. "These detective hours are too much."

"Like nurse hours."

She laughs.

"Be careful," I tell her. Mom being there will make breaking Hank out riskier. Or maybe easier, if I can say I'm visiting the clinic to see her. She pecks me on the cheek and leaves. I stand in the window and watch her car pull away. The night is blue and black, and her headlights cut through in wide beams that get smaller and smaller.

I pick up the phone, dialing the number Myrtle had given me just a few days ago, though it seems like years. I think briefly of calling her, updating her, but decide not to. She'd just be confused and worried, especially with no word on Daphne yet. She's not whom I need to talk to right now.

"Hello, Samuel Blanchard."

"Hi, Samuel, it's Andy. We met the other night?"

"Oh, of course." His voice pitches up in delight. "Why are you calling so late? Is there some big break in the case?"

"Maybe. I need to ask Leo something, if that's all right."

"Oh, how exciting. Leo! Leo, it's the detective! He needs to ask you something for his case."

"What?" I hear Leo's voice in the background, thrilled. He takes the phone. "Hello? Detective? You need me?"

I'm worried he might explode from joy. "I do. I have a question, about the studios."

"Ooooh, did the case take you to Hollywood? Well, no surprise, everything in this town does."

"If there was a doctor who did work for the studios, helping stars with insomnia, stuff like that, and he got one of the actresses he was treating pregnant, how would that go?"

"Oh, terrible. You don't mess with the talent, you know. The talent is property of the studio. They're only allowed to date approved people and, even if they're married, only allowed to get pregnant with studio approval."

"What happens if they get pregnant anyway?"

He makes a clicking noise, a sort of hum. He doesn't want to talk about this. But I keep silent and eventually he relents. "They force women to get abortions. And the doctors know that. If one was going around with a star without the studio's permission, he'd be ruined. Wouldn't be able to get work in LA anymore, there'd probably be an investigation by the medical board, maybe worse. When the studios come down, they come down hard."

I nod, thinking about the rumor from Mom. If I were smart, but stupid enough to have knocked up a rising star, I'd try to avoid letting the studio know. I'd try to fix the problem myself. And if I wasn't the sort of doctor who normally performed abortions, and something went even slightly wrong . . .

"You remember Edward, the guy I was looking for?" I ask Leo. "You said he worked for Mannix."

"Yes, yes, did you find him?"

"I did. What exactly did he do for Mannix, do you know? You said he was a spy?"

There's a long pause. "Yes. Mannix knows everything. So he needs people who can get information. People others open up to. Edward had one of those faces, didn't he? I was always careful around him—I think he joined Mattachine just to make sure I wasn't gossiping, so back then I didn't. Edward was one of his eyes."

"Would he have worked with any doctors?"

"Huh? Edward?"

"Yeah."

Leo thinks for a moment. "Well, actually, yes. I remember he was friendly with one of the doctors we used, now that you mention it. What are you asking for?"

"Was the doctor's name North?"

"Y-yes, I think it was. I feel like maybe I've said too much, now."

"That's a first," Samuel says in the background.

Leo titters. "What is all this about?"

"Dr. North runs a clinic now, curing men like us—torturing us really, giving us drugs that make us vomit for an hour while looking at muscle mags."

There's a long pause, and I look out the window. It's so dark. "That's awful." Leo's voice sounds different, the light gossipy exterior slid off, something harder underneath.

"What is?" I hear Samuel ask.

Leo tells him, and I feed Leo more details. They're quiet so long I wonder if we've been disconnected.

"And he's doing that to Edward?" Leo finally asks.

"Hank. I think Edward put him there, though. Punishment for their breakup."

More silence. I didn't expect Mattachine to have the same reaction I did. I remember that doctor at the meeting back in San Francisco—he was talking about this, just leaving out the details. Isn't this what they want? To blend in? Or maybe that's unfair. I try to remember Myrtle's face during that meeting, while the doctor spoke. Her expression was fixed, I think. Forced. A polite smile stuck on with plaster.

Vera said it was about how they have to blend in until the world sees all of us as normal. They want the world to treat them like it would anyone else—so they think they have to act like everybody else. But torture—that's not what they want.

"Who would do that?" Leo asks finally. He sounds on the verge of tears.

"You just said he worked for one of the hardest men in the industry, that he had a hand in forcing abortions and blackmailing."

"That's true. I just didn't think one of us would . . ."

"I know. But what I've been trying to figure out is how he got the doctor to go along with it. Hank wouldn't go in willingly, from everything I know of him, so they must have kidnapped him. But why would the doctor do that for someone like Edward?"

"Because he slept with a star and Edward knew," Leo says in a gasp.

"And she got pregnant, her abortion went wrong, and she died. If Edward knew about that, would that be enough to make the doctor assist in his scheme?"

"Absolutely." There's a long pause. I hear them murmuring before Samuel comes back on.

"Andy, you're going to get him out of there, right?"

"I'm going to try."

"We want to help."

A chill of surprise creeps over me. I smile. "Do you have a big truck, for carting wedding stuff around?"

"Sure. I mean it's the studio truck, but I have the keys."

"All right. I think I have an idea. I'll come around in a bit. Might bring some people."

FIFTEEN

I talk it over with them, then make another call. When that one is done, I call Gene, just in case.

"Hi." I can hear music behind him.

"Hey, it's later than usual, I was getting worried."

"Sorry, it's been a long day. Going to be longer."

"Oh? What do you have planned?"

"Something dangerous."

He sighs. "Andy—"

"I'll be as careful as I can be, and I will come home to you," I promise. I hope I can keep it. "I just wanted to say I love you first."

"I love you, too."

"Is Lee there?"

"He is."

"You want to tell me you love me, too, Andy?" I hear Lee shouting.

I laugh. "Give him the phone."

"*Her*," Gene corrects.

"Thanks, *her*."

Lee takes the phone. "What can I do for you?" She sounds like she's had a drink. "You miss hearing my singing?"

"I do, but I'm calling about a job."

"Job?"

"It's a little more than what you usually do, so you can say no."

"Sounds exciting."

There's something different about Lee's interest in my job

from that of the folks from the Mattachine meeting here. Less voyeuristic. Lee likes the stories, the intrigue, but he sees it all as real, not just something to watch on-screen.

"I have a neighborhood for the missing girl, Daphne. You remember her description?"

"Sure, birthmark on the jaw."

"Great. Can you find her? She lives in Sea Cliff somewhere."

"What do you want me to do, just drive around looking?"

"Yes. If you can't find her, I'll take over when I get back."

"Sounds boring."

"It is, I'm sorry. It's real detective work though."

She sighs. "All right, but you'd better get back here for your birthday. They are planning—"

She's cut off as the phone is taken from her hand. "No spoiling the surprise," Gene says. "And there will be a surprise, right?" he says to me. "You'll be back?"

"After tonight, I'll probably have to skip town."

He doesn't laugh. "Be careful," he says. "I love you."

"I love you, too."

I hang up the phone and stare out at the night again. I open a window and hot damp air floods in, like an approaching storm. Time to get started.

It's after eleven by the time we're done with the meeting. It took some time to pick everyone up, and then there were personalities on full display. But everyone agreed that rescuing as many guys as we could from the clinic was the priority, and since I had brought them all together, I was in charge. When I spoke up, they listened, even settled down a little, and we mapped everything out. Now we'll see if it works.

I'm up first.

The palm trees that line the path to the clinic rustle at night. The lights inside are on, silhouetting them and casting long thin shadows on either side of me, lined up like men marching to the executioner. I run from where Will dropped me off at the street, trying to work my body so I seem more out of breath than I am. I try the door of the clinic, but it's locked, not normal business hours. I pound furiously, make my face worried. I keep pounding on the door until it opens a crack. Marge stares out at me, bewildered.

"Mr. Mills?"

"I'm so sorry." I push the door open and barge in. "I need to find my mother. I need to find everybody."

She spins, eyes wide. "What?"

"I . . ." I make my face embarrassed, remember how it felt admitting this to Mom. "I don't know if my mother told you, but I'm here on a case. And I have reason to believe someone is going to target this clinic. We need to gather whatever night staff is here and make a plan."

Her eyes go wide. "I should call the police!"

I nod. I expected that. I just have to hope Mattie pulled that part off. "I called my contact at the police department, he's already on his way, but that's a good idea. Call the station, get them all. Then get everyone else down here, please. How many staff do you have on at night?"

She shuffles back behind the desk and picks up the phone, dialing. "Um, me, your mother is filling in, one of the orderlies, and two other nurses. The janitor went home already, he said good night." She puts her ear to the phone. "No one is picking up."

I hide a smile. Good job, Mattie. "That's all right. Just get everyone to the lobby. My police contact will be here soon."

Marge nods, my performance of fear spreading to her. She's sweating. She picks up the phone again and clicks one of the buttons at the bottom of it. An interoffice system. Good. "Mary? Your son is here, he wants us to gather all the staff in the lobby. He says we're in danger!" Her voice goes up a little at the end, and I almost feel bad. I watch her face as she nods. Come on, Mom, don't doubt me. "All right. Yes. I'll call the infirmary." She hits a button on the phone and glances up at me. "She's coming." Marge picks up a mic for a PA system and speaks into it hurriedly. "All staff, please report to the lobby."

I nod, happy, but keep my face etched with concern. Then I turn to look out the window. A large white van rumbles by. Right on time. I yank on my tie once in full view of the window, signaling Will—five minutes.

Mom, the other nurses, and the one orderly walk into the lobby one by one. Mom looks at me confused, but I hold up a finger.

"Hi, everyone," I say loudly when they've all shown up. "I'm so sorry to bother you. I'm Mary's son, I'm a detective. I followed a case down here and I'm afraid it has to do with your clinic. There's a killer who I think is going to come after one of the staff here, tonight."

I let that sink in.

"What?" Mom says, doubtful. "Andy, what are you talking about?"

I expected that, too. There's a sudden knocking on the door. Everyone looks at it confused, so I go quickly and open it. Will strides in past me, in full uniform. Mom might doubt her son, but she won't doubt a cop. I notice the way everyone else perks up, paying him attention. I hope he can sell this.

"You tell them?" he asks me.

"I was just starting to."

"Right." He turns to the staff. "So Detective Mills here has been tracking a killer who goes after nurses." Marge gasps. "He's shown me compelling evidence about some deaths up in San Francisco and a more recent one here. We believe the killer is planning to attack tonight, which is why I asked him to gather everyone together, to be on the safe side." I watch all of them as he speaks. They're confused, worried, but I'm not sure how much they're buying. The uniform helps. "There should be more police coming," Will continues. "We're short-staffed at night, I won't lie. But in the meantime, I think, Andy, it makes sense for you to guard everyone while I do some quick recon."

I nod and point at the door to the patient wing. "Can someone open the door?"

Marge does it quickly, pulling at a key ring on her belt.

"May I borrow that, miss?" Will points at the keys. "Just to make sure I don't have to come back."

"Oh, of course." Marge gives him the whole ring of keys. Good. He vanishes into the patient wing.

"What about the patients?" Mom asks.

I shake my head. "This guy only goes after nurses. They're all in their rooms, right? No one is kept anywhere else?"

"All in their rooms," Mom says, "but what does this have to do with—"

"Then they should be safe." I don't need anyone thinking about Hank right now.

"And awake because of the PA," the orderly says. He's a big guy. I wonder if he watches the second floor. "Some were shouting through the doors asking what was going on."

"I should call Dr. North," Mom says.

"If you need to." I suspected she might. I don't have a plan for him. Hopefully he won't cause too much trouble. "Tell him the police are here already. We have everything under control."

"Why didn't you tell me about this?" Mom asks, picking up the phone.

"I thought there would be more time. I didn't want to worry you."

She sighs, glaring at me as she cradles the phone to her ear. The other nurses are looking to her. I'm not in charge here. I just need to hope I can sway my mother.

"Dr. North?" she says into the phone. "I'm so sorry to wake you. We have a situation at the clinic. The police are here, and my son. They seem to feel a killer might be targeting one of the nurses." She pauses. Her voice isn't as worried as I'd like it to be. She's calm under pressure but this needs to overwhelm her so she stops asking questions. "Yes. The patients are safe. Just the nurses." She nods into the phone. "More police are coming, one is searching for the killer, while Andy protects us. They say they have it under control, but I thought you should be notified. . . . All right, I'll tell him. . . . Yes." She puts the phone down. "He says thank you, and he's on his way to see if he can help."

"Good," I say, hoping he won't get here in time.

"So what do we do?" one of the nurses asks, rubbing her hands together in front of her like she's trying to get warm in front of a fire.

"Just wait and hope my officer friend finds the suspect. Maybe it's best if we all keep away from the windows and doors, though." I motion back the orderly, who was looking out the window. Everyone shuffles toward the middle of the room. They look scared, and I feel a twinge of guilt for scaring them, but not enough to stop me from rescuing the people trapped here.

"I don't understand—who is this man?" Mom asks. "Why

would he kill nurses? And what does this have to do with your case, with—"

"He's a vet," I interrupt again, looking at all the other nurses, my eyes hopping around so Mom can't sense the lie as much. "Korea. When he was over there, a young nurse gave him an injection of something she wasn't supposed to. I'm not a doctor so I don't quite understand what happened, but he was in a coma for a few months, and when he came out of it, he was different. Angry." It's a ghost story meant to frighten nurses. As I look around, it seems to work. Except on Mom. "He's going after hospitals and clinics where other vets are—especially ones he served with." I give her a long look, praying she doesn't know Hank never served. She stares at me a long second and I can feel my heart speed up. I just pushed it too far and her doubts will ruin the plan, I can tell. But she just nods.

I turn around and go to the window, looking out. A white van leaves the parking lot and takes off down the street and I smile.

"This is terrifying," the nurse rubbing her hands says. Her voice isn't quite a scream but it's stretched high and thin, reaching for one.

"My son will keep us safe." Mom goes to her and rubs her shoulders. "He was a policeman, and now he's a detective. He helps people."

I nod, glad Mom and I are in agreement about that—it's just the word *help* we might differ on.

Will comes out of the patient wing, nods at me. I feel a knot in my chest slowly loosen.

"I think we're clear," Will says. "All the patients are safe, I didn't find anyone."

"The only way in is the front door," the orderly says. "Unless he digs under the fence."

I nod. "I know. But this guy is off his rocker. Who knows what he'll try."

I sniff the air. Something is wrong. I glance over at the door to the patient wing. Smoke.

"Fire," I say, pointing. I look at Will confused. He shakes his head, eyes wide. He doesn't know either. Fire was not part of the plan.

The nurses are scrambling away from the door, which smoke is now pouring out of. Outside, I hear a motorcycle peel away at top speed. Damn it, Russ.

Smoke starts to pour in from the other door, to the treatment wing.

"Okay," I say, "everyone out the front door."

"What about the patients?" Mom yells.

She's right. The plan was that if any patients didn't want to leave, we wouldn't make them. Patients might still be inside their rooms.

"You take them out, guard them from the killer," I say to Will, who nods. "I'll help the patients."

Will opens the door and shuffles everyone out except my mother, who stays, glaring at me. "You're not going to stay in a burning building without me."

"Mom—"

"Evander, don't argue with me." She reaches down and tears a strip of fabric off the hem of her uniform, then tears it in half. She grabs a nearby vase of flowers and dumps the water from it onto the strips of fabric, then hands me one. She wraps the other around her face. "You, too. For the smoke."

I do as she says, the fabric clinging to my skin, and together we go into the patient wing.

Fire is everywhere, climbing the walls, cracking and peeling the white paint, turning the carpet to curls of charcoal. It has the chemical smell of gasoline. Russ must have poured it down the hall before striking the match. I thought we were together on this—he'd go after the clinic legally. But he clearly had other ideas. The walls spit waves of fire and heat ripples the air. I crouch low, looking at Mom, who is doing the same. The heat is overwhelming, I can barely take a step without flinching. The walls hiss and crackle. My blood starts to simmer in the heat. This place is going to be ash. The walls bend in a little, and I can feel the air shaking more than it should, the building panting with the effort to stay up. We have to be out of here fast or we'll be buried under it.

I shuffle as carefully as I can down the hall while still moving quickly. Sparks land on me and my jacket starts to smolder. I can feel them through the fabric like bug stings, and they're everywhere, swarming. I smack some out, and my mother gets the rest. I see her eyes squint in a smile over her mask. Then we turn back to the building, making our way to the rooms.

Every patient door is open, and every room is empty. I smile behind the wet fabric. They're all gone. All free. At least down here. Upstairs is where they were locked in.

"They're clear," I say to my mom.

She narrows her eyes at me, her pupils shining back the red flames. She sees something in me. "You knew they would be." It doesn't sound like an accusation, but she'll figure out it is one if I respond.

"Let's check upstairs," I say, and turn away, running up the stairs. There's less smoke up here, and the fire isn't as hot. Every room is empty here, too, every door thrown open and turning black, warping so they can never close again. Below us, the floor lets out a long creak. I jump back to the stair landing, where my mother grabs me.

"We have to leave. Everyone is safe," I shout over the roar.

She nods and we run back down the stairs, down the hall, and into the lobby. Fire has reached in here, too, the doorframes to the wings with halos of flame, the ceiling vanished under the smoke. We keep running until we're on the path outside. I cough suddenly, all the smoke I'd managed to breathe in collecting at once and then forcing its way out, like a ghost leaving a body.

Will has the other nurses and orderly gathered in a circle in the middle of the path. They're staring at the clinic. Fire reaches out from the windows like hands. One of the palm trees is alight. Smoke is everywhere.

"We pulled the alarm," Marge says, pointing at a firebox down the block.

I nod. This wasn't part of the plan, but looking at the building, I do feel a certain joy knowing it'll be mostly cinders soon.

"Andy," Mom whispers, pulling at my shirt. "What is going on?"

I look at the other nurses. They're just staring at the fire. In the distance, I can hear sirens.

"Look, there are the patients," Marge says.

My heart goes hard as stone, beating against my ribs like a mallet. Did we fail somehow?

I look over. In the parking lot are a few patients, but just a handful. They wander toward us, like stunned sheep.

"There were men," one of them tells us. "They said we needed to get out, and that we could leave with them and never come back if we wanted."

I nod, keep my face still, but then try to make it confused. So only some escaped. These must be the patients who wanted to stay. More than I'd hoped.

"Men?" Mom asks.

The sirens grow louder. Down the street, I can see the blinking lights of a fire truck. Everyone goes silent as it pulls up. The firemen hop off it, unrolling hoses, getting to work. One pushes us back, across the street. I meet eyes with Will. It's time for us to go.

"Andy," Mom says, pulling on my sleeve again. She takes me away from the crowd and holds my wrist. "Andy, what is going on?"

I look down at her. The light from the fire flickers on her face, still wet from the mask she made. She'd wanted to save them. To help. What would my wanting to help look like to her, if she could see it, laid out and naked as a newborn. What would she do then?

"It's okay, Mom." I take her hand in mine. "I love you."

"Andy, I don't understand. Is there really a killer? Who were the men in there?"

I squeeze her hand tightly and say nothing.

"Andy," Will says behind me. He's on his motorcycle.

"I lied about Gene," I say to her.

She shakes her head, confused. "What?"

"Gene's not a nurse. And not—"

"Mary!" Dr. North has pulled up, is rushing out of his car. "What is going on?" His eyes are huge, his dreams burning down in front of him, and I don't bother trying to hide my smile.

"This was the work of the killer," I shout, loud enough to tell everyone. "The police will be here soon. I need to go make sure he doesn't escape."

I move toward Will, who has started the motor on his bike.

"Andy." Mom runs after me. "What do you mean you lied about Gene, about—"

I hug her tightly, maybe for the last time. "I love you, Mom. You'll figure it out."

Then I get on the back of Will's motorcycle, and he pulls away. I look back once. Dr. North is standing next to Mom, shouting, but she's just looking after me. For a moment, we meet eyes, and I can see her taking me in, my arms wrapped around Will's waist, leaning into him slightly. Everything I said, everything I've wanted to say, seems to crash on her as there's the sound of something collapsing in the fire. Everyone else turns, but she keeps her eyes on me, her mouth dropping open slightly in understanding as the sky burns behind her.

SIXTEEN

The curtains of the Dahlia Pharmacy are all drawn and dark, but the neon light is still on, casting a pale green shadow on the asphalt, making it look like it might bloom. Will and I knock three times, then twice more, and the door nudges open. Javi looks us up and down before letting us in.

"They don't look too mad," he says to the room after closing the door behind us.

Inside is crowded to the brim. The patients who chose to go in the van with Samuel, Leo, Marie, and Ethel are all sitting on stools or leaning on the wall. A few are sitting on the floor, eyes bright with an energy their bodies don't share. Their drivers stand in a corner, talking among themselves. Vera is walking around handing out glasses of water and pills to the patients. Mattie is taking down their information on a clipboard. The place feels like the end of a party and a hospital rolled into one. Russ and Stan lean against the pharmacy counter, giving us guilty looks.

It didn't take much to bring everyone together. We all knew how evil that place was. But we had just planned a prison break, not arson.

"My mom was in there," I say, walking over to Russ.

He puts his hands up. "I'm sorry. She's okay though, right?"

I nod.

"Good. You can slug me if you want though."

I sigh. "I thought you were going to handle it legally. Sue him or something."

"For what? Nothing he was doing was illegal, except maybe

with Hank." Russ nods at one of the patients. Tall, dark hair, but otherwise not at all how described—he looks like all the other patients: weak, pale. This is not a man who could put up a fight. "Come over here and meet your savior," Russ shouts. Then he turns back to me. "Andy, the law wasn't going to help us. I did what I had to."

I nod and he extends his hand. I shake it. I don't love what he did, but he's not wrong. That place had to go.

Hank leans against the bar. Up close I can see traces of who he was— handsome, strong—but now his skin is too pale and weak looking. It hangs on him like a shroud.

"I don't know you," he says to me.

I smile. "I know. But I've been looking for you."

"Why?"

"Myrtle. You, Edward, and Daphne all stopped going to meetings. She was worried someone was taking you all out."

He starts to laugh, then coughs and drinks from the glass of water he's holding. Vera is next to him a moment later, looking him up and down. "You all right?"

"I laughed. It hurt."

She nods. "You've burned your esophagus. A lot of you have. Drink the water. Honey should help, too. And I'll send you all home with antinausea meds. You need to eat." She looks at me and smiles. "Thanks for letting me help."

"Thanks for helping."

Someone else coughs across the room and she swans over.

"Myrtle?" Hank asks me.

I nod. "I still haven't found Daphne. I have a friend looking for her in Sea Cliff. Don't suppose you remember where?"

He squints. "California Street, I think."

"Great, thanks."

He smiles, still confused. "Thank you. You didn't need to . . . I . . ." He looks like he might cry, and Russ claps his shoulder and squeezes.

"There's one more thing I want to know." I wait until he looks up. "Tell me what happened the night you were taken? To Tommy?"

Russ looks at me, a little surprised.

Hank shakes his head. "I tried—" He coughs again.

"Can I guess and you nod if I'm right?"

He nods and drinks more water.

"You and Tommy were hanging out in the garage, maybe fooling around, I don't know. I'm guessing he went inside for something?"

"More beer," Hank says.

"And while he was inside, Edward and Dr. North pull up. Edward had been there before, right? When you told him you weren't going back with him or going home?"

Hank nods. "I called my parents once for money. He picked up. Told me he'd bring me"—he coughs—"cash without telling them where I was."

"But that night it was two against one. Maybe they had something to grab you, too."

"Handkerchief. Edward put it over my mouth. Got dizzy."

"Chloroform, easy enough for the doctor to get. But before they could knock you out and take you away, Tommy came back. Fought them off, or tried." I glance at Russ, who is staring at us, rapt.

"Edward grabbed a syringe from the doctor's bag, stabbed Tommy with it."

I nod. "Apomorphine. Same stuff they used on you in the clinic. But too much looks a lot like a morphine overdose. Then you fell unconscious and woke up in the clinic?"

Hank nods.

I turn to Russ. "And they dumped his body in that alley. Edward knew Tommy was an addict. He didn't hide it. He didn't overdose. You were right. He was murdered trying to save Hank."

Russ is stone-faced, his eyes wet.

Hank stares at him a moment. "I didn't know he was dead. I'm so sorry, Russ."

Russ doesn't say anything, but he wraps Hank in a hug so tight I worry Hank will snap. Russ buries his face in Hank's shoulder and softly cries. I leave them, the emotion too much for me to handle right now. I'm too heavy with feeling, it's sloshing over my sides and I can't carry any more.

On the other side of the pharmacy, with all the escapees, are the rest of the Mattachines, laughing and talking. They spot me and all walk over.

"Thank you for letting us have a little adventure," Samuel says.

"I haven't had that much fun since I went to one of Barbara's orgies," Marie or Ethel says.

"You said you didn't go!" Ethel or Marie says, shocked.

Marie or Ethel shrugs. "You're only young once."

They both cackle and I turn to Leo. "You won't get in trouble for taking the van, will you?"

He shakes his head. "We'll bring it back now, nice and clean. Martha—or Mattie—is gathering up all their information, so she can get copies of their birth certificates if they can't go back home, and I asked her to get their clothing sizes, too. Samuel and I will do a little shopping tomorrow after work, see if we can get all of them out of those terrible asylum clothes. Dress them for this Hollywood ending you're written them."

"They really can't be seen on the street like that," Samuel says. "Much less the screen."

"But we'd better get that van back. Ladies, you're our ride back from the lot."

I wave at the four of them as they leave. Mattie is speaking to one of the escapees, right next to Vera, who is talking to another. They're pointedly not looking at each other, except when they think the other isn't looking.

Mattie glances up at me and smiles. "So I guess tapped phones have a use."

"What did you say exactly?"

"That we were planning a radical queer uprising at the Boyle Heights police station."

"Who did you say it to?"

She shrugs. "Random number. Just needed to say it on the line, right?"

I laugh. "I guess so. The Feds must have had the local cops in enough of a tizzy they couldn't pick up the phone."

"It's a fun trick, I'll have to remember it."

I look at the patients, some of whom are smiling now, laughing. A pair are holding hands. "And you're getting all these guys their birth certificates?"

"Just trying to get these for them quickly so they can get new IDs, apply for jobs. Get back to having a life." She looks down at the clipboard, all the names there. "Samuel said not everyone wanted to come back?"

"Yeah, a bunch stayed behind, still eager to be cured."

She shakes her head. "A shame. But I'm glad we rescued the ones we did."

"Me, too." I spot her looking over my shoulder, at Vera. "It's nice when folks with disparate views can come together on something."

"It is." Mattie's eyes slide back to mine. Her face is unreadable. She moves on to the next escapee, collecting his information.

Will and Javi have joined Russ and Hank on the other side of the room and I walk back toward them.

"You heading out?" Will asks.

"Actually, I was going to ask if I could crash at the garage." I rub the back of my neck. "I'm not sure I have anywhere to go back to tonight, after what I said to my mom."

"Of course," Russ says. His eyes are dry now, a smile stretched thin over his face. "Everyone else is. Between sofas and bedrolls, we'll put everyone up."

"You look ready to fall over," Will says to me. "Why don't I take you there now so you can sleep? Everyone else will handle things here."

"We're going to take everyone in Russ's car in trips," Javi says. "So it doesn't look too suspicious."

"You see all this in your cigarette smoke?" I ask him.

He shrugs. "You can see a lot of things in smoke, y'know? But smoke blows away. What we did tonight is going to linger for a while." He nods at me. I say good night to everyone and walk out with Will.

"Actually, can you wait one minute?" I ask. He nods and I walk down the street to a pay phone and call Gene. It's almost two in the morning, but he might still be cleaning up. He picks up after one ring.

"Andy?"

"It's me. I'm okay."

He lets out a long breath. "Good."

"I'm going to drive home tomorrow morning. Be back the day after that. Sooner, if I can."

"Just in time for the party."

"Maybe I should delay by a day."

He laughs. "No, you miss me too much."

"I really do."

"So what did you do tonight?"

I laugh. "A lot. I made friends. I'll tell you about it when I'm home. Oh, and tell Lee to look on California Street."

"Okay. Hurry back."

"I will."

I hang up and walk over to where Will is waiting on his motorcycle.

"Good?" he asks.

"Great." I get on the back of his bike, arms around him, and he drives forward into the dark. I don't mind the wind in my face anymore. I'm kind of used to it now. It's strong, all that force pushing into you. But I feel like I'm sturdy enough I can take it. At least if I'm riding with someone else.

At Russ's place, I fall into a sofa before Will even finds me a blanket, and I'm out.

There's not much need for a long goodbye with the Bacchanals. Russ gives me a handshake, Stan a clap on the back, Will a long hug, and Javi tries to kiss me on the mouth before I turn slightly enough so he gets my cheek. He laughs. "I'm not looking for a third boyfriend, just how I say goodbye to a friend."

"Stop by the Ruby next time you take a trip to San Francisco," I tell all of them. "Drinks are on me."

Hank and the rest of the escapees are still sleeping, lying on the floor in Russ's place so close I have to hop between them as I leave. But I see Hank standing in the doorway as I get in my car, and he waves once. I wonder what Edward is doing now. Why he even did any of it. To control Hank? To take advantage of Hank's wealthy parents? Some twisted form of love?

I don't know, and I probably never will. What matters isn't the why, just that Hank and the others are safe now. I hope Edward gets his comeuppance, but I doubt he will. It's not that kind of world, and we've already pulled off enough miracles.

I finally feel ready to eat again about an hour out of LA and stop at a diner for some toast and eggs. I drive all day and part of the night, as fast as I feel is safe along the cliffs. I finally make it back to San Francisco the next day. The windows are down and I can swear it smells better here, though I know that can't be true. The water looks different, and the air feels like an old, loved blanket. I park and take the stairs two at a time up to my apartment. When I unlock the door, Gene is waiting for me, reading in bed.

"You're home," he says.

"I am." I go over to the bed and kiss him. We do a bit more kissing before he finally pulls away. "I have to go get ready for work—big party tonight."

I sigh. "I'd almost forgotten about that. Forgotten my birthday is tomorrow." I wonder about my annual phone call with Mom. Will she even call this year? Ever again? "Seems unfair that I can't spend some quality time with my boyfriend because of a birthday party I don't want." My hands slide low around his torso, slipping under the waistband of his pants.

He kisses me, then pulls away with a grin. "Think of it as another present to unwrap." I laugh as he stands up, slipping on his shoes. "Besides, Lee found your last person. Left the address on your desk."

"Ah." Daphne. I hope her story isn't as sad as the others'. "Then I'd better go talk to her."

"Lee also says you owe him two days' pay for the work."

"Oh?" I say, skeptical. "How long did he spend on it?"

"I think he said two hours the first day and another hour after you got the street name. But apparently it was so boring going door-to-door that it felt like longer."

I snort a laugh. "Let's see if it's the right address."

I stand up and stretch, looking out my window. It's only a little after noon, and the light for the Ruby's sign isn't on. I can see down the street almost out to the water, and I can smell it, too. Home.

Gene hugs me from behind tightly for a moment. "I'm so glad you're back. You'll tell me all about whatever foolish thing you did later?"

"It's my birthday, I'll regale the crowd with stories."

He laughs. "I will hold you to that."

He leaves, and I take one more breath of San Francisco out the window before I remember I'm back and will probably be breathing it in enough I'll be sick of it again within a few hours. Across the hall, in the flourishes of Lee's handwriting, is an address on California Street.

It's a joy not to drive. To stand on the trolley and just to feel my legs stretched out again as I take it all the way over to Balboa Street. The red arches of the bridge pass by like waving hands. The smell fades, or at least my love of it does, but it doesn't matter. I don't even mind the long walk from the station to Daphne's home. The smell of the ocean gets stronger as I walk, my legs aching a little, lazy from spending so much time driving. It doesn't feel as hot anymore, like something has finally come along and taken the burning away and left just a clear open summer.

Sea Cliff almost reminds me of Long Beach, with small buildings all lined up along a main street, most of them Spanish-style, everything geared to walk or drive down to the beach. You can hear the waves and people laughing. It's still hot, the sun beating down like an iron about to press a shirt, and I almost want to join everyone else, throw myself in the ocean.

Daphne's place is a white two-family home, with an arched terra-cotta roof. Hers is the door on the left, and I ring the bell and wait. I wonder if she's out. I can wait. Maybe I will have time to walk down to the beach, at least stick my toe in.

But the door opens. It's the woman Myrtle described, right down to the birthmark. She's in a pretty gray dress with a small cap, and she's putting on an earring as she opens the door, holding it in place and then fiddling with her lobe with both hands as she looks at me expectantly.

"Daphne?"

She nods. "Are you selling something? I don't have much time, I'm just leaving."

"This will only be a moment. My name is Andy Mills. I was hired to find you."

She laughs. "Find me? I'm not lost."

"By Myrtle," I say softly.

He expression goes blank for a moment, then a smile starts to bloom on her face, just the barest breath of one before it wilts. She sighs. "Come in."

She walks inside and I follow. It's a nice house, or at least a nice hallway, with a blue runner decorated with yellow flowers. She turns. I'm not going to see more of the house.

"What do you know about how I met Myrtle?" she asks carefully.

"Mattachine," I say, looking around to make sure no one else is in the house. She doesn't look around or hush me, so I think we're alone. "I know all about it. I'm not really a member, but I could be, if you catch my meaning."

"No one is home, you can be open." She puts her hands on her hips. "I thought I was done with this but . . ." She shakes her head. "Myrtle." She sighs. "I do really care for her, please make that clear when you speak with her."

"So you're not going back to the meetings, then?"

She shakes her head. "It's all just too much. I thought maybe we could attain some recognition, live our lives without always looking over our shoulders, but after the split, all the meetings, I realized it will never be in my lifetime. Probably not for decades. And then I asked myself, 'What sort of life do I want to have? One of struggle and secret community? Or one where I can tell my parents about my life and just relax?'" She crosses her arms. "I'm getting married. A man, an old friend who always thought we should be something more. All it took was a little flirting, three dates, and now we have an appointment at the church to pick out flowers and homilies. That fast, that easy. Can you imagine a life that easy?" Her arms drop and she smiles, only a hint of sadness in it. "Even if I don't feel the way about him I know most wives would, we can have a good life together. Tell Myrtle I'm very sorry, and I really do care for her. But this is what I'm choosing."

She walks past me to the door and opens it. Outside, a car is pulling up. As I leave, an older woman who looks a lot like Myrtle gets out of the car.

"Mother," Daphne calls. "I'm ready, just hold on a moment."

She closes and locks the door behind us. "So nice meeting you," she says to me.

"Who's this?" Daphne's mother asks as we walk to the sidewalk.

"A door-to-door necktie salesman," Daphne says without hesitation. "I invited him in to see the catalog, maybe there'd be something that matches my dress a little for Jerry, but then I decided that was a bit much. Thank you again, Mr. Mills. I'll be sure to browse the catalog more thoroughly."

"Thank you." I nod. She'll be fine in her new life. "And congratulations on your wedding."

"Thank you."

I watch her and her mother for just a beat. Her mother is beaming, lit up even more when I said "wedding." She's taken Daphne's hand, and as I turn away and walk back to the trolley, I know that she's squeezing it. I can practically feel it, the joy, the excitement, the love, all in one tight squeezing of palms. Like a door being thrown open and you're being pulled into a party just for you.

I have one of those of my own to get to. I look at my watch. Not for a while though. There's time to close the case.

SEVENTEEN

Back in the office, I can hear things happening down in the Ruby. The band is here already, tuning instruments. There's the rumbling of moving crates of liquor. I had tried stopping off to see Gene, but soon as I'd opened the door, Elsie had slammed it in my face, then popped out to give me a hug and welcome me home and tell me not to step foot in her bar until she said it was okay. All the doors to the dressing rooms on my floor are closed, and I hear voices whispering behind them. Those doors are never closed. I'm getting scared now, but that's probably the point.

I call Myrtle a little after five.

"Hello?" She sounds sad.

"Hi. Myrtle, it's Andy."

There's a pause. "I thought maybe you were dead."

"I'm sorry, the case ended up being complicated. But it's solved now. I found everyone."

"You did?" It's almost a scream of relief. I hate what I have to tell her.

"Why don't you come over?" Mattie's phones were tapped, so I don't want to go into too much detail in case Myrtle's are, too. And news like this is better to give in person.

"Yes, yes, I can do that right now. I'll be there soon."

We hang up and I crane my ears, listening to the noises that are preparations for my party tonight, trying to determine what kind of torment they have in store for me. I'm pretty sure I hear Lee's laugh from next door. A saxophone honks ominously through the floorboards.

Myrtle shows up only twenty minutes later, breathing heavily as though she'd run up the stairs. Maybe she had.

I nod as she comes in, try to smile professionally, not in a way that's filled with pity. She closes the door behind her without saying anything, then sits down opposite me, scooting the chair as close as it can go.

"So?"

"The Fifth Order wasn't related. I found everyone. They'd all vanished for . . . different reasons."

She shakes her head, confused. "Are they safe?"

"Yes. Hank was in some trouble, but he's with friends in LA now. Edward is"—I work hard not to sneer—"doing well for himself."

"And Daphne?"

I hold back a sigh. "She told me to tell you she really cares for you. But she's getting married. She wanted an easier life. One her family approves of." I put my hand over the desk so Myrtle can reach out for it, if she wants, and I remember Daphne's mother, the way she'd held her daughter's hand, and suddenly remember my own mother's expression as I rode away on Will's motorcycle. I never really said goodbye. She doesn't know I left LA. I don't know if I should call or write or if she'll ever extend a hand to me again. I take a breath. That's a problem for later. We'll talk when she calls tomorrow. And if she doesn't, then that's that.

"That's it?" Myrtle says after a moment. Her eyes are wide open, shock maybe.

"That's what she said. She's left Mattachine, she's—"

"I understand that. But she didn't say . . ." Her lip trembles for a moment and she takes a breath, stops it. "The last time I saw her, I told her that I . . ." She lets it drift off. I don't know how to respond. She shakes her head, and we both pretend she'd never said it at all. "Well, that's all good news." Her voice is professional again. "I'm glad they're all safe."

"Me, too. I'm sorry they won't be rejoining."

Her eyes soften for a moment as she looks at me. "I've had plenty of time to get used to disappointment in my life. How much do I owe you?"

She takes out her checkbook and I do my best to calculate all the expenses in my head.

"You know," I say, after she hands me the payment, "they're throwing a party downstairs in a bit. You can join us if you want. Music, drinks, lots of men and women."

She seems like she's really considering it for a while. She looks at me, mouth open like my mother's was, and doesn't say anything. Then there's another burst of laughter from next door, and she shakes her head.

"Thank you, but no." She stands up, closing her purse. "I just don't think this is my kind of place."

I stand and open the office door for her. "It can be." I don't know why I'm trying so hard. Maybe it was what we all pulled off in LA. Together. We're all better together. "I went to that Mattachine meeting, and I liked it all right. Maybe you'd like the Ruby."

She smiles slightly, and for a moment I think she might say yes. Instead, she shakes her head and puts out her hand, and I put out mine, and we shake. There's only the slightest squeeze, but that's more than nothing.

"Thank you, Mr. Mills. The Mattachine Society will be sure to look you up again if we have need of your services. And I hope you might stop by a meeting now and then."

"Thank you. Maybe I will."

As she walks away, I hear one of the dressing-room doors slam and a burst of laughter. Definitely Lee.

"I know that's you, Lee," I say loudly, then go back into my office.

Lee appears a moment later in a silver dress, with a feathered headdress so big she has to duck to come into my office.

"Welcome back." She smiles. "How was LA?"

"What is going on in there?" I ask, looking at the wall I share with the dressing room.

"I'm just helping some of the boys get ready. We have a special performance for you tonight. New costumes."

I raise an eyebrow. "Costumes?"

She shrugs. "Clothes, whatever you want to call them. Gene tell you how much you owe me?"

"Yes, I'll pay you for one day's work after I cash the check."

"Fine, but no more boring work for me. Just the matchmaking."

I grin. "So you don't want to do any of the exciting work?"

"I want to hear about it," she says, smiling. "Gene said you haven't told him yet, but you did something dangerous."

I nod. "You'll like this one."

"Lee!" a voice calls from the hall.

She frowns. "I guess later. I think you'll be wanted downstairs soon."

"Someone going to come get me?"

Her eyes widen. "Good idea. I'll tell someone to do that. Now stay in here with the door closed until they do."

She waves goodbye and ducks again to get out, closing the door behind her. I go over my books, make sure I charged Myrtle the right amount. Music begins in earnest downstairs, a soft instrumental number. It would be nice to dance to. I'm getting a little antsy. I didn't want this party, but I don't like being kept out of it, either.

The phone rings and I answer it quickly, wondering who it could be now.

"Amethyst Investigations."

"Hi, Andy, it's Russ." He sounds tired.

"Hey, Russ. Something go wrong?" We'd worked it out pretty well, I thought, but I hadn't accounted for the fire. I never said Will's name in front of anyone. The only thing that could really go wrong is if my mother put it all together and decided to point the finger at me. Which is possible, but even if she did, it would be worth it.

"No, no. Just wanted you to know it's all fine. Will has been asking around, no one is filing criminal charges. The patients who stayed behind just talked about men who came to break them out before the fire, but it was dark and none of them gave a good description. No one thinks you or Will were part of it, though the story about the nurse killer has confused things enough they're trying to find evidence of other nurse killings, think maybe it's related. But you're fine."

"That's good." I wonder if I should thank Mom. If I should call her instead. "How are Hank and the rest of them?"

"They're doing well. Vera has everyone patched up, eating easy solid foods, drinking water with honey in it, though I'm not sure what that does. Some of them are making plans—Mattie and One are hiring a few, some are moving out East, or up to San Francisco. And one wants to get a motorcycle and start riding with us."

"Yeah? That's great news."

"I think they're going to be fine. I mean, not totally fine, how could they be, but you know how it is. We saw war. Some of them did, too. It's like that."

"I get it."

"I know. And Hank is . . . Well, he got some news. He tried calling home, to tell his parents about Edward, get a little vengeance. They begged him to go back, go to some new clinic, told him he was crazy—because Edward is marrying Hank's sister."

I let out a low whistle. Poor Ginny. With the clinic gone, Edward must have predicted Hank's next move and done what he needed to ensure he'd get to stay part of the family and keep all those comforts he felt he deserved.

"Yeah," Russ continues, "he's staying here. I think for a while. He wants to try to catch his sister alone, maybe if she goes back to college, talk to her, warn her."

"Tell him good luck. Ginny seemed pretty smitten with Edward—though I don't think Edward even acknowledged her when I saw them."

"It's a bad situation. I hope Hank can talk some sense into her."

"Yeah." I sigh. Another wedding. Daphne, Edward. He's being welcomed into the family while Hank is being kicked out. Hank is willing to give it all up to be himself. Edward will always be whoever gets him what he wants.

"We all talk about Tommy a lot, too. Soon as Hank is feeling up to it and Javi's foot is better, we're going to do a day ride to Badger Flats and do a little memorial for him. We don't have his body or anything, but we'll bury his jacket there."

"I like that. Tell me when you go, if you want. I mean, I don't want to impose."

"I'll tell you," he says, almost laughing. "And we're going to take you up on those drinks next time we're in San Francisco. You're part of the club now, Andy."

"You going to get me a jacket?"

"Nah, but there's a patch in the mail for you. We thought it would look good on your hat."

I laugh just as the door opens, Gene smiling just beyond. "I think I gotta go now. Thanks for calling, and say hi to the guys for me."

"Will do. We'll talk soon."

I hang up. Gene hasn't said anything; he's just standing, waiting, his face all mischief.

"Okay. I guess let's get this over with."

He laughs and takes my hand, squeezing. "It's going to be fun," he promises. "Just put on this blindfold."

I sigh and let him wrap it around my eyes. We take the elevator down, my hand in his as he guides me. The Ruby is silent, but I can hear breathing. I'm not sure how many people are here, but it's more than the half dozen I expected.

There's a drumroll. I reach up to take off the blindfold, but Gene takes my other hand. "Not yet," he whispers.

"Presenting," I hear Elsie say, from the stage and with a mic, "the Ruby's finest act—Vanda Mills and the Evanderettes!"

Oh no. Gene tears the blindfold off me to the sight of Lee onstage, in the same getup as before, towering headdress, and behind her, a group of male impersonators, all dressed like me.

"This is for you, birthday boy," Lee says, then motions the band and starts singing "Guilty," the male impersonators doing backup, swaying, their faces sad in what I assume is a parody of me. All around me are familiar faces: Elsie and Gene, of course, but also Pat, Pearl, Shelly, who owns the bar named for him, even my old navy friend Helen.

When they're finished with "Guilty," Lee—or Vanda for the night, I guess—sings "Happy Birthday," and Elsie brings out a huge purple cake topped with enough candles I wonder if there's a fire extinguisher on hand. Gene and Elsie start handing out slices and drinks, and everyone wants a moment to wish me happy birthday, to thank me for those blackmail photos I gave back or the fake relationship I helped create that lifted suspicion from them at work. So many people I've helped in small ways. All reaching out, shaking my hand, kissing me on the cheek.

Elsie finds me to hand me a slice of cake, shoveling a forkful in my mouth when I try to demur.

"And you thought no one would come," she says, looking around the room. We're to the side, and other people are dancing, laughing.

"You offered them free booze."

She laughs. "You think I'm not charging? That guy there is handing money to Gene right now. What kind of detective are you?"

"Not very good, I guess. How'd you even get a cake that big into the elevator?"

"Carefully." She throws her arm over my shoulder and pulls me tight into her. "I'm glad you made it home in time. Would have been weird to throw this without you."

"Thanks for throwing it."

She grins. "Anytime."

"I'm still not sure I des—"

She lifts the plate of cake up into my face. "Shut up, eat your cake, and listen." I wipe my face as she points out at the crowd, hand sweeping over everyone. "You helped every person in this room. Every single person is someone you helped with matchmaking or a case, or you returned a blackmail photo, or just someone you bought a drink for, or who saw you take a punch during a raid and felt a little safer, a little more protected. I made the guest list myself. These people are here for you."

I look out and realize she's right. I know everyone here, and they all fill the Ruby so tight I can't see the floor. It feels, somehow, like the way it did in the Dahlia after we helped everyone escape. I wonder whom we rescued here.

"So don't give me your sad-sack, don't-deserve-it spiel, okay?" She wipes some frosting off my cheek.

"There was this guy in LA," I start slowly. "He was part of the motorcycle club. Gay. A cop." She raises her eyebrows. "But he warned people about the raids. He helped me out on the case—helped a lot of people escape this . . . terrible place."

"You think he was better than you?"

"I think I could have been him." I shrug, look down at my plate of smashed cake. "If I'd been better."

"We all could have been a lot of things. But we are who we are. Look around. You're a hero now."

I let a small smile creep over my face. "I think hero might be a bit much."

She sighs. "Fine, you're just some guy. Happy?"

I laugh. "Very."

We look out at the dancing crowd for a moment. "Tell me something," she says, without turning to look at me. "Was he cute?"

"What?" I stare at her.

She turns slowly. "This heroic gay cop. Was he cute?"

"I'm with Gene," I say, shaking my head, hoping the dark lighting hides my blush.

"I'm with Margo—I'm not asking if you slept with the guy. I'm asking if you thought he was cute. I think other girls are cute all the time. Margo and I compare sometimes."

"Yes, he was cute. Or, I don't know if *cute* is the word. But attractive."

"When was he attractive?"

"What?"

"In uniform or out of it?"

"I didn't get him out—"

"Civvies, Andy, calm down. I'm not accusing you of cheating. Just answer the question."

I think back to Will and me smoking, him in uniform, the heat. "In uniform. We were smoking outside. He didn't have a jacket on, or hat, just the shirt, tie, pants, sunglasses."

She laughs suddenly.

"What?"

"Sunglasses?"

I nod. "So what?"

"And you saw yourself in the reflection?"

"I—yeah. I don't get what you're saying."

"I'm saying I think maybe, just maybe, Evander Mills has started to love himself a little." She stands up, offers me her hand for a dance. "Or at least finds a reflection of himself cute."

I take her hand, standing up. "I don't think—"

She makes to shove my plate of cake in my face again and I stop talking. She smiles, nods, takes the plate from me, and puts it back on the table we were sitting at. "Let's dance."

I dance with her, and Gene and Lee, and so many other people. At midnight, they all toast to my official birthday and sing "For He's a Jolly Good Fellow."

People start clearing out after that, and I finally have a chance to just sit and talk and tell Gene and Lee and Elsie about my adventure in LA. They take it in with varying faces, Lee fascinated and loving it like a movie, Gene's brow furrowing every time I did something reckless—which was a lot.

"You rescued a whole clinic of people," Elsie says. "That's amazing, Andy. I don't know why you object to being called a hero."

"It was dangerous," Gene says, reaching out and stroking the top of my hand over the bar. "But it was the right thing to do. I'm glad you're okay. And very glad you didn't tell me what you were planning."

"Didn't want to worry you," I say, lifting his hand to my lips.

"That's a good story," Lee says. "You should make it into a movie."

I laugh. "I'm not sure any of the studios would do that."

Lee shrugs. "Maybe not, but I'll imagine it anyway. Who do you think would play me?"

Elsie laughs. "You're not even in it."

"I'd be in the movie though," Lee says. "To give it some star power. I'd probably have to play myself."

We all laugh. The bar is mostly empty now, and Gene starts cleaning up.

"Leave it," Elsie tells him. "I'll do it. You and Andy go upstairs, everyone brought presents that I left in your room. Get some sleep."

She and Lee each give me a kiss on the cheek before I take Gene's hand and we go upstairs.

"You worried about your mom?" he asks me in the stairwell. "If she'll turn you in?"

"Russ called, doesn't look like she did, but . . ." I shake my head. "I don't know if she'll ever talk to me again. If she'll call tomorrow."

He squeezes my hand tight. "It's okay if she doesn't, you know. I mean, it hurts, but sometimes I think it's for the best. Like it might just cause me pain if I still talked to my mom, because every conversation would be about trying to change me, trying to get me to go to a place like that clinic."

"Yeah, maybe you're right." I don't say it convincingly, but he doesn't add anything else.

Inside, my apartment is filled with gifts—wrapped boxes with bows, bags, cards. I shake my head. The place is covered in them. I laugh at the sight.

"You want to open all these now?" Gene asks, sitting on the bed.

I smile at him. "Actually, there's one present I want to unwrap first."

He grins.

When Gene wakes up, I've been in my office for about an hour already, just staring at the phone. Between ten and noon, that's when she calls. He walks from my apartment across the hall through the open door and sees me sitting at the desk. I try to pull my eyes away from the phone as he comes in, but I do it too slowly. He walks over and sits on the desk in just his jockeys.

"Hey, why don't we go get breakfast?" he says.

"I'm just going to give it a little while longer." I don't know what I'm hoping exactly. That she calls and says she understands, that she calls and doesn't understand, that she calls just to say goodbye? Most of the time we don't get goodbyes, I know that better than most people. Seen so many relatives of victims, crying, and the same phrase: "I didn't even get to say goodbye." But Mom isn't dead, and neither am I.

"You could call her," Gene suggests, running his fingers through my hair.

"She calls me for my birthday."

He's quiet and I can't make myself look in his eyes. I know what I'd see, and I don't want pity, not yet. Not until noon.

"I'm going to go shower." He kisses the top of my head. "Happy birthday."

I smile at that and watch him walk back to the apartment. Everything feels so easy, now that I'm home. The party last night, all those people. I really have made some kind of difference in the world. And maybe I even deserve the friends I have, despite whom I used to be. I've changed. People can do that.

He showers and comes and sits across from me in my office, reading aloud from the latest Narnia book for me.

When the clock on the wall turns to noon, I sigh. "I don't think she's calling."

He reaches across the desk and I give him my hand. "It's okay. I promise, you can survive. You have friends, you have a family."

I smile. He's right. I have a family. I have my people. Even if Mom never calls, I have everyone, and we're all here, together.

"I'm going to go wash up," I say, standing.

And then the phone rings.

ACKNOWLEDGMENTS

Publishing a book is like forming your own gang, and I couldn't be happier to be riding along with this one. Driving from Forge to Minotaur was a bit of a gearshift, but I'm so thrilled by how welcoming and kind my new club is. We should totally get jackets.

I need to start by thanking my amazing agent, Joy, my ride or die, whose sidecar I will always happily get into and have been in for two decades at this point. Can never thank her enough, she's family.

And next I must thank the president of this motor club, who drove me over to Minotaur, my editor, Kristin, who continues to give me brilliant insight and point me in the right direction so that each of these novels works not just as a whole but as a collective. She's a genius. And thank you also to Jill, for working with us to make this book amazing.

The whole gang at Minotaur has been so kind and I'm so thrilled to be working with them, and so grateful for all they've done: Kayla, Sara, Hector, Paul, the library marketing team, Steve, Greg, and their fearless leader, Kelley. Thank you so much to all of them for the work they've put into keeping this series going.

Special thanks to Colin, who did not only this breathtaking cover, but the covers of my two other books out this year! At this point he's done the covers for half my books! I'm so lucky we're friends and so lucky to have him making these amazing covers for my books. And thank you to David for designing this cover so beautifully, an evolution of the previous covers, different but recognizable.

Likewise thank you to my audio team, led once again by the amazing Emma, and my astounding narrator, Vikas, who not only brings each of these characters to life so beautifully, but also will watch the movies I tell him have the most in common with the characters!

I always have to thank so many folks from outside Macmillan: my amazing film agent, Lucy; SallyAnne, who continues to help me find my voice; my writing group: Robin, Laura, Jesse, and Dan, for the continued support and feedback; and of course to all my writing friends: Dahlia, Josh, John, Margot, Hank, Chantelle, Liz, Dan, Dawn, Sara, Deborah, Sujata, Steve, Nekesia, Robin, Wanda, Adam, Caleb, Cale, Adib, Julian, Sandy, and probably a million others. Writing is a community sport.

And, of course, thank you to all the amazing booksellers out there constantly advocating for books like this and for me to write more of them—John, Krysten, Julie, Leah, Bea, Barbara, Jenni Mariana, Ryan, David, Bill, Laynie-Rose, Susan, Emily, Liz, Beth, Kaitee, Derek, Elizabeth, Laura, Kinsey, Sophie, and so many, many more. If I were going to pull a heist and burn something down, you're the folks I'd trust to lead the way.

I jokingly referred, in early drafts, to this book as "Mattachine, Motorcycles, Medicine, and Mommy." While the last of those comes purely from my imagination, the other three required some research, and I have a lot of people to thank for helping me with that.

First, on the Mattachine Society, and their schism. All of that is real history, but the specifics of the history are often blurry, especially about the time around the schism (though the meetings where the schism occurred are well documented). In many cases,

ACKNOWLEDGMENTS

I found contradictory information from different sources—even primary sources often contradict one another, as such interviews were often given years after the events had occurred, and people remember things differently. In the end, I just went with whichever version of history made for a better story. However, the primary book I used was *Behind the Mask of the Mattachine*, by James T. Sears. I also greatly enjoyed the *Queer Serial* podcast, hosted by Devlyn Camp, which gives a great overview of the history.

Relatedly, the One Institute, who once published *ONE* magazine, is still around today. They were only an archive for a while, but are now back to their activist roots, making them the oldest active LGBTQ+ institution in the country. The magazine stopped publication in 1967, but the One Institute and Archives at UCLA still have so many amazing documents and pieces of history. Today, One works as an educational institution, not only maintaining the archives and curating exhibits, but mentoring queer youth and helping to teach kids today about queer history. They're a fantastic nonprofit worthy of a donation, which you can make at OneInstitute.org. I also highly recommend the book *Letters to ONE*, edited by Craig M. Loftin, a collection of real letters written to *ONE* magazine during the fifties and sixties. It'll give you a sense of what it was to be queer back then. And if you can, find an image of that amazing bright green gay marriage cover from '53. The FBI raided *ONE* in August of '53, so that particular issue went out late—but it still went out.

As for motorcycles, the Bacchanals I made up, but they are heavily inspired by real-life gay motorcycle club the Satyrs, founded in 1954, which has remained active since. They're the oldest continuously operational gay rights organization in the United States, and they are not the only gay motorcycle club out there, not by a long shot; I also drew inspiration from the Oedipus, Blue Max, Spartan, Warlocks, Barbary Coasters, and Empire City Motorcycle Clubs, and there are so many more I stumbled across or found one photo of to add to my collection. I had the pleasure of speaking to various gay motorcycle club members (and riding buddies), and I thank them for all their stories, photos, and kindness in explaining things to me, especially Peter, Jonathan, Chaz, and Scott. They gave me the sorts of details that brought the Bacchanals to life. Several of them are also writers, and I recommend checking out their books if you're interested, including *My Leather Life* by Peter Fiske, and the articles "Longing and Belonging" and "With an Eagle on the Back" by Jonathan Boorstein, both in *Rider's Digest*. These guys have experienced and studied all this far more than I have, and they're way smarter than me. There is also a documentary about the Satyrs, called *Original Pride*, which I found helpful and moving, and which you can find on YouTube.

I want to emphasize that nowhere in my research did I find evidence that the Satyrs or any of these queer motorcycle clubs were involved in drug use. That part is completely fictional for the sake of a noir story. These clubs have been amazing gay rights groups that have helped many folks find community and self-respect in a world that didn't want them to have either.

I also found the online archives of the Leather Museum to be incredibly helpful for both Mattachine and motorcycles—their online audio recordings of interviews are a fantastic resource.

Finally, medicine. There have been so many different theories on how to "treat" homosexuality over the years that when I began that research—often from medical papers on the history of treatments—I was quickly overwhelmed (not to mention depressed). There were a lot of "treatments" to choose from, almost all of them horrifying. In the end, I decided, instead of trying to find a murder in all that medicine, to work backward and run my ideal murder scenario by my dear friend Alexis, an actual doctor who understood everything far better than I. She quickly helped me come up with the right drug and what it would be used for, in "curing homosexuality" and in murder. I can't thank her enough for her help.

Conversion therapy, as "curing homosexuality" is often called, is still alive and well. In the United States, over a dozen states have no laws banning conversion therapy for minors—minors often forced to go to clinics like the one in this book or else be disowned by their parents and kicked out of the house. And though twenty-six states have laws banning conversion therapy, a *Time* magazine report in 2023 found that it was still practiced in some form in forty-eight states, despite the laws. A Trevor Project study the same year showed that 10 percent of queer people had been through some kind of conversion therapy practice, and many more had been threatened with it repeatedly. As of earlier this year, several states that do ban conversion therapy are now facing lawsuits from organizations attempting to have the bans overturned completely. This is still ongoing. Though the very real practice of combining nausea-inducing drugs with pornography is no longer the primary form of conversion therapy, study after study has shown that all forms of such therapies have no real effect aside from traumatizing the "patients"—as should be expected, as in the end, all forms of conversion therapy are just forms of torture. It's terrible how much things haven't changed since the fifties—but that's partly because so few people know that this is still happening or what it looks like. Every voice that speaks out against it can help. If you find this as horrific as I do, please look into your state and local laws and write your representatives, urging them to ban conversion therapy—especially on minors—and then urge them to enforce those bans.

Though this book was ripe for inclusion of major figures in queer history, I intentionally avoided that. Those are real people with real history, and you should read all about them, but queer history is already covered up and rewritten so often, I didn't want to participate in doing that any more than the story warranted. So all the characters are fictional. Mattie may mention Harry Hay and W. Dorr Legg, but they're not on the page. Harry Hay did have a house in Silver Lake though, and you can still see the steps leading up to it, now called the Mattachine Steps.

As always, I want to credit Nan Alamilla Boyd's *Wide-Open Town* for all my knowledge of queer San Francisco. But this time we also went to LA, so I must thank my dear friend Sarah for all her LA history and helping me pinpoint where everyone would be.

I also want to thank Trina and the team at the LA Museum of Neon Art, who gave me a tour of all the best period signs and introduced me to Doc Kilzum, the best metaphor an author could ask for.

There are so many other bits and pieces of research I accomplished online, from people just posting photos and memories to folks who kept track of street constructions. Thank you to all those historians out there.

And to Chris for being Chris.

ABOUT THE AUTHOR

Rachael Shane

LEV AC ROSEN writes books for people of all ages, including the Evander Mills series, which began with the Macavity Award–winning *Lavender House* and continued with *The Bell in the Fog* and *Rough Pages*. His most recent young adult novels are *Emmett, Lion's Legacy,* and *Camp*. Rosen's books have been nominated for Anthony and Lambda Awards and have been selected for best-of lists from the *Today* show, Amazon, *Library Journal, BuzzFeed, Autostraddle, Forbes,* and many others. He lives in New York City with his husband and a very small cat. You can find him online at LevACRosen.com and @LevACRosen.